Praise for Glenn Rolfe

'Rolfe is a rising talent in the horror field. Fans of
The Lost Boys film will enjoy this, and Rolfe puts his
own spin on the standard summer bloodsucker tale.'
Booklist on *Until Summer Comes Around*

'An intense tale reminiscent of classic works by
Jack Ketchum or Stephen King.'
Booklist on *August's Eyes*

'Rolfe is the real deal, folks, and anything
he writes is well worth checking out.'
Gord Rollo, author of *The Jigsaw Man* and
The Crucifixion Experiments

'A major new talent rises from the Maine woods...'
Nate Kenyon, award-winning author
of *Sparrow Rock*

GLENN ROLFE

WHEN THE NIGHT FALLS

This is a **FLAME TREE PRESS** book

Text copyright © 2024 Glenn Rolfe

FLAME TREE PRESS
6 Melbray Mews, London, SW6 3NS, UK
flametreepress.com

US sales, distribution and warehouse:
Simon & Schuster
simonandschuster.biz

UK distribution and warehouse:
Hachette UK Distribution
hukdcustomerservice@hachette.co.uk

Thanks to the Flame Tree Press team.

The cover is created by Flame Tree Studio with
thanks to Shutterstock.com.
The font families used are Avenir and Bembo.

Flame Tree Press is an imprint of Flame Tree Publishing Ltd
flametreepublishing.com

A copy of the CIP data for this book is available from the British Library
and the Library of Congress.

PB ISBN:978-1-78758-809-7
ebook ISBN: 978-1-78758-811-0

Printed and bound in Great Britain by Clays Ltd, Elcograf S.p.A.

GLENN ROLFE

WHEN THE NIGHT FALLS

FLAME TREE PRESS
London & New York

PROLOGUE

Life won't wait was something I remember my dad saying to me when I was a kid. He didn't like me lounging around the house playing Atari all day. Dad didn't have video games when he was young, so he didn't understand the joys of Pac-Man or Galaga. He wanted me and my sister, Julie, up and out of the house in the summer. "Go do something," he'd say. Dad said a lot before we lost him. I miss him like crazy. What I wouldn't give to sit down and have a beer with him, watch a Red Sox game, or just talk to him. We never got to have an adult conversation. I often imagine what that would've been like.

I still think about the summer we lost him. I can't not think about it. You had to be there, trust me. It's not every summer you fall in love. It's not every summer you lose your role model, and it sure as hell isn't an annual thing killing a vampire.

But that was then.

Ten years later, I was twenty-six and still living in Old Orchard Beach, Maine, serving the town as a member of the fire department. I had a severe case of scoliosis growing up and wore a back brace for most of my teen years. I was close to needing surgery but stopped growing just in time, I guess. I probably shouldn't have been able to join the OOBFD, but the chief had been friends with both my dad and my uncle Arthur in high school and he did me a solid in getting me past the physical. I was strong for my size and my back never bothered me anyway.

Two years into the gig, I was ready to do something else. It wasn't the job alone that had me burned out, pardon the bad pun, it was my life in general. Dad's old *life won't wait* mantra no longer rang through my head. In the summer of 1996, I didn't care anymore. May 15th, I gave my notice at the station and decided to spend the summer living off my savings. I needed time to figure out my next move. In truth, I'd never been more lost. And maybe that's how these damn things happen. I'd saved enough people in my twenty-six years on Earth; I wanted – nix that – *needed* someone to save me. If you had told me then that it would be her, I wouldn't have believed you in a thousand years. But that girl had never left. She just stayed in the shadows. And when I needed her the most, November finally came back around.

PART ONE:

WHAT IS, WHAT WAS, AND THE INFINITE SADNESS

CHAPTER ONE

Rocky always knew when she was near. The briny perfume of the Atlantic, mingled with the scent of summer sweat and subtle death. In the years since he'd last seen her, he'd never forgotten that smell. It was a sense that triggered his instant and total recall to the most magical moments of his life. Where the beach met romance and where every whispered promise was kept and guarded by hearts not quite ready for that sort of thing. *Love* had always been for movies, top-forty radio hits, and for grown-ups ready for a life ever after. It was an emotion that was too precious and carried too much weight for teenagers walking locker-lined hallways afraid someone would point out any of their imperfections. Yet, even back then, as he was turning sixteen, trapped in a back brace that made talking to girls next to impossible, a force descended upon his little beach town and, for better or worse, tied Rocky's heart to its own.

Rocky had been having dreams like this one tonight for nearly ten years. And though she was always there, a darker presence within the shadows, November Riley never revealed herself. Even his nightly visions wouldn't allow them to be together.

Tonight's version of the dream was like all the others. He stood at the end of the pier where they'd last spoken, gazing out at the angry swells waltzing in the ice-cold ocean, winter's snow cascading down from a stormy sky. He'd fallen in love with a monster and paid the price. A penance that saw him bound to loneliness, stuck in a dream, and wondering if the universe would ever set him free.

He was ready for the part of the dream where the shadow moves and he sets out after her in a mad dash that ends with him falling from the pier and into a depthless sea, but in tonight's dream, it was different. Standing in his starting position, he *heard* her. Somewhere in the frosty midnight air, her voice called his name. It was faint but there, just above the crashing waves. She felt. So. Close.

Rocky awoke, certain November would either step from the shadows of his bedroom or call to him from beneath the streetlight next to his house on East Grand Avenue. Asleep or awake, the feelings of anxiety and anticipation were enormous. His heart and mind were exhausted.

Rocky slid his feet to the floor and climbed out of bed. The town was quiet for a change. He hated it. These hot summer nights, it was the motorcycles, muscle cars, and loud drunk people singing out of tune that soothed his busy mind and lulled him to sleep. As he went to the window, he heard the waves.

At least I'm not dreaming.

The street was still dark and empty. He took a deep breath, ran his fingers through his shoulder-length hair and decided he needed some water.

Rocky turned on the TV on his way to the kitchen sink. A commercial played while he grabbed a glass from the dish strainer and filled it at the faucet. He held the drink to his lips as he recognized the nickname mentioned on the TV, the Beach Night Killer. A shiver barreled along his spine from the back of his skull down to his ass, creating a cold mess in the pit of his stomach.

He carried the glass into the living room and stared.

Paper clippings, local news reports, and tabloid trash headlines ran in a quick series of snapshots across the screen as the deep, ominous voice of NBC's Corey Davison spoke of the ten-year anniversary of the night that almost ended Rocky's life. Premiering in two days, Dateline's three-part series – *Summer of Death: The True Story of the Beach Night Killer.*

Rocky grabbed the remote and shut the TV off. He stood in the dark, a mix of shock and rage battling within him. He'd refused the producer's interview request. He'd threatened them. Told them if they even thought about airing the documentary, he'd sue. Apparently, the producers didn't give a fuck.

Sitting on his sofa, he downed the water and placed the glass on his coffee table. He wanted to throw it. Watch it smash against the wall, the television, the whole damn world. In two fucking days this town would be buzzing with all this shit. His story, his past, the murders his town was just now getting beyond…it was all about to come back like a fucking once-cured disease.

He tried to go back to bed but couldn't shut his brain off. How many nights had he spent with nowhere to go and no one to turn to but the night? Rocky spent most of his free evenings drinking at Duke's Tiki Lounge or watching old comedy VHS tapes trying to put this all behind him, to put *her* and Gabriel in his rearview mirror for good.

Turns out replacing someone so *unique* wasn't that easy.

He'd dated, but those relationships never developed into anything serious. How could they even compare? He'd even considered signing up for a session with his sister Julie's therapist, but Rocky didn't think he'd have the guts to dig down as deep as necessary. There were just some things most people wouldn't understand no matter how many certificates lined their walls.

He thought of his two years with the Old Orchard Beach Fire Department. In that relatively short amount of time, he'd braved his fair share of conflagrations and helped as many people as he could without any care for his own safety. He couldn't tell anyone else that it was less about bravery and more to do with a lack of self-care, but people only saw what they wanted to see. They saw him as a hero. But he'd given his notice and walked away from the station just before Memorial Day.

Lost somewhere in his thoughts, Rocky fell back to sleep.

★   ★   ★

She watched him wander from his bedroom to the kitchen, to the living room, and back to bed as she always did. It was a routine he usually did a few times before exhaustion finally took hold of him. Rocky rarely slept through the night, and she knew why. It was the same thing that tied them both to this town, to this street, to each other. It was the summer of 1986, and all the love and death that went along with it. It was one immense moment after another that didn't care if they were too young. Was it fair? Was that even a worthwhile question? When did the universe ever care about *even-steven*? November hoped Rocky would move on. That one day, he would meet someone and that he'd be able to let November go. Maybe then she could move on, too.

For now, she'd hold on to that string and wait to see if it would bring love back to them.

★   ★   ★

Rocky opened his eyes against the glare of the sun barging through the window. He'd forgotten to close the shade last night and now the brightness attempted to burn his retinas from his head. He swept his arm across the bed, found his blanket, and pulled it over his head until he was swallowed in the comforter. For a moment, all was good, and then he remembered the commercial from last night.

Summer of Death: The True Story of the Beach Night Killer

CHAPTER TWO

She really didn't mind the sunshine, but Kat hated the heat. She preferred winter's icy lips to the sweaty gross caress of summer. Hot weather, like today's ninety-five-degree forecast, made for maggot-filled stomachs and curdled-milk chasers. Being a creature of the night was certainly more attuned with playing the part of a night owl, or prowler. Either one worked. Killer worked, too. Kat didn't hang her hat on the latter, but she wasn't stupid. Vampires needed to feed, and human blood was the crème de la crème among what the world had to offer. It didn't just sate you, it empowered you. Lifted you into the night and made you nearly invincible. Of course, you had to be careful. As with anything so intoxicating, the edge always wanted to lure you over. *Too far* happened before you ever had a goddamn clue.

Her creator was the perfect example. After years of careful seduction, selective feedings, and living more than fifty years as a monster in the world, he fell to the hunger. In the end, all his intellect and all his self-control were not enough. He fell as many had before him, caving in to the desires. He burned through his humanity and became a thoughtless beast. He was cornered and shot to death on the outskirts of a shithole town outside of Vancouver. Could Kat have saved him? No, but she may have been able to prolong his life. To what end, though? Once a vampire is that far gone, there's no sense. There's nothing left to salvage.

Vampires in real life weren't exactly like their movie-star counterparts. For starters, they weren't immortal. They died of old age, head wounds, heart failure and diseases just like humans. The sun didn't burn them to a pile of ash, but it did dampen their supernatural gifts. This was where monster movies got some things right. Like in

Dracula and *The Lost Boys*, vampires were physically stronger than humans, and thanks to the effect of blood – especially human blood – they could move undetected by the human eye, like ghosts. And hell yes, they could fly.

Because they could walk in the sun, Kat chose to venture away from her Canadian roots and hunker down where a monster was least likely to be discovered – just down the hill from the Hollywood sign. It was on the streets of Los Angeles that she found Vincent. He was one of a million failed actors/wannabe rock stars littering the sub-Hollywood streets, a vagrant numbing his failure with whatever junk he could squeeze into his hardening veins. She could lie to herself and say she saved him from a wasted life, but that was only that, a lie. She was lonely. Kat needed companionship. She'd taken plenty of lovers and fed upon nearly just as many, but it was the emptiness in the spaces in between where the aching became too much.

Vincent wasn't the perfect match for her, far from it, but he was right for that moment, a moment that had since become nearly a decade long.

"What are you looking at?" Vincent asked. He was sitting in a pair of jeans and shitkicker cowboy boots. He wore his hair long, as he had when she found him. He still had the look of a wannabe L.A. rocker, but that was the only thing of natural beauty about him. Kat wasn't sure if she despised him now or if she was just bored.

"Where's Fiona?" she said.

Vincent turned away, feigning disinterest in his little pet's whereabouts. He and Fiona thought Kat was stupid. She knew there was something brewing between them. If they hadn't fucked yet, they soon would. She hadn't decided how she felt about that, either.

Vincent looked over his fingernails. "I think she was going to grab something for dinner."

"I told you I didn't want her going out alone yet. She's not ready."

"And I was when you turned me loose?"

"I was always near."

He harrumphed at this.

It wasn't a lie. Kat watched Vincent from above for months before he was actually out hunting on his own. He should be doing the same for Fiona.

Fiona was only twenty-two and the poor thing still thought she was a creature from a bad TV movie. She was lucky Vincent had stumbled upon her when he did. Bringing her in to their company probably saved the girl from one kind of terrible death or another. At least with them, she had guidance. What she did with the knowledge they bestowed upon her was up to her. Eventually, she could stay or go out on her own.

Kat looked at Vincent. He was now enthralled by something on the hotel television. She couldn't see what it was. "You really should shut that off and go find her. At least make sure she's not being reckless."

"Kat," he said, sitting up and leaning forward. "You might want to see this."

She got off the bed, pulling her long black curls into a ponytail as she crossed the room.

A barrage of hypnotic flashes crossed the screen. Kat caught glimpses of a seaside beach town, a Ferris wheel, a roller coaster, followed by *Missing* posters featuring teenagers, girls, boys, and then a face…the images halted. Two familiar cold, black eyes gazed back from the screen followed by a series of local news channels reporting about Gabriel Riley, The Beach Night Killer. Kat and Vincent had talked about this particular serial killer before. It had happened in the eighties over on the coast of Maine, but every so often a late-night radio show would discuss the oddities surrounding the killings and the death of Riley.

No sooner had the thought crossed her mind than a man in a brown dress coat and a mustache appeared on the screen talking about rumors of Riley being a true movie monster come to life.

A vampire.

"That's him, all right," Vincent said. His knee was bouncing as he watched.

Kat placed a hand on his shoulder. "You see it, don't you?"

There were only a limited number of images of the young man. The main picture they used was a mugshot from Riley's lone arrest a year prior to the summer slayings. Kat and Vincent had studied the photo at least a dozen times since they'd met. Something about the eyes gave the monstrous rumors a level of credence.

The song used in the commercial for the upcoming program played up the recent fear surrounding musician Marilyn Manson. One of his songs played in the background as Gabriel Riley's face faded and the host walked the beach where it all went down.

The *Morning Show* host came on sitting with the man in the clip who'd been walking on the beach.

"Tune in tonight with Corey Davison for *Timeline's Summer of Death: The True Story of the Beach Night Killer*." She turned to the man sitting next to her. "Thank you, Corey. I'm already getting the chills." Turning back to the camera she said, "Up next, find out what superstar John Travolta has cooking. He's going to bring his great smile and dance moves to our set to teach us how he makes his favorite hot wings. Stay tuned, we'll be right back."

"Vincent," Kat said. "Go find Fiona."

CHAPTER THREE

Vincent stepped onto the street and lit a cigarette. It was fucking sweltering out here. The street was relatively empty. A city bus was just departing from the stop at the end of the block; two other vehicles – a white box truck and a little red Toyota pickup – were heading in his direction. Other than that, and the few resting vagrants between himself and the bus stop, Dez Street was deathly still.

Vincent's right heel stuck to the cement.

"Aw, are you kidding me?"

Gum on his boot. The two bums closest to him were whispering to one another. He stepped over them and muttered, "What the fuck?"

The two stopped and glared at him.

"Do you mind?" the one with a long, raised scar across his big nose said.

The other one's eyes were too close together.

"No," Vincent answered. "I don't mind at all." Vincent checked the street and watched as the box truck rambled on farther down the road and the Toyota turned right, disappearing onto Iris Avenue. Coast clear, Vincent reared back and kicked Eyes Too Close in the face. The man's head knocked back; his hands flew into the air. Blood exploded from his nose, splattering the concrete wall behind him. As Scarface tried to reach out and grab for him, Vincent clutched the bum by the collar of his filthy army jacket and forced him to the ground, the back of Scarface's head smacking the concrete with a quick *thwap*.

Both men were moaning as Vincent stood and dropped the bubble-gummed heel of his boot to Scarface's jaw and pressed down. Bones cracked beneath his foot as Vincent dragged the sole and heel across the man's already ruined face.

"Asshole, leave him alone," Eyes Too Close said, blood oozing out from between the fingers steepled over his broken nose.

Vincent turned to face him, flashing his mouthful of sharp, jagged vampire teeth. Eyes Too Close sucked in a breath, flattened himself to the blood-spattered wall and turned his eyes away.

Vincent dropped to a knee. The sun at his back did its best to weaken his supernatural strength but was unable to temper his vicious disposition. Stabbing his long thumbnail into Scarface's grimy throat, he punctured the skin and squeezed. Crimson juice oozed out like the man's neck was a grapefruit. His body jerked and spasmed. Gurgling sounds erupted from the dying man's throat as blood bubbled over his lips. Vincent buried his teeth into Scarface's throat and watched from the corner of his eye as Eyes Too Close continued to stare at the wall, his body trembling. It was always a treat to see what happened to people when they realized they were face to face with a monster. Vincent stared at the quivering man, daring him to look, to see the life drained from his street companion.

Scarface stopped moving.

Vincent let go and brought his crimson-covered thumb to his mouth. Sucking the lifeforce and reveling in its charge, he leaned into Eyes Too Close's ear and whispered, "Be grateful I don't do the same to you, you blood bag piece of shit."

He smelled urine as darkness blossomed around Eyes Too Close's crotch.

Three other vagrants farther down the street avoided eye contact as Vincent began to whistle, his thumbs hooked in the belt loops of his jeans, his long hair flowing freely. He found Fiona three blocks away at a diner called Cassie's Café.

He ducked inside, made his way to the third table from the door, and slid in beside her on the red vinyl-covered bench seat.

His hands caressed her pale cheeks and he kissed her mouth.

She moaned, tasting Scarface's blood on his lips.

When they broke the kiss, she bit her lip and asked, "What have you been up to this morning?"

"I was just about to ask you the same thing."

A smile stretched across her gorgeous face. Vincent could not stop thinking how much she looked like a redheaded Julia Roberts. She nodded toward the counter behind them. He turned and looked and saw the plump fellow eating what appeared to be a fruit salad. She seemed to like the big boys. The plumper the better. She claimed they were juicier. He loved her sick sense of humor.

He also prayed to whatever freak ruled this universe that Kat never uncovered his true relationship with Fiona. At least not anytime soon. And fuck, if she ever learned the true way Fiona became a vampire, well, that one he was taking to the grave.

She slid her hand beneath the table and clenched his thigh.

Vincent was ready to tell her to scrap whatever she had planned for this morning, so he could take her right here, right now.

Fiona's target got up, dropped his payment on the counter and headed out the door.

"You wanna come with me?" she asked.

Vincent leaned in and ran his nose across the side of her neck, inhaling her scent. Kat's orders for him to bring Fiona back to the hotel to watch the Gabriel Riley special evaporated, vanquished by his arousal. "Yeah, sure."

"You only get to watch, though," Fiona said. "This one's all mine."

CHAPTER FOUR

The slightly distorted voice on the radio sang that nothing seemed to kill him.... Rocky felt the flesh on his bones melting as he sat in the Congress Street traffic. The air conditioning in his Accord came and went as it pleased. His sister, Julie, often asked why he refused to drive a new car. The fire department had paid okay, but he could never bring himself to spend that kind of money on a brand-new vehicle. He'd given up on cool cars. He could see his uncle Arthur handing him the keys to the old Buick. The one he'd surprised him with ten years ago. His eyes teared up as the Soundgarden song gave way to a No Doubt tune he'd already heard far too many times this summer.

"I'd pay *her* not to speak," he muttered to himself as he reached forward and flicked the tuner. From Maine's alternative rock station to the Stephen King-made-famous 102.9 WBLM, aka 'The Blimp', Rocky almost laughed aloud as the chorus from Van Halen's 'Best of Both Worlds' blasted through his cracked speakers.

He leaned forward and looked out the windshield and toward the heavens. "Are you fucking kidding me, right now?" It could all be coincidence, thinking of his long-gone car from Uncle Arthur, and the Van Halen album of 1986. He could almost hear the arguments with friends playing back now: *Diamond Dave is the true voice! Van Hagar sucks!* But after falling for the girl who bought him a copy of the *5150* album, Rocky's favorite VH singer was cemented. Sammy Hagar could sing a ballad *and* a rock song. Proof positive on the speakers right here, right now. The brief sadness brought on by the thought of his uncle had passed as he finally reached the traffic light and pulled right on Forrest Avenue.

Just down the road he caught the ramp to 295 and headed south.

A small Igloo cooler sat on the floor of the passenger side. After pulling into the angry summer traffic full of Mainers pissed off about having to share the highway with invading outlanders, Rocky reached down, pawed through the ice, and drew out a cold Miller Lite. He popped the top with his forefinger and poured the beer into his travel mug. He swallowed the lager and while it didn't erase the heat, the sweat running from his hairline into his eyes, or succeed in convincing his AC to start working, it was enough to make the drive tolerable.

He'd just spent the last hour bitching to his lawyer, 'Sweet Baby' James Frost, about the network and their shitty special on his nightmares. A lot of good it did. 'Sweet Baby' James (as he'd overheard the secretary call him to another woman in the waiting room; both flushed and giggled like a couple of school girls) told him they had no case. Rocky had refused the interview requests; therefore, he'd not be in any of the shows. He could try to plead that the special would cause distress, but the cost of the most likely losing battle would not be worth it.

Rocky finished the first beer before he got past Scarborough. He popped a second and let it take the edge off. He got off the exit and hit Route 1. More bumper-to-bumper tourists versus locals met him, but he had enough of a buzz to keep his frustration at bay. He cranked up the radio. Metallica had never been one of his favorite bands back in the day, but this new song was different. Hauntingly beautiful, yet still heavy, 'Until It Sleeps' continued to rumble through his speakers as he took a left at the Dairy Joy.

He pulled into the Saco & Biddeford Savings to make a quick withdrawal and heard his name before he'd even finished parking.

"Hey! Rocky!"

The booming voice startled him. Franklin Tibbets strode to his window. The guy's beer belly was threatening to bust through a t-shirt that read: *You Wish*.

"What ya been up to, Rock?"

Franklin Tibbets was a volunteer at the fire station. He wanted to be a full-timer, but the guy got winded while fetching a cheeseburger. He came to Old Orchard Beach via Rhode Island the summer after Rocky came home. He worked on cars out of his own garage on Smith Street. He'd done some minor fixes on Rocky's Accord.

"Not much, Franklin. How about you? How's business?"

"Can't complain, man. These outlanders are helping me make some serious bank. How about you? You really finished down at the station?"

"Did Scott tell you?"

"Yeah."

"Yeah, afraid so."

"Think you could put in a good word for me?"

"Already did."

It was a lie. Outside of Rocky and Scott Jorgenson, everyone else in the department hated Franklin. They made fun of him to his face, but whether he knew it and pretended not to, Franklin never stopped showing up and hanging out. Hell, the guy even came down every Sunday during football season to grill for everyone. The rest of the department was a bunch of macho assholes, another reason Rocky was a) leaving and b) never hung out with any of them besides Scott.

Franklin smiled behind his permanently chapped lips.

"Thanks, Rock, I mean it. Thank you. You're a real stand-up guy. I don't care what Duke says about you."

"You'll earn your spot soon enough, Franklin. Listen, I gotta go in and grab some cash. You take care of yourself, all right?"

"It's after five, Rock. They're already closed."

"No shit?" Rocky looked at his watch. "Man, the day went by fast. Well, I guess I'll have to stop in tomorrow."

"You need me to loan you a few bucks for the night?"

"Ah thanks, man, no, I'm good. I didn't really need it anyway." Rocky was just going to pick up some beer money to head over to Duke's, but he could skip going out tonight.

Franklin tapped on the hood of the car. The scent of onions and body odor wafted in on the slight summer breeze, causing Rocky to make an ugly face that he hoped Franklin didn't see.

"All righty then. Bye, Rock. Thanks again."

Rocky gave him a nod as Franklin backed away. Before he'd even pulled the Honda out of his parking space, Franklin was bellowing after someone else he knew.

Rocky pulled out and headed down Old Orchard Street. He needed to stop at a store and pick up some beer. As much as he didn't want to, if he was staying in, he was going to sit down and see what kind of bullshit story they were going to try to sell and sensationalize on the TV special.

Fucking vultures.

He got home to find a note waiting for him.

Before plucking the piece of paper from the door, he stepped back and looked down each side of the street, half expecting to see November drift in and out of the swarm of people. The white piece of letter-sized paper was folded once in the middle and attached to the door with Scotch tape. He pulled it from the door and unfolded it.

Hey Rocky,

Sorry we missed you. Me, Caroline, and Olivia were in town and thought we'd swing by and see what their favorite uncle was up to. They really wanted to see the fire station again. Maybe next time. We hope you're having a good day. Stay safe!

Love Jules + the Girls

He hadn't told anyone besides the guys at the station, Duke at the Tiki Lounge, and now Franklin, that he'd left the fire department. His nieces would be bummed. Jules would probably give him grief. Rocky crumpled the note and stuffed it in the pocket of his cargo shorts.

A few hours later, Rocky settled onto his ugly, stained Salvation Army couch and set the chilled six-pack of Miller Lites on the coffee table. Checking his watch – it was eight fifty-four – he twisted the top off the first beer and downed it in a few swallows. A loud belch blasted free as he set the empty on the table and twisted the top off a second. He downed this one as quickly as the first and decided he'd sip the third, at least until the show pissed him off.

"An exclusive prime-time special.

"In the summer of 1986, a small beachside town in Maine experienced what can only be described as a nightmare come to life."

Audio clips of local residents played over scenes of the pier, the Ferris wheel, telephone poles with *Missing* posters:

"It's tragic, it's scary. I have two kids of my own."

"We don't have stuff like this happen here. This…this is like a bad dream."

Gabriel Riley's mugshot appeared as the camera slowly zoomed in on his eyes. Craig Davison's voice grew grim.

"That summer a killer arrived amongst the millions of regular tourists. A killer named Gabriel Riley."

"Fuck it." Rocky downed the rest of the third beer and was buzzing hard as he finished off the sixer and sat through the hour-long show mesmerized, enraged, and afraid. It all came rushing back, a wave ready to rise and crash over his head.

Drunk and lying on his sofa, Rocky remembered it all.

CHAPTER FIVE

Following Rocky's sister, like she had this afternoon, wasn't her norm, but Julie's little visit had November curious. Had Julie seen the commercials? Did she need to talk to Rocky about it? To plan on how to best handle the onslaught that was sure to come after its premiere tonight. November had already spotted a few intrigued twenty-somethings poking around. She heard their questions, their intentions, their naivety.

"Was Gabe Riley a man or a monster?"

"Was he a Dracula?"

"Do you believe in monsters?"

"Where were you when the killings started piling up?"

The audacity of some of these people. The thought of making a few of them into snacks passed through her mind. It was enough to bring a smile to her face. A rarity. People would forever remember her brother as the Beach Night Killer. A psychopath who murdered innocents and left a crimson stain on the tourist trap's history, but November knew Gabriel before. When he was loving and sweet, curious and brave. Her big brother, her best friend. Within two years, he lost who he was and fell to the monster in their blood. By that summer, he no longer sounded, looked, or loved like the person he was before. His lust for blood and power corrupted all that had been good within him. It was heartbreaking. When he took their mother, November buried him in her mind and soul. The creature that tried to kill her and Rocky got exactly what he deserved.

The TV special was on now, but she had no interest in reliving the trail of death left in her brother's wake. Instead, November stayed out on the beach. She reached into her purse and pulled out her headphones and Discman. Skipping ahead to track four, she hit play and let the jangly guitar and Steven Tyler's voice trickle into her ears. There really was something wrong with the world today. Dressed in a long-sleeved white shirt and cutoff jean shorts, and her Chuck Taylors (matching green, no longer the mismatched Punky Brewster of the eighties), November returned the compact disc player into the bag and made her way down the shore.

There were far worse places to be stuck in this world. Old Orchard Beach was beautiful. The summer people were all about their vacations and paid her no mind. Occasionally, she'd catch the eye of some man or woman, but love and all things connected were long-gone notions she buried down deep. Loneliness is all that she deserved. The guilt over what she'd taken from Rocky and his family would never allow her to walk happily ever after.

If Rocky could forgive me....

Not even then. And she was pretty sure his ability to forgive wasn't quite strong enough to reach that level. And to make it all the worse, he too was trapped in this isolated hell. They were both alone among the living. Were they walking, talking, breathing ghosts? In a way, yeah. Their growth as people was permanently stunted by the horrors of that summer.

The Ferris wheel rose above everything else with the gates of the seaside amusement park. The carnival ride was a landmark to many but even more so to her and Rocky, albeit for darker reasons. November watched the wheel spin and the buckets rise into the sky, but she only heard the screams from Rocky's sister as November bit into their mother's neck, the final threats and posturing of Gabriel, and Rocky's rage and pain, along with her own as they all fought for their lives.

The wheel spun against the stars but there was nothing shining. Not anymore.

In the end, they'd finished off Gabriel, and made it out alive. Changed and scarred, but still breathing. Were there any such things as ghosts? Maybe not, but everything that died that night walked hand-in-hand with her every day since. If that's not a ghost, she didn't know what was.

November spun the volume dial on her Discman, tuning out the rest of the memories, and walked like an apparition herself into the night.

CHAPTER SIX

"Why don't you take the money from the jar? You know it needs an oil change."

Eddie turned the radio down and looked at his watch. It was nearly ten in the morning. He'd promised Karla that he'd be over to take her to McDonald's for lunch. He didn't have time to take the Dodge in for an oil change. Besides, Dad usually had Franklin across the street do it for them.

He scooted off his bed and grabbed his sneakers, hopping on one foot while he tried to get the right one on. He had to put a hand out to catch his balance. The TV/VCR combo atop the bureau teetered as he got his other shoe on. Eddie grabbed his wallet from beside the combo and walked out to the hallway.

"Ma, I'll talk to Franklin about getting the oil changed this weekend."

"Edward Steven Mulligan," she said, hand on her hip, her green eyes suddenly peering over her thick glasses at him. "Do you understand how bad it is for your car's engine to go without timely oil changes? Hmmm? Do you?"

"Yeah, Ma, I do."

"I don't think that you do. Just take it to the Midas station on Route 1. It's not going to take your whole day. You can go see Candy Whatserface later."

Eddie plucked the key ring from the ceramic bowl on the kitchen counter, walked over to his mom, still standing with one hand on her hip and the other raised up in exasperation. He could smell the Virginia Slims on her as he kissed her cheek.

"Her name's Karla, Ma, not Candy Whatserface. I'll talk to Franklin before I leave and get the oil change set up for this weekend. 'Kay?"

He didn't wait for her response, he just opened the door and started out.

She followed him, stopping at the porch. "Fine, Edward, but if something happens to that engine, you're not using the truck or your father's station wagon. You hear me?"

He waved her off as he got in the car and started the engine. After pulling backward onto Smith Street, he swung the car around, and braked.

"Hey," his mother said, "I thought you were going to talk to Franklin *before* you left?"

Eddie put on his round John Lennon sunglasses and smiled. "I will. As soon as I get back. Promise. Love you, Ma."

He left her shaking her head on her way back into the house. Eddie knew Franklin wasn't home anyway. He'd seen him leave about an hour ago. Probably over to the fire station. Franklin Tibbetts was the biggest wannabe fireman you would ever meet. Nice as hell, but the guy would never cut it. You had to be in reasonably good shape and have at least a fleeting aspiration to play Superman in real life. Franklin was neither fitness guru nor aspiring savior. He was more like Roseanne's husband, Dan Conner, on the TV sitcom – a solid dude just trying to live his best life and drink a few beers while working in his garage.

As he headed toward the square, Eddie wondered if Karla would still date him when school got back into session. She was a fucking cheerleader, for Christ's sakes. As far as Eddie was concerned, he was her bad boy for the summer like the guy in *Grease*. Whatever the case, they'd had some damn good summer lovin'. He'd be a little sad. He really did like Karla. She was funny and knew a lot more about serial killers than any other girl he'd ever met. Her knowledge on the dark subject had surprised him when they started talking about Gabriel Riley, Old Orchard Beach's Beach Night Killer. And when that conversation turned to Ted Bundy and John Wayne Gacy, and she turned out to know even more about the Zodiac killer than he did, Eddie almost fell in love. *Almost.* Their romance would meet its cold reality of an ending September 3rd, no doubt. They were going to be seniors, and there was no way she was going to waste her senior year or prom night with a grungy, true-crime-lovin' hooligan who was not even considering post-high school education. Karla would go back to one of her jocks and take whatever scholarship offer to whatever out-of-state school she could. She hated Maine and made it perfectly clear that she wasn't sticking around a second longer than she had to. Eddie, on the other hand, liked his gig at the record store he worked in, Bullmoose Music. He had to drive to Brunswick every day, but the store was so cool. His boss, Brett, was awesome, and the whole staff had welcomed him with open arms back in June. In Eddie's mind, he could see himself sticking around for a long time. Brett was talking about opening more locations and he would need managers for those when the time came. Was it as glorious as, say, Tower Records in New York or Los Angeles? No, but it was the closest you were going to find outside of the real big city. He really loved it there. Being surrounded by music, playing CDs all day, and talking about bands hardly seemed like something that could legally be called 'work'. Karla would have bigger and better things on her great horizons. Eddie would be fine. Working in a record store and living by the beach sounded like the perfect life to him.

Still, Karla was special. A sappy love song came over the radio that made his heart hurt a tad more as he turned onto Karla's street. Eddie shook the sentimental lyrics from his head and tried to focus on having fun, at least for these next two weeks. Whatever the future held for them, well, that was for the universe to figure out.

He pulled into her driveway next to her sister's Accord and changed the radio to WBLM. A nice, vapid AC/DC song pounded to life as Karla came out through the screen door, her summer dress swaying. Eddie's heart continued dancing to some silly beat that was discovered and reserved only for lovers. Karla smiled and he knew that September was going to fucking hurt.

"Hey," she said, leaning in and pressing her lip-glossed mouth to his, "you need to park on the curb."

"Why?"

"I have something spectacular to show you."

"Um, yeah, sure." Eddie put the car in Reverse and backed out onto the curb like she instructed. He shut the car off and got out.

Karla held out a hand, her fingers wiggling, gesturing for him to grab hold.

"What is this?" he asked, taking her hand. She raised the clicker for the garbage door and tapped the button. "What's up?"

"You'll see," she said, giving his hand a squeeze.

The white door opened, revealing a brand-spanking-new red '96 Ford Mustang.

"Whoa." His jaw dropped as Karla pulled a set of keys from her purse and jingled them in front of him.

"My dad got it for me."

"Are you for real?" he said. A strong dose of excitement and descending self-esteem tangoed through him. There was no way a gorgeous, cool girl this fortunate would be his for much longer.

Shut up. Just fucking enjoy it while you can. Christ.

Karla held the keys out to him. "Do you want to drive?"

"Uh…is your dad cool with that?"

She moved to him, wrapping her arms around his neck, staring into his eyes. "It's my car, and I can choose who gets to drive it. Besides, my dad is out with his brother. They're probably drunk as skunks out on my uncle's boat on Sebago Lake."

"Well," he said, kissing her, "in that case, let's hit the town."

She kissed him back, handed him the keys, and let out a *wooo* that would make "Nature Boy' Ric Flair proud as she skipped around to the passenger side of the new car.

As they pulled out onto the road, Eddie put it in Drive and stepped on the gas. The tires squealed. Karla *woooooo*ed again and her fists tapped the ceiling.

Set to turn right, toward the I-95, Karla placed a hand on his wrist and looked into his eyes. "Let's go to the beach. I want to show off."

He knew she meant cruising on East and West Grand. That's where all her friends would be hanging around. Where they'd all see the two of them…together.

"Are you sure?"

She leaned across the seat and gave him a long, open-mouthed kiss. As their lips parted, she said, "I love you, Edward Mulligan. And I don't care who knows it. Take me to town."

He turned left, aiming the Mustang toward OOB.

CHAPTER SEVEN

Best summer ever.

Jonathan Roux poured two fingers of Knob's Creek into his glass and set the bottle down. He whispered, "Cheers," and swallowed it in one satisfying gulp.

"Ahh." He wiped his thumb across his lip and grinned about the reports he'd spent the evening looking over. This was the Hotel Avalon's best season yet. They'd been sold out every weekend since the last week of May and nearly every weeknight, as well. He had his parents' inheritance to thank for the opportunity to buy the place, but it was his experience in the business and his luck with putting together and keeping an excellent staff that put the Avalon among the top hotels in Old Orchard Beach.

He poured a second drink.

Knock, knock.

"Come in," he said, sliding his tumbler of bourbon just behind the stack of *Lodger Monthly* magazines.

The door to his back office opened. Nina Sanni ducked her pretty head inside. Her cocoa skin looked smooth as silk and made her emerald eyes pop. Nina was cool as hell, and she was one helluva desk agent, as well. The total package.

"Hey, Mr. Roux," she said, "are you sure you don't wanna come out tonight? The 'phin is supposed to be mad crazy tonight. You know DJ Poppy?"

"No, Nina, can't say that I do."

"Well, he's this amazing DJ from the Brooklyn club scene and he's here. Tonight."

"Thanks, Nina. Sounds awesome. It really does. You and your friends be safe, yeah?"

Nina bowed her head, and then brought her chin back up, a sly grin on her face. "Okay, Mr. Roux. But if you ever want to join us, the offer always stands."

"Believe me, if I didn't already have the finest woman in town coming to pick me up, I'd dance the night away with you. Go on. Have fun."

"Night," she said and closed the door.

Temptation was always lurking, especially in the hotel business when you were surrounded by beautiful women day in and day out, but Jonathan wasn't lying. Maggie would be here any minute. They loved taking strolls on the beach after he got out, no matter the time. She was his reason for everything. Life before her had been empty. He'd never jeopardize what they had, even for a hundred Ninas.

He intended to ask Maggie to marry him next Wednesday at the office where she worked. She'd been burned by several exes and told Jonathan on multiple occasions that she didn't intend to ever get married. She wasn't religious, she didn't have a mom hounding her to tie the knot and give her grandbabies, and she had too many friends who'd suffered through nasty divorces. She told Jonathan she loved what they had as is and saw no advantages to adding a wedding certificate.

Would it make anything better? No. But Jonathan was old-school, and he wanted to make Maggie Mae Miller his wife. He wasn't afraid of breaking up or protecting his assets or bankroll. He believed in their relationship. Early in their courtship, he promised himself that he wouldn't ask her for at least five years. January 7th marked six years since their first date, and everything between them was amazing. She told him she was pregnant two months ago. They were going to name him Elvis. Both of their fathers had been huge fans of the King of Rock 'n' Roll. The unexpected baby was a surprise that they hadn't shared with anyone else yet. Jonathan felt that a wedding would slide perfectly into that 'unexpectedly awesome' category.

He pulled the ring from the drawer in his desk and gazed upon it. He couldn't help but smile. He'd already devised the proposal. He'd come up with it five months after that first date. He and her boss were both huge Phil Collins fans. Jonathan was going to come into her work playing 'Groovy Kind of Love' on his acoustic guitar, and have her co-workers join in as he approached her cubicle. Once there, he'd finish the song and get down on one knee, present her with a bouquet of peonies and the ring, and ask her to be his forever.

Holding the ring in his hand, he wondered if he'd be able to wait until Wednesday. He closed the little black box and put it in his pocket.

Jonathan stood as the lights went out.

What the hell?

He stepped out to the front desk and found the lobby in total blackness.

"Marc?" he called. Marc Hebert was his night auditor. The guy had never been late in his three years at the Avalon. He was the epitome of reliable; besides, Nina would have mentioned Marc calling in or being late.

"Marc? Are you here?"

The shocker wasn't the power outage. They'd had surges in town during high-heat days like today, or during harsh winter storms, but the generator should have kicked on by now.

Beyond that, the truly disturbing aspect was the complete and total silence.

Not even one guest tromping down the stairs complaining, calling the desk to see what was going on.

Something was terribly wrong.

"Hello?" The darkness seemed to swallow his voice.

A door – the east stairwell – opened.

He turned but saw no one.

The skin at the nape of his neck pulled taut.

To hell with this.

The lobby entrance was blocked.

Even in the shadows, Jonathan could see a shape between him and the front exit.

"Can I help you?" Jonathan said.

"I'm going to need to borrow your hotel for the next few weeks." The coolness in the man's voice made Jonathan's stomach turn.

"Ha," he half-laughed, trying his best not to sound frightened. "Excuse me? Are you a guest here?"

The shape in the entranceway was gone.

Jonathan was breathing like he'd just run a 5k at full speed.

He went to the front desk and felt beneath the computer, finding the black flashlight they kept there for times like these. He clicked it on. When he spun back to the lobby area, the bright yellow beam shone upon two people: a man with long dark hair and a woman, her hair like curly fiery embers.

"All right," he said. "Enough is enough. I'm calling the police."

He grabbed the phone and held it to his ear. There was no dial tone.

"Yeah, that's not going to happen," the man said.

The nearly six-foot intruder was suddenly standing right beside Jonathan.

"Impossible," Jonathan whimpered as he stumbled toward his office and tripped over something on the floor.

He fell face to face with Marc Hebert, his tardy night auditor. The flashlight beam spilled across Marc's pale face. Marc's brown eyes were open and staring off into nothing. Blood oozed from the ruined flesh of his throat.

"M-M-Marc...oh, oh my G-God."

Marc's body was yanked away, revealing a second body.

The body looked as though someone had sucked the air out of it. In its current state, it could be any woman, any guest from the hotel, if not for the fresh Elvis tattoo on her forearm.

Her name fell from his lips. "Maggie."

"She was delicious," the being behind him said.

Jonathan's gaze was locked on to his girlfriend's dead body, his eyes sticking to her tummy and their unborn baby.

The monsters stepped between them.

Jonathan rolled to his back and aimed the flashlight at the killers standing over him.

"Jesus, what the hell are you?" he cried.

The two fiends opened their mouths and descended upon him.

The Avalon Hotel's current guests, those not fed upon, left the hotel after finding notes beneath their doors claiming the hotel was closed effective immediately. The empty desk and office offered no refunds and did nothing to find them new accommodations. Cancellation notices and full refunds had been dealt to all its future registered guests, claiming the hotel had been sold and would be closed until further notice.

Jonathan Roux had apparently sold out and left without a trace.

CHAPTER EIGHT

Franklin closed the hood of the Dodge Caravan. Even for an eight-year-old vehicle, having to swap out a cooling fan seemed a bit premature. The best Franklin could figure, it may have been damaged in the fender bender Arletta LePage got into earlier this year. She rear-ended some outta-stater back in June. Said they "just slammed on their brakes". Huh, Arletta was a space cadet soccer mom. Hot as hell, but flaky as all get out. She was probably messing with her makeup and not paying a damn bit of attention.

Franklin finished wiping what grease he could from his hands, picked up his can of iced tea, walked down to the edge of his driveway and plopped down in the lawn chair there. Across the road, he saw the Mulligan kid and his girlfriend in a brand-new red Mustang. Ugliest cool car Ford ever made in Franklin's opinion, but the kids seemed proud of it. They were making out like crazy. Franklin smiled and raised his glass. Good for them. The car was still fugly, though.

Next door to the Mulligan house was Allan Jeffries' place. The only Black guy in the neighborhood. He was always nice to Franklin, so if he liked dudes, whatever, good for him. Pink flamingos lined Allan's walkway; the guy also had some pretty flowers in his fancy little garden. Jeffries' yard was just as nice as the Younglings' at the other end of the street. Nathan Youngling, however, was about as opposite of pretty as you could get. The fat old asshole thought he was a gift to the Earth sent from above. Rich thanks to his many years as head of the Saco & Biddeford Savings in town, since retired, he now rode around in his BMW with his nose up in the air. He looked down on regular joes like Franklin. Fuck him. His wife was a zoned-out Prozac popper. She followed Nathan around like a half-asleep living doll.

Franklin wished they'd sell the house and move to Kennebunkport to be with the rest of their kind.

The night was clear, warm, and perfect for people-watching. Right now, just sitting here reminded Franklin of one of his favorite movies, *The 'Burbs*. All he needed was a set of creepy neighbors to move in next door. Instead he had Patty Beverly. She was just the sweetest old lady, had a couple cats and an ugly little pup, he couldn't recall the dog's name, Cutie or Cookie, something dumb like that, but he loved Patty. She always brought him molasses cookies. They were freaking de-lish.

Franklin found himself humming along with a Bob Seger song playing on the radio in the garage as his gaze drifted to the headlights turning onto the street. A beautiful classic Volkswagen van, bright yellow like the Beatles submarine, rolled up the road. He raised a hand and waved as the vehicle passed. To his surprise, the brake lights came to life. The Volkswagen van sat idling. A sick feeling niggled into Franklin's stomach. The windows of the van were dark, but he could see forms moving, shadows undulating behind the glass. The VW sat perfectly still in the road. Were this any other vehicle, at any other time, Franklin would be on his feet and headed toward the van to see if anything was the matter. His ass was cemented into the lawn chair. A bare-naked Heather Locklear couldn't get him out of his goddamn chair. A cold sweat broke over his skin like the temperature surrounding him suddenly dropped. He gripped the arms of the cheap lawn chair, his clammy hands slick on the plastic edges. It was stupid, but he'd rather look like an ignorant fool than step any closer to this vehicle.

The sound of two car doors shutting across the street broke the trancelike gaze Franklin had on the van. The Mulligan boy and his girl were at the edge of the Mulligans' driveway, staring at the idling van. Neither got any closer.

The brake lights vanished, and the van rolled along. And just like that, whatever weight that had been pressing down on Franklin's soul seemed to abate and dissolve.

He managed to peel his hand free from the arm of the chair and give a wave to the Mulligan kid and his girl.

The kid nodded before the cute young woman grabbed him by the hand and dragged him to the light (and safety) of the porch. They went inside the house and Franklin suddenly felt too alone out there beneath the summer night sky. He found himself looking both ways down the street as he climbed from the chair and headed for his garage. WBLM, the local classic rock station, played 'Don't Fear the Reaper'. While he loved the song, right now, it made his skin crawl. He switched the radio off and pulled the garage door closed.

He stood for a few more minutes watching out the little window, expecting the yellow Volkswagen to come back.

Franklin never wanted to see that classic van again.

CHAPTER NINE

Jeremy grabbed his formidable friend in a headlock.

"You better let go, man." Ben was never one to be manhandled. Jeremy knew this but the opportunity to show his best friend that not only could Jeremy hold his own, but maybe, just maybe he could get the upper hand, at least from time to time, had him pushing the limits. The play was a dangerous one as Ben's temper could blast a hole through concrete, but with his hands clasped around Ben's neck, Jeremy pushed a little more.

Ben tried to pull free but couldn't. Jeremy smirked and tightened his grip. His boots knocked over the spray paint. His half-finished Shadowrun character's silhouette, viewable by the light of the full moon above, made his smile grow.

Ben growled and raised Jeremy off his feet, tossing the two-hundred-plus-pounder like a man half his size. Jeremy's moment of dominance was over as Ben's head slipped from his grasp and Jeremy found himself plummeting to the paved parking lot of the abandoned seaside hotel.

"I told you to let fucking go," Ben said, spitting to his right, his breath coming in angry gasps. "Why don't you fucking listen?"

Jeremy propped himself up on an elbow and started laughing.

"Yeah, it's gonna be real funny when I knock the shit out of you. Get up and finish this before the cops see us." Ben rubbed his throat with one hand and motioned toward Jeremy's graffiti with the other. "Fucking nitwit."

Jeremy got to his feet, patting Ben on the back as he walked by him.

Ben shrugged him off and started pacing. "Don't fucking touch me. I'm pissed."

"Sorry," Jeremy offered as he bent and snatched up one of the cans of paint. He had a bad habit of pushing people's buttons, especially when he knew them as well as he knew Ben. It was borderline asshole-ish, but Jeremy felt like getting people uncomfortable did more good than bad. Did they temporarily hate him for it? Sure. But his good friends, his real friends, like Ben, were loyal. And Jeremy felt like Ben, of all his friends, 1) needed it more than others, and 2) understood what he was trying to do and grew with each challenge.

"I'm leaving," Ben said.

Jeremy knew he'd pushed too far, and Ben usually needed space, a couple hours, sometimes a day or two to get over Jeremy's antics.

"Sure," Jeremy said, shaking the can. "See you for football Sunday?"

"Yeah," Ben said, pulling his keys from his pocket. "You fine walking home?"

"Of course."

As Ben opened the door to his Oldsmobile, Jeremy said, "Hey."

"Yeah?"

"What do you think really happened to this place? Who closes during the summer in a beach town and vanishes?"

"Who knows," Ben said. "Maybe someone died?"

"No. I don't believe it. There's something really messed up about this. Look at it. It's beautiful. The Avalon is one of the nicest hotels in town."

"Yeah, I don't fucking know. Maybe you should go the Better Business Bureau and find out. I'm going home. I have to work in the morning."

"Later," Jeremy said.

Ben nodded as Jeremy went back to his art. The Oldsmobile started up, the headlights spilled their dim glow across the otherwise empty lot and drifted out and away from the suddenly abandoned hotel as Ben backed into the road and took off.

Alone, Jeremy sang a Monty Python song, wistfully finishing his latest masterpiece. He'd found this spot the other night when he started camping at the KOA over in Saco. He'd decided when he got back from his two-year stint with the Army that he was going to live by his own rules. Being ordered to keep your appearance and clothes a certain way had knocked who he really had been out of his head and heart. It was difficult. He figured it usually worked the other way around and brainwashed people, clean-slated them and sent them back into society well behaved and conformed, perfect soldiers for society. Well, that was true of the non-combat service soldiers. Men like his own father, who'd served in Vietnam, on the other hand…well, they just never developed beyond that scarred point in their lives.

The first thing Jeremy did with his money when he was out was buy an RV. His mother tried to keep him at home, but he needed to be out and on the move. He decided he was going to work his way across the state before heading out across the country. The next thing he did was grow his hair out and dye it purple. His friends here in Maine seemed to think he was going crazy, but he knew it was just scary to some people to see such sudden changes in someone you think you know; it was jarring. Ben seemed to get it the most. He'd crack a joke about the hair or nomadic lifestyle and that'd be it. It was funny. Ben would benefit the most to just let the hell go and break out of the mold. The guy was still walking as straight a line in life as he could. No rocking the boat for that guy. Well, he did hang out and smoke cigarettes while Jeremy went about his other new favorite hobby – spray-painting abandoned buildings. The teen version of his friend wouldn't have stuck around for that, let alone drive him to the places.

Headlights and the sound of a running engine caught his attention. He let his finger off the spray nozzle and glanced toward West Grand Avenue. Maybe Ben had decided to come back. Only…the vehicle sitting in the road was not an Oldsmobile. A memory of being a kid left alone in the backseat of his parents' car while they ran into the grocery store slithered to the front of his mind. When a blocky, green Dodge van rolled up into the empty space next to his parents' station wagon and the strange man in sunglasses and a fat walrus mustache glared at him from behind the steering wheel. Jeremy had pissed his pants that afternoon. Just the threat he perceived as a child left alone to the elements of life…. Alone to the elements of life, just like he was now. And the fear that filled that seven-year-old version of himself in the backseat of his parents' wagon was suddenly here with him now. He swallowed hard as he waited to see what the vehicle was going to do.

His heartbeat pulsed in his neck.

The thought of how that pulse in that particular spot on the human body could be a beacon…to the wrong sort of element…drifted through his head.

And just like that, the vehicle, a yellow van, drove away.

Jeremey hurried to his backpack, brought it to where his paints were and loaded them in as quickly as he could. He was done here for the night, maybe forever. He zipped the pack and shouldered it. As he hit the edge of the lot, the headlights came back from the opposite direction.

You don't know that that's the same vehicle.

But part of him did. The primal part of his consciousness that sensed danger was telling him that beyond a shadow of a doubt, this was the same van. This was one of the elements in life he was very much vulnerable to…. It also screamed in his mind for him to run. And he did.

Standing like a shadow beneath the streetlight at the end of the road, a slender figure started his way. Jeremy stopped and looked back at the van behind him. It hadn't moved.

"Hell with this," he said, and ran back into the hotel parking lot and stopped.

A second figure appeared to be admiring his art.

"This is pretty shitty, you know," the man said.

Jeremy's heart thrummed harder against his chest as he looked around for an escape route. Glancing over his shoulder, he saw the van now blocking the street. The slender figure now stood in the lot to his left, guarding the fence leading to the side street.

How'd they move so fast, so silently?

His only option was the hotel. Were the doors even open? He cursed himself for not checking before, but breaking and entering wasn't on his list of things to do. Now he had no choice. He bolted for the front entrance. He expected to hear footfalls in pursuit but heard nothing save for his own breathing and boots on the pavement.

He slammed into the door, which refused to budge. There were large chains around the bars of the door and an enormous padlock.

The strangers, the ones he could see, hadn't moved. On the ground at his feet lay a small pile of broken bits of tar. He bent and grabbed the largest chunk and slammed it against the glass pane of the door. The glass splintered and he did not hesitate to smash it two more times before it shattered. He could feel wetness trickling from several spots on his hand. Ignoring the wounds, Jeremy raced blindly into the darkness within. He managed to find the stairwell door and rushed in, using the handrail to hurry up the steps.

He needed to hide. Would they follow him?

He stopped at the third floor and used the wall to work his way down the hallway. Each door he tried was locked. Halfway down the hall, between the two moonlit windows at either end, he leaned his sweat-drenched back against the wall, his head swiveling back and forth.

He tried to control his breathing and listened. There was complete and suffocating silence.

Good, he thought. *Just leave. Just leave and leave me alone.*

The seconds turned to a minute, to two minutes. His pulse began to settle. His sight had acclimated to the shadow-filled hall. They were gone, or they didn't feel like breaking any laws to...to what? Scare him?

How had they moved so fast? Unless they were many. Maybe that wasn't the same girl who went from the streetlight to the parking lot. Maybe the van was full of these assholes. Safe or not, Jeremy wasn't heading back out until he was certain the coast was clear. He started toward the window that ended by the street.

He could just make out the edge of the parking lot. The van was gone.

Jeremy gave a nervous laugh in relief. And turned to see the silhouette of the man who'd commented on his art at the opposite end of the hallway. Jeremy burst through the door to his left and was halted by a shape in the blackness.

It was the slender woman. He wagered on his own size and strength and tried to drive through her. Instead, he was grabbed by unseen hands and flung hard into the wall. Something in his shoulder snapped as he fell to the stairs and tumbled down to the next landing.

"Don't worry, it'll only hurt for a few seconds," a woman's voice whispered just before dagger-like nails sunk into the side of his head just above his ear and pinned his other ear to his shoulder. Pain exploded in his neck as the woman punctured his throat with her bite.

The undead.

The thought was snuffed out as the pain in his neck increased, like something was impossibly trying to suck his soul through the tiniest holes in his flesh. Jeremy's scream filled the stairwell.

He cried out for what felt like eternity. A numbness floated over the pain. And it was…nice. A morphine bisque warmed his insides, his neck, and finally, his mind. He felt the monster pull free from his throat and his body being dragged up the stairs. His head thumped over each step, but it didn't hurt, nothing did. A ridiculous smile split his face as he was dragged into the moonlit end of the hallway.

Three pale faces hovered above his own.

This is…the end.

Closing his eyes, Jeremy welcomed his death. It was warm and nice…until it wasn't.

Something fist-sized pierced his chest. The pain cut through the numbed haze and ruptured every possible nerve in his body. He felt sharpness as something burst through his chest cavity and he knew what it was in search of. He tried to scream again but his shriek was quickly cut short. His eyes shot open as he saw one of them holding part of his throat in one hand. Another held his still-beating heart.

The vision of these two beasts feeding upon parts of him was suddenly overshadowed by the male figure grinning like the Cheshire cat before baring its curved, blade-like fangs and biting into the open wound across the front of his neck.

His brain registered the pain and the sounds for another thirty seconds or so and then, Jeremy was finally spared his last anguishing moments of life.

CHAPTER TEN

"Where the hell are you going?" Vincent said. He was buckling his belt as he came out of the bathroom.

Kat reached into her bag and pulled out a notebook and a handheld voice recorder. "Katherine Collins, reporter, *The Scene*. I'm here in the beautiful seaside town of Old Orchard Beach, Maine, where ten years ago, a man by the name of Gabriel Riley slaughtered more than a dozen locals and tourists. But was Riley really just a man?"

She cocked an eyebrow at him. Vincent queered his mouth and shook his head. "Too fuckin' early for this. You look great, though. You seen Fiona this mornin'?"

Yeah, she thought. *Right after I saw you crawling away from her room last night.* Kat kept the thought to herself. The girl was his to train and keep track of, no proof they were doing more than that. Not yet anyway.

"No. I don't think she's awake. Probably still in whichever room she chose."

Vincent pulled a cigarette from his pack on the nightstand and lit it. He blew the smoke from the side of his mouth and nodded. "How many you think you'll find today?"

She'd made a list of locals who had been here during the murders and were still listed as current residents. She crossed off any over the age of sixty and any under twenty-five. She also scratched off any who were in college or serving in the military during that time. The list was still large, but she was certain she'd whittle it down by the end of the day. The star, the person responsible for the death of Riley, one Rocky Zukas, was at the top of the list. She was hoping to bump into him as soon as possible. The fire department was her first planned stop.

According to what she'd found on him through various phone calls, he'd been working there since coming home three years ago.

Kat placed the notebook and recorder in her bag, tossed it over her shoulder and headed for the door. "Hopefully, the right ones. The less time wasted the better."

Vincent walked to the window across the room. "I don't know. I'm in no hurry." He looked back, grinning. "Last night was a shit ton of fun."

She knew that they'd feed while in town, the unlucky bastard they'd taken last night just happened to be in the wrong place at the wrong time. She couldn't deny the thrill, the rush, and the chase the kill had given her. That kind of hunt was long overdue. It was always best when they were terrified. The way their blood pumped wildly through their veins. The way their breathing quickened right up until the point that their hearts began to slow, and death came calling.

A surge of energy from the fresh memory ran through her like a current sparking in the dark.

Vincent smirked. He saw it. She knew he felt it, too. Caffeine had nothing on what quenched their thirst.

Vincent took a last drag off his cigarette, shoved the window open further and tossed the butt out into the daylight. "Have fun."

"What are you going to do?"

"I'd go back to bed, but I just feel too goddamn good. Maybe I'll go for a stroll."

"Just be smart."

He strutted across the room and kissed her cheek. "Aren't I always?"

No, you aren't, especially with little miss nightmare along.

"Stay on top of her," Kat said, regretting her choice of words as soon as they slipped past her lips. "She's your responsibility. We want to stay quiet, at least for a few days."

Vincent turned on the television. A music video of Marilyn Manson riding a black, oiled-up pig came on. Kat dug this version of the song, but still preferred the original Eurythmics version.

She walked out the door and into the hallway. The hotel was perfect. Secluded, empty, yet right in town. Vincent had found the place. What he lacked in restraint he made up for in preparation. He'd grown in that aspect. He always seemed to know what he was doing. He always set things up just like he wanted them. It made him reliable. It was always his inability to stay on task once they were in the middle of something that kept him under her thumb.

Kat stepped from the back exit of the Avalon. They'd parked the van on the next cross street. Better to keep things optically copacetic. The police had discovered the remains of the body two days ago. Vincent dumped it on the shore – well, most of it. The man's hands and feet he left outside the arcade. What Vincent found amusing surely scarred some snotty punk kids and put a gruesome end to their summer vacation. The find was kept from the papers and TV news, at least so far. An unidentified body found on the beach. That was all they said. No report of murder or dismemberment. It was a dumb move, but one they would probably get away with thanks to the timing. No way did the town want to scare the flood of incomers on their way from the TV special.

Kat unlocked the van, climbed behind the wheel and started the old VW. The fire department was on Saco Avenue, surrounded by a few maple and pine trees. She smiled. The sign at the corner read:

Town of Old Orchard Beach
"It's a Shore Thing"

She parked the van in the mostly empty parking lot, killed the engine, grabbed her bag, and headed toward the front doors. Two men – one fat-gutted with a black t-shirt and dirty jeans, and the other, a sturdy-looking, mustached man in a navy-blue shirt with *OOB Rescue Squad* emblazoned over the right breast – stood outside the closed bay door. She recognized the chunky one from a couple nights ago. He'd been sitting in a driveway drinking and watching his neighborhood. He also saw her that night. Kat wondered if he'd say anything or if the fear would keep his mouth shut.

Both men turned to greet her.

Kat gave a toothy smile. "Hi, guys."

"Hey," the mustached one said, taking her in as she stepped toward them. "Something I can help you with?"

T-shirt and Jeans saw her and dropped his gaze.

He remembers.

"Yeah, I hope so. Is Rocky Zukas working today?"

Moustache placed his hands on his hips. "'Fraid Rocky doesn't work here anymore, ma'am. Are you a friend of his?"

Doesn't work here anymore? She wasn't ready for that.

"Oh, yeah, sorry, I haven't talked with him in a while. Do you mind if I ask what happened?"

T-shirt and Jeans refused to lock eyes with her, preferring to look everywhere else instead.

"Not sure, really," Moustache said. "He just looked tired of it. Happens sometimes."

"Do you happen to know where he lives? I'd love to catch up with him."

"I can't give you his home address, no offense. You seem nice and all, but if you stop in at Duke's along the pier tonight, or any night, really, you'll probably bump into him. Pretty thing like you, I'm sure he'll say hello."

She smiled and opened her notebook and jotted *Duke's* and *pier* onto the page.

"What's up with the notebook?" T-Shirt and Jeans asked, averting his gaze as soon as it caught her own.

"Oh, I have the worst memory. Better to write it down. Thanks, guys."

As she gave Moustache another smile and turned, T-shirt and Jeans spoke again. "How did you say you know Rocky?"

She turned back. "We went to school together, but it's been forever since we last talked."

"Funny," the man said. "*I* went to school with him. I don't recall ever seeing you before."

This guy was annoying the piss out of her. She tried to keep the irritation from her face, though her smile faltered slightly. "Oh, I didn't go here very long. Probably no one would remember me. It was like half a year in sixth grade."

Damn it, she was giving this asshole too much information. He was going to call her on the bullshit again.

Only, he didn't.

"Huh," he said, dropping his gaze to his shoes again. "Probably right."

"Try Duke's," Moustache said. "You'll find him."

"Thanks again," she said.

From the van, she watched as T-shirt and Jeans slapped Moustache on the shoulder and hurried toward the sidewalk. He stopped at a silver and blue motorcycle parked at the curb. After donning a white helmet, he kick-started the bike and pulled into the road.

She considered following him. She imagined running him off the road and tearing the shit out of him in the ditch.

Later.

He obviously knew Rocky. He may even be friends with him. She could see him going to Rocky now and giving him a head's-up about the lady asking about him. The urge to hurt this man or to follow him faded. She'd find Rocky tonight. Duke's seemed like the best way to bump into him without looking like a total creep.

Kat started the van and moved on. There were others to talk to. Ending the evening with a drink with her star target would do just fine.

CHAPTER ELEVEN

In her small apartment two towns over in Biddeford, November sat in the darkness listening to 'Let It Be'. The simple piano resonated with warmth and hopefulness. Paul McCartney's voice soothed her fears and the hurt, and made the loneliness bearable, if only for four minutes and twenty seconds.

The dramatic current coursing through her heart was fit for a more epic turn. There was no grand, gothic castle. No ocean between her and Rocky. It was, however, the nineties. Kurt Cobain had delivered John Lennon-level impact with both his talent and his untimely demise. While their deaths were different, the shock and despair shook a generation to its core. The economy was in the toilet, drugs were destroying young lives across the country and depression seemed to be all the rage. And there was a shit-ton of rage. You could feel it building, but it wasn't just a horde of angry young men this time; the ladies were suddenly roaring. Alternative radio was ruled by anthems of female empowerment.

November could identify with the frustrations she was hearing vocalized over the airwaves. It was so many things all at once. At twenty-six, she was in a world that might as well not even know she was there. She'd become invisible...and worse, she'd accepted it. The juxtaposition of being alone with everyone was something she saw and connected with in these female rock superstars. November cherished interviews where these larger-than-life gods let the door open just a crack and exposed the vulnerable, frightened kids inside, dropping lines about not knowing who to trust. Who loved you? Who wanted to fuck you? Who wanted to use you? November had no one, so maybe even someone who wanted to fuck her over would have been better. Being a monster did not help. Living with what she'd done to Rocky only made it worse. She knew it wasn't like she had a choice at the time, being barely sixteen and victimized by her ruthless brother, but facts can't negate facts. She'd done terrible things.

November turned off the stereo. She had to head out to work. She slipped into a pair of Vans and set out for Whitman's Funeral Home. The job was something to keep her busy. She'd vacuum, dust, wipe down furniture and showroom caskets, and do whatever general touch-ups the Whitmans asked. It was quiet, she was always alone, and she could listen to her Discman. A welcome cool breeze wrapped around her, prickling gooseflesh to life on her arms as she drifted down the sidewalks. Being ignored and unseen wasn't always insufferable. She appreciated being left to her thoughts on these evening strolls. However, loneliness was a permanent fixture. Her gaze stuck on couples holding hands, heads on shoulders, getting lost in each other's eyes, and her heart gave its dim thumps somewhere in the cold cellar of her chest, reminders of *him*.

Sighing, she crossed her arms over her chest and bowed her head, leaving the lovers behind.

Standing in the setting sun, surrounded by people in Mechanic's Park that she would never know, November stared at the Saco River. She often had thoughts of jumping in and just letting the undertow take her. The moments of wanting to die swelled within her constantly. She was not immortal. Death could be achieved with ease, and with it all this baggage, all this weight. But there was one reason she never did it. Rocky.

She checked her watch. There were two things in her life that gave her some purpose or sense of meaning. One was the two days a week she spent cleaning the funeral home. The other weekly joy was the three hours on Wednesday overnights from twelve to three a.m. when she got to DJ at WMPG, the little college radio station. Phone calls and requests were few and far between, but occasionally, a listener would contribute, suggesting a song that might fit the night's playlist. November had discovered a handful of artists thanks to those few listeners. She never gave her name, preferring to call herself Midnight, and her show Midnight's Moods. As far as she could ascertain, she had at least three loyal listeners. A guy named Jason, and two girls, Nancy and Stevie. The trio didn't phone in every week, but often enough for her to remember them. Jason liked hair bands and seemed to be pining over someone as he constantly suggested power ballads. Nancy tended to love Smashing Pumpkins and Nirvana, while Stevie was more enamored with the crop of ladies screaming out their souls – Alanis Morrisette, Gwen Stefani, Liz Phair, Sarah McLachlan, Tori Amos. The trio of listeners kept her playlists varied, which she loved. Along with her own eighties favorites and newer tracks, Midnight's Moods were many. The small audience gave her a sliver of connection with the real world and the humans in it.

She reached the bus stop just as the large, silver Southern Maine City Transport bus came to a stop. She liked to take the bus into Saco, especially in the daylight hours. Howy Lomeyer waved from behind the wheel. He was one of the only humans she had any sort of regular contact with. The large Black man was cool as hell.

"Hey, Howy," she said, stepping onto the city transport.

He looked at his watch and said, "Hey, girly, you just made it."

"I know."

"What was you, on a date?"

"Yeah, with four pretty cool lads from Liverpool."

"Lemme guess, John, Paul, George and Ringo?"

"You got it, Howy."

"Ah, I gotchoo, girl. Love, love me do…."

She smiled as he crooned, and made her way to the back of the bus.

November closed her eyes and leaned her head against the

window. Within minutes, she nodded off.

"Hey, girly!"

Howy's voice woke her.

"It's your stop, sleepyhead."

She stood and walked down the aisle. "Thanks, Howy. Have a good night, okay?"

"You, too, girly."

November stepped onto the sidewalk and started toward Whitman's. It was just at the edge of the Saco–Old Orchard Beach town line. She wondered what she'd do if Rocky ever drove by her. Would he recognize her? Would he stop? He'd probably convince himself it wasn't her and keep going.

A yellow 1960s Volkswagen van cruised by, seeming to slow as it passed her.

The hairs on November's neck and arms lifted. Two hooded figures stared in her direction. A man and a young woman. The vehicle stopped.

Her heart stammered in her chest.

Unsure of the reason for the skin-crawling vibes, November stopped in her tracks, prepared for anything. A third person, another woman in the back, smiled a pearly white grin as she reached up and pulled a dark shade down between them. The man in the front passenger seat turned his attention to the road ahead of them. The sunshiny VW bus rolled forward, and November saw the mother and child up ahead at the edge of the crosswalk.

See, they didn't stop to look at you. They don't know. They let the mother and child cross the road.

To get to the other side.

But they looked at me like…like….

They didn't recognize her. No one did. Vampires don't walk in the light of day. Hollywood had given her the best sleight of hand imaginable.

Still…it felt like the man and woman had…*what?*

Seen me. The real me.

The vintage van, warped by the heat coming off the blacktop, turned up the center street and was gone.

In the warmth of the afternoon sun, November shivered.

CHAPTER TWELVE

As he drove home in the crappy five o'clock traffic, coming from yet another useless visit with his lawyer in Portland, Rocky's blood boiled in his veins. He'd made himself sit through three nights of that goddamn Beach Night Killer special and he couldn't shake the feelings of helplessness and anger the program had instilled in him. Being the surviving victim of something so heinous wasn't easy on the best of days, but the show had done just what he thought it would, and now every asshole reporter was calling him, hounding him for his side of the story.

Poor timing caused Rocky to have to stop at the train tracks. The dinging and red blinking lights always drove him nuts. As the black-and-white-striped arms came down, blocking traffic from the tracks, he saw the yellow Volkswagen van on the other side. In it, a woman in shades seemed to be singing along to something. Her head stopped weaving and her mouth fell still as she pulled down her sunglasses and stared across the tracks right in his direction. Their eyes met just before the train broke the spell.

A strange sensation trickled through his body, accompanied by the urgent need to see her.

"Come on, come on already."

Tapping his thumbs on the steering wheel, he was chewing his lip in anticipation. He watched the moving boxcars until the caboose came into sight.

And there she was. She had her sunglasses back in place, but she was still staring at him. His mouth went dry and he swallowed hard. His stomach felt funny, swimming with slick, cold vibes. The railroad crossing arms raised, and the VW crossed the track. Car horns blared to life behind him, but Rocky just followed her as she drove past. She appeared to laugh on her way by.

"Buddy, get the fuck out of the way!"

Rocky waved a hand at his rearview, acknowledging the loudmouth behind him as he put the car in Drive. He glanced in the rearview, looking for the yellow van again, but it was already gone.

For a few minutes, the world stopped, and he forgot who he was and why he was so upset.

Rocky walked into Duke's and made his way to the bar.

Duke Peleke was an Old Orchard Beach transplant by way of Hawaii, but he'd been here since the late seventies. He opened the little tiki bar in the summer of 1980, two years after the Blizzard of '78 destroyed the old pier. Duke's was a staple of the OOB scene and had been here ever since. He closed for five months out of the year, from November to April, when he flew home to the islands to spend time with family.

"Aloha, bruh," Duke said, grinning from ear to ear.

"Duke," Rocky said, taking up a stool at the end of the bar as a group of couples fed each other shots. "A Miller Lite and a shot of Jager."

"Coming right up, boss."

"Oh shit, are you fucking kidding me?" the girl next to him, a brunette with heavy eyelids, said. "It's him. It's the fucking...the fucking guy."

"Who?" said the square-jawed bro beside her. The jock leaned back and eyeballed Rocky.

"The fucking guy from the thing. The serial-killer shit."

"This guy's a serial killer?" the jock asked, his face all screwed up in disbelief.

"No, he got away. He survived. That's you, right?" she said, leaning in close enough for him to smell the whiskey pouring off her like Chanel Old #7 on the Rocks.

"No, I don't think so," he said, taking his drinks as Duke placed them down. Rocky gave Duke a nod and downed the shot.

"You sure?" the drunk girl said. "'Cuz...you look just like him, I think."

"Babe, this guy ain't nobody. Look at him. He's just some local drunk."

"He's right," Rocky said. He held up the beer. "Sorry. Cheers?"

"Yeah, I guess maybe you're right." She turned back to her group of friends, and they all laughed.

This fucking bullshit was going to get old quick. He didn't want to have to wear a disguise to come out to his favorite spots, but if this kept up, he wouldn't have much of a choice.

Rocky finished his drink in peace; Duke dropped off two more Miller Lites and another shot. "That one's on me, bruh. Sorry you gotta deal with this hassle. Guess you were right."

Rocky lifted the shot glass. "To the rest of my summer."

"Hold up," Duke said. He grabbed another shot glass and poured himself one. "Okole Maluna!"

"Okole Maluna!"

They clinked glasses and downed the shots.

Duke had taught Rocky the Hawaiian saying for 'bottom's up' the first night he stopped into the little lounge to drink his sorrows away. That had been shortly after hearing about Rocky's cousin Axel's death. Axel had been Rocky's best friend all growing up. Sex, drugs, and rock 'n' roll found a way to take him down way too young. His cousin passed away the Christmas after Rocky came home from the crappy apartment they'd shared in New York City. Axel had contracted AIDS somewhere along the way and became another rock 'n' roll casualty.

This bar had been the church Rocky came to for salvation and Duke was the reverend who helped guide him through the hurt and the guilt. He'd come close dozens of times to telling Duke about November, but as far as he could recall, he'd been able to keep that little secret. Even in the aftermath of that final showdown with her psychotic, murderous brother, no one ever heard or printed her name.

November had managed to stay out of the special, as well. She was a specter. Was she ever really there? His heart felt her presence. The story told and the big rumor being stoked to life right now was that there had to have been a second killer. Someone tied to Gabriel Riley. It was only a matter of time before someone tried to track down the killer's family. If they had tried, the paths only led to dead ends. Vampires had remained undetected by society for a reason. They were stealthy out of necessity.

Sometimes, like right now with the alcohol spilling into his system, Rocky wanted to let it go, let it out, to tell someone about that summer, about November. Julie told him he could always call, but he didn't want to pin back dead skin and keep those old wounds open for her either. She had Jase and Henry.

The bar filled in around him, the drinks continued to free him slowly, a river forever winding and pulling him along as the night stretched out into another hazy prologue to some eventual nightmare.

Rocky slid off his stool and had to grab hold of some dude's shoulder to keep from falling on his ass.

"Sorry," he muttered. The guy glared at him and then went back to his conversation with the three girls on the other side of him.

Lucky dog.

Duke's was so full, it felt like it had to be the only bar open on the pier, which of course wasn't the case. Still, Rocky had to walk sideways to make it to the bathroom. Once he got to the tiny corner room, he had to wait in line behind three dudes the size of lumberjacks, only their flannels were still wrapped around their waists. Two of them had stolen Billy Idol's bleached-spike look, while the third was stuck in the hair band days.

Rocky was next in line when he just happened to glance over his shoulder.

His heart skipped a beat.

A beautiful woman walked into the bar. Her hair was long black curls. Dark eyebrows knit over eyes that seemed to search the place until they found him. Rocky froze, his mouth suddenly dry.

She gave him a sly smile.

"All yours," one of the Billy Idols said, holding the bathroom door open for him.

"Oh, thanks," Rocky said.

He glanced over his shoulder before entering. The stunning woman was gone.

Rocky shook his head and walked in.

After relieving himself for what felt like an hour, Rocky found his way outside. He needed fresh air. A walk home seemed about right.

The seaside town was in full bloom, the Ferris wheel standing like a sentinel over them all. The scents of pizza, burgers, Lisa's Pier Fries, cigarettes, gasoline, and spots of marijuana filled the humid air as he made his way off the pier and started toward West Grand Avenue. He stopped at the fence of Palace Playland, the little amusement park that Old Orchard held dear, and was transported through time. Ten years gone in the blink of an eye as he found himself back in that night with Gabriel trying to kill him. The vampire laughing and toying with him, confident in the fact that a crooked-backed weakling like Rocky couldn't possibly stop him.

He stumbled onward; the rest of his thoughts swam in the booze-induced fog and carried him home. He didn't remember walking through the door, stripping out of his t-shirt or his head hitting the pillow, but that night, Rocky slept a dreamless sleep.

★   ★   ★

Kat kept her distance, although she was certain he was too intoxicated to notice even if she had been right over his shoulder. She considered catching him before he walked out of Duke's, but she wanted their first conversation to be a sober one.

He was much better looking than she'd thought he would be. Not that it mattered, but having seen him, she did feel something she hadn't in a while. *Hunger* of a different kind. She would try to be at the bar before him next time, maybe chat it up with some other locals and the Hawaiian bartender, maybe see if she could ingratiate herself before he arrived.

His little house was cute. She'd watched him fumble the key into the lock and spill inside. Kat turned and faced the ocean. The East Coast was different. She'd lived near the Pacific her entire life – her ocean sang differently. She couldn't quite place the variance; it was just something about the way the waves crashed. She wanted to get a closer look. Inspect the night tides of the Atlantic.

Heading back toward the living, breathing city, Kat saw a path leading between two buildings. An empty parking lot on one side, and a garage on the other. Kat hurried out of sight from the streetlamps and kicked off her sandals as she hit the sand. She bent and plucked them from the ground, relishing the feel of the cool sand between her toes. The ocean swooshed and swayed in the night.

To her left toward the pier, a band played an eighties ballad she'd forgotten about. Drunk lovers shared the shore holding hands, propping one another up, kissing and laughing. The moon sat high above the black ocean, a brilliant orb in the night sky watching over all below.

It was a beautiful summer evening just like this the night she'd been changed.

Theodore Campbell had proposed to her at Long Beach on Vancouver Island. She'd said no. Ted was a nice guy; he had a great job working for his father's beer company and he was the most chivalrous man she'd ever encountered. The problem was Ted could transform into a fucking asshole when he was upset. He'd never struck her, but he'd broken two televisions, kitchen chairs, and shattered more pint glasses than she could handle. He swore he'd never hit her, but Kat always felt crossing that line for Ted was right there; it was a pulsating possibility sitting with them, just waiting for its turn. It was for that reason and probably others she hadn't dug up and examined properly that she declined his proposal. And that was the moment he snapped. She clearly recalled the darkness settling over his gaze. A flame of hope and his happiness doused by her unthinkable rejection, and the realization that all his energy and commitment to her was all for nothing. The tightness in her stomach at the way he looked at her in those moments…she could still feel it even now, all these years later, her gifts and her power nullified by a sliver of life that was dead and buried. Ted worked himself up, muttering to himself, his hands clenched, pacing back and forth and kicking the sand. All the while, Kat sat and waited. She remembered feeling like she deserved whatever he was about to unleash. She'd love to kick that girl's ass now for allowing her mind to fuck with her in that way. She owed Ted nothing, yet….

She sat silent.

When he finally stopped and spoke, she knew it was coming, like a tsunami wave, towering and unstoppable, the force of his rage and hurt was at her shore.

"What? You have nothing to say? After everything I've done for you…for *us*?"

She didn't respond – she couldn't. His hands clenched her upper arms, and he lifted her from the ground, his teeth gnashed, his nose crinkled, and he struck. Backhanding her once, twice, three times before she stumbled away, tears flowing freely as Ted approached for another round.

It was then that another monster came to her rescue. The western sky was blood orange and growing darker by the second when the shadow slammed into Ted and took him off his feet. An *oomph* and a moan were quickly replaced by the sound of something sucking, drinking, draining. Ted's body shivered and shook, and then ceased all movement beneath this dark shape. It was a man, yet it was more than that.

And when it rose, turned to her, her ex-lover's blood covering its chin and all down the front of its shirt, her fear subsided.

"I'm sorry," he said. "I could watch no more. I could not allow it."

And she knew he'd been there and witnessed Ted's own change from mere man to angry monster.

"Please, forgive me."

She could only nod *yes*.

"Would you...." He turned away shyly, almost afraid to ask. "Would you wish to come with me?"

And as surely as she knew the answer to Ted's question that night before they'd arrived here, she knew also, that yes, yes, she would go with this stranger. It felt like fate. Like destiny. She took his extended hand and allowed him to enfold her in his arms. Ted lay at their feet, dead. And Kat felt a new world, a new life about to begin. And as the vampire was at her neck, she welcomed it with every ounce of her body and soul.

The man at Kat's side now looked familiar. He stunk of booze and cigarettes.

"I said, hey there, honey...."

This was the man who feared her, the man from the fire station. He was drunk and brave, and more evident – stupid.

Kat turned from the gorgeously gentle crashing of waves and faced him, staring into his red-rimmed eyes.

"Yes, can I help you?"

"I seen you, you know. The other night. Be-before you came hunting for Rocky."

"Hunting?" she said. "That's an odd word choice, don't you think?"

He had a blue Igloo cooler in his hand. He dropped it to the beach and bent to pull another can of beer from its insides. After popping the top, the man wearing a too-tight Guns N' Roses t-shirt guzzled the beer. "Well, ain't cha?"

"What? Looking for an old friend?"

He harrumphed and finished the drink before crumpling the can and dropping it to the sand.

"You're one of them," he said, pointing one of his stubby sausage fingers in her face.

"One of what?"

Surely, he couldn't tell what she was, right?

"A fucking reporter come to rehash that old psycho killer bullshit with *my* friend."

Oh, yeah, that makes more sense.

"Wow," she said, stepping back and putting a hand on her hip, biting the corner of her bottom lip. "What gave me away?"

Suddenly, he didn't seem so upset or disgusted. His eyebrow went up. His top lip exposed big front teeth. His left hand fumbled around the neckline of his t-shirt. He looked love-drunk and goofy.

"You're pretty for a reporter," he said.

"What does that even mean? Aren't most reporters cute?"

"Um, the TV ones, I guess, but not like you."

"Aw. Thanks. What was your name again?"

"Franklin."

"Do you live nearby, Franklin?"

"What? Ah…." He seemed to have lost his words.

"I'm a huntress," she said, stepping toward him, her gaze locked upon his. "You said as much."

"Oh, ah, that."

"Maybe I found what I was really looking for," she said. Her hands found his hips and pulled him close.

"You want a beer?"

"Maybe later. Do you have someplace we can go that's a little more…." She looked at a couple of women walking fifty yards down the shore. "Maybe a little more private?"

Franklin moved his hands to her hips. His alcohol haze surrounded her. It was almost cruel what she was doing – putting her face to his warm throat, his face red and filled with the very thing she wanted at that moment more than anything. The craving, the hunger came over her, pulling at her from the inside.

"My place is just…just a few streets over…across the avenue. We can be there…I mean, if you want, in, like, five minutes."

She put her lips to his ear and whispered, "Take me."

He bent to take his cooler.

"Leave that," she said, tugging at him.

Kat wasn't sure she could wait. Even if his house was five minutes away. The hunger was upon her like a creature all its own. A lust, insatiable, unstoppable, an all-consuming desire burning inside of her. Franklin's stupid plump and blood-filled body was agonizing to hold.

Arm-in-arm, she helped him maintain his balance as they left the sand and the waves behind, stepping onto blacktop, and into a darkened alley between two businesses. His palms were sweaty. The pulse in his neck throbbed like a beacon demanding her attention. She couldn't take it any longer. She needed to taste him.

Kat slammed Franklin against the wall and placed her mouth to his neck. Her lips rested just over his carotid artery.

Thud-thud-thud-thud.

She let the rhythmic beat intoxicate her. Adrenaline pounding in her veins, a song to make her weak in the knees...she gave in and punctured his throat. Franklin moaned as she drank the hot, coppery nectar. Any intention of 'just a taste' was out the window. Kat could not stop. She heard nothing but the slowing of his heartbeat, the drawing of his lifeforce and the gulping sounds from her own throat as she devoured everything this man had to give.

"Get a room," a drunk girl's slurred voice echoed down the alley. The group of young men and women accompanying her laughed like idiots as they passed.

Kat could drain them all.

The thought began to grow, even with her teeth still in Franklin's neck. That was one thing about the bloodlust – the craving. It could pull you over the edge in an instant. If you didn't watch yourself, the fall was quick. The distance from the edge and the bottom of the well closed in a heartbeat.

Coming up for air, she stumbled backward and watched Franklin's dead and drained body crumple to the ground. She felt lost in the throes of an ecstasy ten times as strong as the best orgasm. Every fiber of her being hummed like a Japanese bullet train, the blood coursing through her, strengthening her, overtaking her—

NO!

She'd lost all sense of where she was. As best she could, Kat rose and looked down both ends of the alleyway. Late-night summer people ignored them, most too caught up in their own misadventures to witness the monstrous things happening, but her luck would run out.

Kat grabbed the dead man beneath his armpits and lifted him off into the night sky. To the top of the four-story building. By the lights of the pier and the Ferris wheel, beneath the glow of the nearly full moon above, the roof looked like an empty stage. The end of this play, the tragic end of the wanton man and the devil he mistakenly took into his arms, would be Franklin's final curtain call.

She needed to dispose of the body. It could not be left here to rot in the sun. It would certainly be discovered too soon. Realizing these types of things was a necessity, although in the blood haze, it could be as challenging as a drunk driver navigating streets unknown for the road back home. For some vampires, being irresponsible with your kills proved just as fatal.

Kat remembered exactly where Franklin lived. He'd been afraid of them the other night as they drove down his little lane.

Smith Street.

Once she'd delivered the man's body to his own bed and ignored the urge to feed further on other midnight stragglers, Kat returned to the hotel. Vincent and Fiona were both MIA, but she didn't care. She crashed on her bed and rode the rhythmic waves of contentment to sleep. And she slept and she dreamt, and she thought of one man, and she smiled.

Rocky Zukas.

CHAPTER THIRTEEN

Fiona

Fiona Campbell came to be a monster one cold-ass autumn day in late October of 1994. She was in freshman year at Columbia College in Vancouver and ready to set the world on fire. She'd been the singer in bands since her sophomore year in high school. First, it was an all-girl hard rock band called Fire and Ice. Her kinky, fiery orange curls were the fire to the ice of the twins – Destiny and Dina (drums and guitar, respectively) – and their nearly white-blonde hair. Their bassist, Joanna Chen, with her short black hair, was an outlier for the crew, but nobody cared about bass players. Joanna was cool, though, and she eventually turned Fiona on to bands like Bad Religion and Hüsker Dü. Fire and Ice disbanded and Fiona and Joanna started a punk band with Bryan Oswald (whom they called Ozzy) and later Ozzy's cousin Fink on second guitar. Their band, Rathole, played every dive in Vancouver, and eventually worked their way as far south as San Francisco. Fiona was only seventeen at the time, but Joanna, Ozzy and Fink were all nineteen. Rathole recorded two eight-song demo cassettes and were almost signed to Sub Pop, the label that put out Nirvana's album *Bleach*, but a devasting fight over a stupid boy broke up the songwriting combo of Fiona and Joanna. That stupid boy was Ozzy of all people. Rathole wasn't the first band to fall victim to a romantic triangle, but it was a painful blow to Fiona's rock 'n' roll dreams. Joanna and Ozzy were married and ran off to Los Angeles. Fiona didn't give a fuck. If they OD'd or got rich and pregnant or just got regular jobs and faded into suburban USA life, Fiona did not care. Last she heard, Fink was strumming away for a grunge band in Portland, Oregon.

Rathole crashed and burned on the brink of something, maybe nothing, but that would've-could've bullshit ate at her night and day. By the time Fiona left her semi-happy home, her mom and dad remained locked in a loveless marriage but refused to give up on a lucrative union. Fiona moved into her dorm room at Columbia College, fifteen minutes from where she'd grown up; she was in an anger-fueled depression.

She was equally hellbent on getting the best grades, writing the most soul-shattering lyrics the world was going to hear, and sleeping with the most professors on campus as she could. It was all going perfectly well until Professor Roland Torrance took more from her than she had been willing to give. She wasn't fucking these guys for grades, she didn't need to, so when Roland asked for anal sex and she refused, and he got her blitzed and asked again and she still refused, and he decided her being with him was all the green light he actually needed, well, that was when it all began to fall apart. He told her she was his girlfriend, although his wife might have had something to say about that, and he told Fiona it wasn't rape if they were an item. The fire and brimstone, cocksure punk rock bitch had seemingly evaporated overnight. When it came to shitty relationships, no one was out of range.

It wasn't until she met Vincent two days before Halloween that she realized she'd been locked into a sexually, physically, and emotionally abusive relationship. And Vincent gave her the ability to end it with her abuser.

Vincent appeared on campus that day in sunglasses, long flowing hair, torn Levis and a leather jacket. She thought he looked like the lead singer or lead guitarist in a Pearl Jam or Soundgarden knock-off band, but he was so, so, so much more.

He took off his sunglasses and their eyes met. And to her own surprise, Fiona drifted across the courtyard and introduced herself to him.

"I see it," Vincent said.

"Excuse me?"

"You're hurt."

And she was speechless. It could have been a line. Some crazy stab-in-the-dark type of line from some freakshow wannabe rock star or pervert creepo. It wasn't and she knew it, as sure as she knew breathing was automatic and necessary and love was pain. She knew this mysterious man had gazed upon her and in an instant *knew* her. And cared.

"Meet me back here at midnight. I will gift you something that will give you back what you've lost."

"What? What do you mean? What have I lost?"

He leaned to her ear, his scent an odd mix of sweat and something she couldn't place, something pungent yet luring.

He whispered one word: "Control."

Fiona skipped the rest of her classes that day. She ignored the beeping from her pager. It was hard but Fiona dropped the pager, the controller gifted to her by her abuser, into the trash can outside of her dorm and hid in her bedroom, lights off, her roommate, Skylar, away on a family emergency in Toronto, and waited for midnight.

It was ten past eleven that night when Roland came looking for her.

"Fiona," he said. His voice like smooth silk crawled under the door on the intricate leg hairs of a thousand little spiders. "Are you there?"

She knew that door should remain closed.

"I'm here," he said. She could imagine him out there with his forehead against the door, calm, steady...the way he always entered any and every moment. "I know you can hear me, Fiona. Come, huh? Open the door."

She was on her feet before she could think twice.

Hand on the doorknob, her resolve of the last few hours fell like autumn leaves.

She reached up and undid the latch of the deadbolt and began to twist the knob when the door flew open, smashing her in the nose and knocking her backward.

"Where the hell have you been?" He raged his way inside and slammed the door shut.

"I'm sorry."

"Where is it?" He was grabbing and turning over everything in the room. Her books, her bills, her CDs, the bowl of apples, her nightstand. He stopped, towering above her a giant man, an ego, a god in his own mind. "Where's your pager?"

"I'm sorry," she squeaked, a flood of disgust and shame and fear and stupidity swallowing her.

"Get up."

Her lip quivered. Her spine threatened to pull away from the rest of her useless, cowardly body.

"I said, get. Up."

Sweat dripping from his brow, the vein over his right temple pulsing, demanding she get the fuck up and obey his command.

And she did.

Tears flowed down her pale cheeks as he gripped her by the arms and gritted his teeth, his forehead creased like cracks in the thick glass in the aquarium keeping you safe from the coal-eyed shark on the other side, waiting to explode and devour you. Blood dripped from her nose now like chum in the waters off Amity Island. She felt lost at sea. Isolated with the great monster.

Roland smooshed his lips into hers before turning away and heading for the refrigerator. He grabbed the vodka from the freezer and the cranberry juice from the fridge and poured two drinks in red plastic cups he pulled from a stack on the small counter between Fiona and her roommates' beds.

He handed her a cup and began to drink his own.

The compulsion to do as he said, the need to lubricate her own anxiety and the unexpected urge to toss it in his fucking face made her shake.

"What the hell, Fi? Haven't you done enough to ruin the night already? Shit, my wife's gonna be asking me what the hell I've been doing all night. It's almost twelve and you're still going to waste what little time we have together doing what? Pitying yourself? Your life? Just fucking drink, huh?"

The edge of the cup found her lips. She allowed the mostly vodka concoction over her tongue. And the poisonous bite was good.

"Yeah, that's my girl," he said. Roland finished his drink and tossed the cup to the floor before unbuckling his belt and dropping his khaki pants, his engorged penis rocking toward her. "Finish that, put it down, and blow me."

Fiona swallowed, let go of the cup, dropped to her knees, and did as she was told. After a few minutes, she swallowed again.

He walked to the counter and brought the vodka over to her bed where she lay naked and broken.

"Open your mouth," he said.

She knew what was coming. He wanted her good and drunk.

The clock on her wall behind him began to ding. Once, twice, three times.

It was midnight.

"Are you fucking kidding me, Fi? I've got, like, twenty minutes. Max. And you're still trying to spoil our time together?"

He was hard again, his member a monster that was never sated. The meanness in his gaze arrived like a tornado over a town that has been wrecked again and again yet is incapable of stopping the storm about to touch down.

"Turn over."

The door creaked open.

"What the fuck?" Roland said.

"Fiona," Vincent said, stepping over the threshold. "You missed our date." He looked at Roland, who was hurrying to get his pants up.

"Get the hell out of here," Roland said.

"Oh, I'm afraid that's not going to happen." Vincent stepped inside and closed the door.

"Are you blind *and* fucking ignorant?" Roland stood between Vincent and the bed. "Can't you see we're busy here? Get out before I call the police."

Fiona didn't see him move, but Vincent suddenly had Roland by the throat and was holding him in the air. She got up on her elbow and saw Roland's feet off the floor.

"You..." Vincent seethed, "...are in the wrong place." He looked over his shoulder at the clock on the wall and then back at Roland, who was now pissing himself. "At the wrong time."

Roland croaked out something unintelligible and was tossed into the wall, where he fell to the bed beside Fiona.

"Fiona, my dear," Vincent said, holding his hand out to her. "If you wouldn't mind."

Fiona slipped her hand into his and allowed him to help her to her feet. "Is this man bothering you?"

She looked from one man to the other.

"Let me put it another way. Is this piece of garbage hurting you?"

"Fi, who-who is this guy? Tell him...t-t-tell him you're fine."

"Shut up," she said. "Shut up. Shut up, shut up...you...." And she began to cry.

"May I, with your permission, Fiona, show this cowardly little man how *he* has been making *you* feel?"

"Fi," Roland whined, trying to crawl out through the wall behind him.

Fiona turned her back to him and gazed into Vincent's eyes. "Yes, please."

Vincent leaned forward and kissed her cheek, his lips cold but soft, gentle. "Why don't you get dressed and meet me at the diner just off campus, Myron's. You know it, yeah?"

"Yes."

She heard Roland's screams as she started down the stairs and headed out across the courtyard. Fiona gazed up at her window and gasped at the crimson splatter that hit the glass. Roland's shirtless form slumped against the window, his mouth crying out. She could hardly hear his muffled cry from down here. Vincent appeared in the lit room behind him and in a flash both men were gone, only the trail of bloody droplets remained.

She ducked her head, hugged herself tightly and hurried on twig-like legs away from this new mystery man and the boyfriend, no, the abuser she'd allowed to corrupt her life for the last two months.

Two things hit like brass knuckles to her soul: one, she was free. This stranger had been sent to set her free and return her to herself. She got an image of the man with no name, the Clint Eastwood character from the westerns her father used to watch every weekend while he drank his afternoons away. The second thing that hit her was that she was not only *free* but *found*.

Unless her hero stood her up.

It had only been fifteen minutes when the bell above the front doors to Myron's rang and Vincent ducked inside, his beautifully wide smile and his dusky gaze upon her. He took the bench seat across from her. The waitress, a skinny but pretty brunette with straight hair hanging below her breasts, placed two steaming mugs of coffee in front of them.

"Are you ready to order?" asked the young woman with the name Delilah on her name tag.

"I'd like some poutine," Fiona said. "And a burger."

Delilah scribbled her order on a small spiral-bound notepad. She looked up at Vincent and asked, "And you?"

"Just the coffee. Thanks."

Delilah watched him, seeming to study his features for a few seconds longer than she needed to. Fiona felt the gentle nudge of jealousy.

Jealousy?

The waitress was gone while the impossible feeling spiraled into fact within her heart and mind.

Sirens split the otherwise quiet night. Several firetrucks sped past the large diner windows.

"I hope you don't mind," Vincent said, his voice just above a whisper, the warm beverage held just beneath his bottom lip. "I burned down your dorm."

The statement drifted in the air between them like some unexpected yet welcome new scent, an aroma that stole your attention and made your mouth water like nothing ever before. An immediate line from a book or song that didn't just exist, it lived and breathed and changed your path in life.

"Oh," was all that managed to fall from her mouth.

"After you finish your meal, I'd like you to take a walk with me."

She didn't answer. She didn't need to.

He had two refills on his coffee while she finished her food. She did not miss the fifty dollars he put on the table to cover their orders. She took his arm and together, they strolled down to Mesa Park. Fiona was not afraid. She should have been. Anyone with a brain would know you don't go with strange men who just killed your boyfr— *abuser* into the park in the middle of the night. Yet here they were.

"Here's good," Vincent said. "Please." He gestured for her to take a seat on the wooden bench that faced the open field. The moon above was brilliant, full, which she had not noticed before, and bathing the empty lawn before them in a luminescent blue-white light.

"I need to tell you something and it's going to sound…a little crazy."

He didn't look at her, he just stared at the moon.

"Whatever it is," she said, nearly out of breath for some reason. "Just…just tell me."

She wanted him to gaze upon her, needed it even.

"I am not like you. I am not like anyone else you've ever met."

"Okay."

"Do you trust me?"

It was a bizarre question. The answer should absolutely be *No, of course fucking not. I just met you and you killed my abuser and set my dorm on fire.*

"Yes," she said.

Please look at me.

"I'm a vampire."

Her heart began to pound in her chest, an angry monkey in a cage, shaking, rattling, intent on breaking out.

Vincent turned his body toward her, took her hands in his, and met her gaze.

Yes.

She was answering a question he hadn't asked.

He didn't need to.

Vincent placed an arm around her shoulder and dragged his nose across the side of her neck, inhaling her, his tongue darting forth, tasting her.

Fiona's breaths came in sharp bursts, her body tingling at his touch. Waves of blood were pummeling through her.

"Do you want this?" he whispered. The subtle vibration of his voice just below her ear made her wet.

"Yes, yes...."

He opened his mouth and bit into her neck.

She moaned as he suckled at her throat.

Fiona wanted him, every inch of him, all over her, inside her, but within a few seconds, a numbness crept over the excitement, and she weakened. She was putty in his arms as he continued drawing from her neck.

Limp, she let him lay her down on the bench. She felt drunk as he pulled the sleeve of his jacket up his arm and bit into his wrist.

"Drink."

His hot blood dripped like fat, delicious raindrops on her lips. Her body arched as she came to his wound and latched upon his flesh with her mouth. Colors exploded in her mind: deep reds, soft pinks, orange and bruised purple sky.

It was magic.

And then, he pulled away.

She wanted more, but soon felt content with what was her first official feeding.

"I'm going to need you to rest, and then I'm going to need you to feed on your own. In a few nights, I will introduce you to Kat. We're going to keep you a secret at first, but I promise I'll take care of you."

Fiona couldn't speak.

And when he lifted her in his arms and flew them into the night, she believed it to be a dream…a wild, magical dream.

CHAPTER FOURTEEN

Jason Marlon wished they could stay here forever. His breakup with Laura Kemper back home was still oozing pus from the ravaged and ruined wound left in his chest. Midnight, the amazingly vulnerable girl on the radio, was maybe not healing him, but making it hurt a little less. Jason's parents had invited him to come along to Old Orchard Beach. More like threatened not to help him with his second semester at University of Rhode Island if he didn't join them. It wasn't as harsh as it sounded. They knew he'd mope and pine over Laura if he didn't come. It wasn't that hard of a decision. Jason loved the ocean and getting his degree in Geological Oceanography was something he was serious about, at least he hoped. This summer break, a few hours away from school and Laura, was a remedy that only a mother would prescribe.

Having the Hersoms as neighbors was another blessing.

A shared love of Stephen King novels made Jason and the sixty-three-year-old horror fiction-loving Mary Hersom instant friends. Mrs. Hersom and her husband, Gil, were the warmest, friendliest couple Jason had ever made friends with. They came over for dinner every Saturday and welcomed Jason and his parents over every Wednesday. Mary and Jason had been sharing notes on Stephen King's incredible serial novel, *The Green Mile,* since that first dinner. The conclusion to the book was set to release in two weeks, and neither of them could wait. Would John Coffey walk the Green Mile or would justice prevail? Getting a new volume of this story each month from King was an amazing experience. Jason loved the anticipation it built. Of course, it wouldn't matter if the story sucked, but this was King. Well, to be fair, Jason hadn't really liked the last few books from the master of horror. *Insomnia* and *Rose Madder* were just okay, by King standards.

Provided King stuck the landing, *The Green Mile* was really looking like another great American novel. Mary had even convinced Gil to read the installments. Gil despised horror, but he was caught up in this prison story right along with them. It was a monthly discussion between the four of them (Mom loved it, too). Dad refused to join in. He claimed he was too busy. Truth was that Dad was a magazine man. *Rolling Stone, People, Popular Science, National Geographic*, those were Derek Marlon's jams. Bring up Bruce Springsteen, NASA, the *Titanic*, or George Clooney and Julia Roberts and Dad would talk your ear off.

Tonight, Jason had finished a King book he'd never read, *'Salem's Lot*. The vampire story that took place in a made-up town outside of Portland, Maine. He'd finished last night and wanted to return the hardcover, first pressing of the book to Mary. She cherished her hardbacks and had shelves of them to prove her devotion to the grand master's works.

Jason had hardly reached the front porch when the screen door opened, and Mary Hersom appeared in a sleeveless white blouse and peach-colored shorts and sandals.

"Hey, Mary," Jason said, holding the book beneath his arm.

"Finished it, I presume."

"I did."

"What'd you think?"

"It was amazing. And fucking terrifying."

She laughed and tapped the wicker sofa on the porch, gesturing for him to have a seat. "Well, that's just the way we like it, ain't it?"

"Yeah, I guess it is."

"Have a seat, Jason, I'll grab us a couple of iced teas."

He did as he was told.

Holding the book on his lap, he stared out at the Atlantic and OOB's summer tribes clustered along its shore. Once again, he was taken aback by the beauty here. The tranquility, even amidst the throngs of tourists, of which he and his family were counted. This place felt like a coming-of-age movie come to life. He wondered if Stephen King had ever written a book about the area. He didn't think so and wondered why the hell not. The scene was rife with magic.

"Here we go," Mary said, reappearing through the screen door and handing him an already sweating glass of iced tea.

The book on his lap, Jason took the proffered drink and guzzled down a third of its sweet contents. "Ah, nothing better on a hot summer afternoon."

"I couldn't agree more," she said, taking the seat next to him. She reached over and tapped the cover of the book.

"Between us, this is my favorite of his."

Jason held the book, staring at the cover. "Do you ever wish you could read it again for the first time?"

"Oh, heavens yes," she said. "Wouldn't that be lovely. To experience that thrill again."

For some stupid reason, Jason thought of Laura. And the first time she told him she loved him. How wonderful it felt. How the world could have crashed all around them and he wouldn't have cared.

As if she could read his mind, Mary touched his shoulder. "Isn't that girl on the radio tonight?"

The corner of his lip lifted. He'd told her about Midnight a couple weeks ago. He didn't know why. It was just so easy to talk to Mrs. Hersom about anything. The universe was truly a mysterious place. How his mom demanded he come with them, how he relented, the strange wonderous alchemy of the seaside town that could remind him of what was lost while at the same time offering him a ridiculous, impossible sense of hope for all that could be coming his way. New things. Good things.

"Yeah." His cheeks felt hot. "I mean, it's not like I'm gonna meet her or anything, but she just seems so...so...."

"Cool?"

"Yeah."

"Well," Mary said, taking the book from him, "there are still more than a few summer nights left, and if she's on that local college station, she can't be too far away. Maybe you should call in and ask her out."

"Oh." He let out a nervous laugh. "I can't do that."

She held the book to her chest and cocked her head at him. "And why not?"

"I don't live here, for one. And I have no idea how old she is or if she has a boyfriend…."

"Hogwash. Those are what we call poor excuses. What have you got to lose? She says no thank you, and you get to stay home, but at least you can say that you gave it a shot."

She wasn't wrong. He'd thought about it. Hell, after Midnight went off the air until he fell asleep, it's *all* he thought about. He dreamt about her twice this week and he didn't even know what she looked like. One dream they were at a pool party with her friends and while they were swimming, he and Midnight were sequestered away in a pool changing room and he kissed her, but she screamed. All her friends rushed to the changing room, and she told everyone what he had done…. He couldn't remember how that one ended, but in the next dream, they were out on an icy pond, and she fell through. He rescued her, pulling her from the frigid water. After getting her back inside some cabin, and while she was wrapped in blankets, they kissed in front of a fireplace.

"How about this," Mary said. "You call in, request a song, ask her out for an ice cream or to the drive-in over in Saco, and I'll make you your own batch of my peanut butter cookies."

Her cookies were amazing, but the thought of rejection was strong.

"*And* I'll give you the money to buy us each our own copies of the next book in *The Green Mile*. I'll even drive us into Portland to pick them up the day it comes out."

She wasn't going to relent. And that was a damn good deal.

"Okay," he said. "But if she says no thank you, I want two batches of your peanut butter cookies."

She reached out a hand and he shook it.

"Deal," she said.

"All right, I should probably get going," Jason said. "I want to get a swim in before dinner. Thanks again for the book. It really was amazing. Maybe my new favorite."

"I knew you'd enjoy it. I'll expect to hear what Ms. Midnight says no later than lunch tomorrow."

"You bet," he said.

He got up and was two steps to the ground when she called out. "Jason."

He turned. "Yeah?"

"I have a good feeling. This is your summer."

"I hope so. Thanks, Mrs. H. Tell Gil I said *hey*. Have a good night."

"Will do. You too, dear."

He managed to get in some good swimming to kill some time. The water was finally starting to reach a reasonable temperature. Not warm, but no longer freezing. His ankles didn't die instantly when he stepped in, and he could go under and not come up shivering. He even got smiles from two girls who looked his age as he stepped onto the beach. And when he smiled back, they didn't laugh.

It was a good sign.

He had a burger and a vanilla milkshake from Bill's Beach Shack and people-watched until around nine thirty. It was finally dark out when he decided to watch *Pulp Fiction* for the fifth time this summer. He put the VHS tape in and let himself get taken away.

He nearly dozed off near the end but woke up in time to see Pumpkin pull Jules's Bad Motherfucker wallet from his loot bag.

The clock on the wall flashed 11:52 at him.

Jason shut the TV and VCR off and turned on the radio next to his bed. The acoustic strum and slide guitar welcomed a beautiful voice that just melted from the speakers every time he heard it. The song was 'Fade Into You' by Mazzy Star. He'd never heard it before Midnight's Moods, but the song kicked off every show. Jason had looked for the album at the store but hadn't had much luck locating a copy yet.

"That was Mazzy Star, of course, welcoming all of you to another edition of Midnight's Moods. I'm your host for the next two hours, Midnight, and I hope you guys and girls out there will hang with me for a little while. If there's anything you want to hear this hot summer night, give me a shout: 207-555-

9876. *Speaking of hot summer nights, let's liven things up with something from my favorite Van Halen record, shall we?"*

Jason listened to the entire show, the phone in his lap most of that time, his knees bouncing with anxious energy. It wasn't until she asked for her listeners to toss her those last-minute requests that he finally sucked it up and dialed the station.

He got a busy signal three times. It went through on the next try.

She picked up and he could hear the Gin Blossoms playing in stereo.

"Hey, 91.2 WMPG, what do you wanna hear?"

His mouth was dry.

"Hello?" she asked.

"Um, hey, Midnight, right?"

"Yes. Wait, is this Jason?"

"You remember my voice?"

"Listen, don't go getting all lovestruck, I only have, like, three regular callers. You're the only guy in the bunch."

"Oh," he said.

"What do you need to hear tonight?"

He hadn't even considered a song. He rubbed his sweaty right hand on his pillow. A thousand fucking songs and bands and he couldn't think of one!

"Jason? I only have a few more seconds. We're winding dow—"

"'Wonderwall'," he blurted out.

"Oasis? Nice choice. I think I can fit that in. Anyone you wanna dedicate it to?"

Here was his chance.

He took a deep breath and, he wasn't sure why, but he closed his eyes. "I kind of wanted to send it out to…you."

The Gin Blossoms faded into a female voice he didn't recognize. Otherwise, it was silent on the other end of the line.

"I'm sorry," he spit out. "Is that too weird?"

"No, that's…that's really sweet."

He had to do it now. No turning back.

"I was also wondering if...if you weren't seeing anyone, if you might wanna go to the drive-in this weekend?"

This time the silence rode a wave he never thought would crash into existence. He even wondered if she were still there. If not for the music in the background, he would have been convinced that she'd hung up on him.

"I really shouldn't."

"Oh," he said, trying to keep the dying puppy collapsing in his soul out of his voice. "That's okay."

"But maybe, maybe, yeah, maybe we could do that. Um, how old are you, Jason?"

"I'm twenty."

"Okay...can you hold for a minute for me?"

"Um, yeah, sure."

After a minute or so, the song playing faded, and he heard her come back to the air.

"So..." she said. "I got one last request tonight and it's a song I'm really digging. And our listener has sent it out to...me. I know, gushing over here. Sorry. You'll have to excuse me, it's my first dedication. A girl's allowed to gush on air. Anyway, thank you, Jason...hopefully not Voorhees. Here's everyone's favorite new Britpop band, Oasis, and their latest."

Chords filled the space between them.

"Hey," she said.

"Hey."

"So, we're talking the Saco Drive-In, I presume?"

"Yeah."

"And what are we seeing?"

"I don't know."

"You don't know?" she said.

"It doesn't matter."

"Okay. Well, where do you want to meet up?"

"Do you have a car?" he asked.

"Actually, no."

"I can get one. Do you want me to pick you up somewhere?"

"Let's just meet at the food stand. What will you be wearing?"

He glanced around his room and saw his Jaws ringer t-shirt on the floor.

"I'll be in a *Jaws* t-shirt."

"Okay, Jason. I'll see you. Which night?"

"Friday," he blurted out. He hoped he wasn't sounding too anxious.

"Okay. Friday night, Saco Drive-in, food stand, *Jaws* t-shirt and whatever movie is playing."

"Yeah."

"Okay. Thanks for the song. See you Friday, Jason."

She hung up.

Jason sat perfectly still for the first time in two hours. He was smiling like an idiot in love. He didn't have a car, but he'd get one. If his parents were busy, he had a feeling Mary would help him out.

There was no way he was going to be able to fall asleep now. Not without help.

Jason snuck out of his room, making his way to the kitchen and his parents' fridge full of beer. He looked around, not that they'd give him grief, he was going to be twenty-one in October, and they didn't care if he had a few beers if he wasn't driving. He snatched two cold bottles of Budweiser and the leftover Chinese from yesterday and scuttled back to his bedroom.

He turned the TV on and was going to watch MTV until he fell asleep, but he stopped on a channel showing a group of young people at a drive-in. The red-haired girl on the screen was gorgeous. He'd seen this a few times, but it took a minute for the name of the film to come to mind. *The Outsiders.*

Two beers and a bellyful of Chinese food later, Jason remembered a burning cabin and the Karate Kid getting hurt. He was back in dreamland. Tonight, Midnight ran from him, afraid he would try to kiss her again…. Tonight, she looked like Cherry Valance.

CHAPTER FIFTEEN

Vincent had Fiona pinned against the side of the van when he heard a bottle hit the ground and roll across the pavement.

"What's that?" Fiona asked.

He pulled his lips from her clavicle and turned to see what she was looking at.

A man in jeans and a dark button-down shirt was bent beside an orange Camero.

"I don't think our friend should be driving anywhere tonight," Vincent said.

Fiona kissed Vincent's cheek and said, "Can we take him home?"

He wasn't sure where Kat was at the moment. She hadn't come home yet by the time he and Fiona decided to step out to check the nightlife for themselves.

"Come on," he said, guiding her to the passenger's side door and opening it for her. She ran a finger under his chin as she climbed into her seat. Vincent closed the door and headed around to the driver's side. He got in and started the van. Without turning on the headlights, he drove across the street to where the man had yet to get into his own vehicle.

They pulled the van up beside him. Fiona leaned out her window.

"Hey there," she said.

The man looked up and gave her a crooked smile. "Hi," he managed.

"Is that your car?" she asked.

"Um, yeah," he said, trying his best to stand up straight.

"What's the matter? Your friends all pass out on you?"

"Huh, oh yeah." He laughed like a drunken idiot.

"You look a little too tired to be driving. Why don't you let us get you home?"

"Um, us?" he said.

Vincent appeared at his side, taking the man by his elbow, startling him.

"Whoa," the guy said. "You snuck up on me."

"Come on, sweetheart," Fiona said. "Let Vincent help you in."

Vincent opened the side door and took the man by the back of the neck, guiding him in.

"Maybe you guys are right," the man said, climbing in and flopping in the seat. Vincent shut the door and returned to the driver's seat.

Fiona turned to face the man. "What's your name?"

"Jeff," he said.

"Well, Jeff," she said. "I'm Fiona, this is Vincent. We're staying just down the road. Why don't you come crash with us?"

"Oh, I don't know," he said, his head still bobbing.

She reached back and placed her hand on his knee. "You can stay with me, can't you, Jeff? Just tonight?"

Vincent adjusted the rearview mirror to see the look on Jeff's face.

Jeff smiled and looked toward Vincent. "I don't wanna, like, intrude, or nothin'."

"Oh, Vincent is just a friend. He might hang out for a bit, but he won't bother us."

Jeff let out a half laugh. "Um, I guess that's cool, yeah."

"I thought so," she said. She turned to face forward and gave Vincent a sly grin.

They pulled up to the curb on the back side of the empty hotel parking lot. Fiona got out and helped Jeff to the door.

"This is where you're staying?" he asked. "It looks closed."

She opened the door, wrapped her arms around his neck and kissed him. Jeff's hands found her hips as they stumbled into the darkened hallway.

Vincent slipped in behind them.

"Why are all the lights off?" Jeff asked as they broke their kiss.

"You won't need to see anything," Fiona answered.

"Hey, what the fuck?"

Vincent squeezed up behind Jeff; he and Fiona held the man between them.

"We're going to have such a wonderful time."

"I don't know what you two are into, but I don't think I—"

Vincent lowered his mouth to the man's neck. The scent of some pungent cologne crawled up his nose, but he could feel the warmth of Jeff's blood flowing in waves just beneath the skin. Vincent plunged his fangs in.

"Uhhh…" Jeff moaned, his knees weak in an instant.

Fiona bit her lip, before lunging forward and biting into the other side of his neck.

Vincent and Fiona's hands met as they both sucked on the blood bag between them. Vincent felt the surge of fresh blood, the ecstasy of its gift being swallowed in large gulps. He didn't want it to ever end. Fiona's nails dug into the back of his hand.

Vincent pulled himself from Jeff's neck with a gasp.

"Let's get him into a room before we make a mess."

Fiona pulled free as well. "How about we get him in a room so we *can* make a mess?"

With Jeff weaving weakly between them, Fiona brought her face to Vincent's, her blood-covered lips an inch from his own. He felt intoxicated. He and Fiona hadn't given in to their carnal desires, not fully. They'd been close a dozen times already, but the fear of Kat finding them was always just enough to keep Vincent from crossing the line.

"Come on," she said. She pulled Jeff in his blood-loss stupor to the first room they came upon and shoved the door open.

"No," Vincent said. "Not down here. Let's go to the top floor."

He took Jeff and lifted him from the ground. Up the stairs they went, Fiona right behind.

On the fifth floor, he shoved Jeff through a door halfway down the corridor. Fiona was close beside him as Vincent got the blood bag to the bed and held him still, offering the throat to Fiona.

"Drink," he said.

Fiona buried her face into the man's throat. Vincent joined her, sinking his teeth into Jeff's wrist.

Worlds moved and crashed in his heart as the fresh blood flowed. Fiona pulled her mouth free; blood spattered the comforter and sprayed across Vincent's chest. She tore open the man's shirt, exposing his chest. She suckled onto his still-beating heart and moaned.

Vincent placed a hand on her exposed thigh and felt her trembling. She placed a hand over his and began to bite into Jeff's flesh.

Vincent released the man's wrist and began making punctures down the length of his arm. They didn't have to be safe or worry about being seen. This was their playground. And the blood was everywhere.

Fiona lapped at Jeff's ruined neck and Vincent joined her, their tongues dancing, weaving in and out of the open gash until they found each other.

A tremor erupted within Vincent, his body a live wire of lust, hunger, and a desire so heavy he couldn't think straight.

He shoved the dead man aside and pulled Fiona to him. He felt her breasts against his chest. He moved his hand beneath her skirt and slid it up her thigh. She kissed his neck and wrapped her arms around him. His breath came in shuddery quakes as he ran his hands up the side of her body and grabbed her top and pulled it up over her head, tossing it to the floor. His hands came back and found her breasts. Vincent brought his mouth to her nipples, tasting the sweat and blood. Every particle in his body tingled with a current made twice as powerful from the fresh kill.

Fiona undid his button fly as her desperate hands dug into his jeans and pulled his manhood free. Her hand covered in warm blood, she stroked him into delirium.

"I want you. I want you. I want you." She said it over and over.

Vincent's restraint was gone. There was only this moment, here and now. He flipped her onto her back and leaned in, their tongues meeting just as hungrily as the rest of their bodies. She sucked on his bottom lip and bit it until it bled. He pulled away and kissed and nibbled his way down her neck, her chest. His tongue flicked her nipples. Her body writhed beneath him as he continued south, tasting the blood and sweat on her tight belly before moving his face between her legs.

She dug into his shoulders as she squirmed and cried out with pleasure at his touch. After a little while, he felt her orgasm as her thighs spasmed on either side of his face. Vincent climbed upon her and thrust inside her.

They lay in the blood, sweat, and sex. Fiona had dreamt of this since the night they met. The night he gave her back her power, her confidence, her sense of identity. They'd kissed and touched, but he'd never crossed the line with her. Never given in to the desire that had been starving for attention. Jeff's dead body at their feet, they lay naked in the afterglow.

"What are we going to tell Kat?" she asked.

"I don't think she needs to know. Besides, she's going to be busy while we're here."

He turned to her and traced her lips with his fingertips.

"Are you satisfied?" he asked.

She leaned over and kissed his chin. "For now," she said. She shoved Jeff with her bare foot. "We should probably clean our mess."

Vincent got up and disposed of the body. Fiona removed the sheets and blankets from the ruined bed and tossed them down the laundry chute. It's what they had agreed to do with any bloody garments until they were ready to go home. They had already decided to burn the hotel down before they left.

She wondered how long it would take for Kat to discover what they'd done. She wasn't stupid. Fiona wondered if her fucking Vincent would really change anything. Where was Kat tonight? Had she found someone to feed upon? Or maybe she was also letting go with somebody new.

CHAPTER SIXTEEN

Rocky wasn't the first to notice Franklin Tibbetts' disappearance – that was Scott Jorgenson from the fire station – but he was the first to drive over to the man's house and try to see for himself whether Franklin had left town or if maybe something bad happened to him. He pulled into the driveway and was instantly called to by the kid next door.

"I ain't seen him come in or out in the last few days."

"When was the last time you did see him?"

The kid, maybe fifteen, maybe older, walked across the street and joined Rocky next to his car. "Maybe a week ago? Me and my girlfriend were just getting here. He was sitting over there in his lawn chair drinking beer."

"A week ago, huh?"

"Well, I mean, I don't just stare at his house and wait for him, but yeah, it was last week. I remember. There was this yellow bus that rolled down the street real slow. Gave me the creeps."

"Like a school bus?"

"No. It was, like, a hippie van."

"You don't like hippies?"

"No, it wasn't that." The kid's thick eyebrows came together above his nose. "It just drove really, really slow down the road. And I couldn't really see the people inside, but I could see their shapes."

"It was a Volkswagen van, right?"

"Yeah, I think so."

Rocky thought of the yellow Volkswagen on the other side of the tracks that day. The strange feelings that crept over him. The mesmerizing woman behind the wheel. He kept his thoughts to himself.

"Have you seen the van since?"

"No."

"What's your name?"

"Edward, Eddie to my friends. Say," the kid said, "you're Rocky Zukas, right?"

Shit.

"Yep."

"You were the kid that survived the Beach Night Killer."

Rocky stuck his hands in the pockets of his jeans. "Yeah, I guess."

"Aw, man. Sorry, it's just my parents were watching that thing on TV and I saw it and I couldn't stop watching. I usually love that kind of stuff, you know, *Unsolved Mysteries*, serial killers, stuff like that. My girlfriend is really into it, I mean, she'd freak if she knew I was talking to you right now. But the BNK stuff, man, I don't know, it seems too close to home. Pretty crazy that something like that actually happened here." Eddie finally seemed to read the room, so to speak. "Say, ah, what are you gonna do here? You're friends with Franklin, I guess, right? You gonna try to break in?"

"I am a friend, and I wouldn't do that."

"I mean, I won't tell anyone. Hell, if he doesn't answer the door, I'd be happy to sneak in for you. You don't think he's dead, do you?"

"Christ, kid, I hope not. Let's go knock and find out. Maybe he'll come out all flustered and half awake."

"Dude," Eddie said. "More like half baked. He used to get so mad at me and my friends when we were little. I'd always be losing my balls over here and knocking over his shit. He'd come out stoned or drunk and bitch at us."

Rocky could imagine it. He and his cousin Axel used to bother their neighbors, too. One time, he'd thrown a perfect spiral to Axel at the edge of their property and the football went sailing off Axel's fingertips and flew into Mr. Briggs's garage window. The window didn't shatter, but it cracked in a crazy spiderweb design. Rocky had to use the money he'd been saving up for a Nintendo to pay for a new window. Mr. Briggs accepted Rocky's payment but didn't exactly forgive them. He'd yell at them anytime they came anywhere near his yard after that.

Rocky doubted Franklin would hold the same kind of ugly grudge, but who knows, maybe he was a dick to the neighborhood kids.

Eddie followed him to the front door. Rocky gave three quick knocks. There was no movement within. He knocked again, harder this time. Nothing.

"Let's look in the windows."

Rocky glanced around, wondering if any of Franklin's other neighbors might be watching. There was some morning traffic going to East Grand Avenue, but no one would be paying them any mind. Down the other way, the houses were all quiet.

"Okay," Rocky said. "Why don't you take that side of the house and I'll get this side. Make sure no one's watching you."

Eddie nodded. The kid was wearing a strange grin. Rocky knew what he was feeling. The mix of nerves, fear, and the slight thrill of voyeurism tended to land funny on your face.

He ducked around to where the kitchen was, but the windows were too high. He scanned the yard for something to give him some height but decided to come back to these windows if the others – *when* the others, he reminded himself – turned up empty. The living room was next. He cupped his hands around his eyes and peered inside. There were some empty beer cans on the coffee table beside a stack of magazines. There was also a fork and a plate that looked cleaned off. Some clothes littered the back of the couch, but otherwise, everything looked copecetic. He moved on. He was just starting to lean into the next window, when Eddie appeared around the corner, startling him.

"Jesus, kid. What is it?"

"It's not good," the boy said.

Rocky was sure now that they'd find Franklin dead on the floor. He'd seen enough death in this life to know the setup to the punchline. It was a feeling that pulsed under your skin, tightened your flesh, and squirmed like an insect brushing against your naked leg under the sheets in the middle of the night.

"Let's see it."

He followed Eddie around the back corner of the house as the kid, now white as a ghost, led the way in silence.

"There," Eddie said, pointing at the sliding glass door on the back patio.

Rocky gestured for Eddie to stay back. The boy nodded and looked away, checking for nosy neighbors or avoiding whatever might be lying in wait behind the glass.

Rocky crept up the patio steps. He didn't even make it to the door before he saw what had upset the kid. Trails of crimson spray, like a bad piece of art in some fancy New York gallery, spackled the cream-colored wall on the other side of the sliding glass door. Rocky grabbed the handle and gave it a tug. It was unlocked. The door gave a *gasp* as it pulled free from the seal. He slid it open and waited for the scent of putrefaction to assail his nostrils. It wasn't the unmistakable death scent that welcomed him, but an odd odor from his past.

One warm day in early May back when he was nine or ten, one of the first days in Maine, when you could feel the warmth of the sun return and knew you'd finally be okay outside in just a t-shirt and jeans, Rocky had gotten the urge to build a tree house or at least a new fort. That particular winter had been long and agonizing, delivering mountains of snow and ice and trapping kids inside for what felt like eternity, although it was probably only five months. Rocky remembered the heat on his arms as he stepped outside in his Superman t-shirt and how good it felt. He never wanted to go inside again. He wanted to run free and stay out until the darkness stole the sun from the sky. He would build the best fort ever, but first he needed a hammer and nails. His father had left a metal toolbox outside. Lost beneath the snow for a three-month stretch, it was now sitting next to the back steps, sunken into the muddy, thawed ground. Rocky crouched down. The toolbox had started to rust in the wetness and gave off a metallic scent that stung his nose. That same smell was present here as Rocky stepped inside Franklin's deathly silent home.

"Hey, Mr. Zukas," Eddie whisper/yelled from the patio. "Should we call the cops?"

"Not yet," he said. "And don't call me Mr. anything. Stay out there and let me check this out."

The kid remained quiet.

There was more blood dried on the linoleum floor in the crease next to the wall. Rocky followed the trail to the living room, where it stopped abruptly and seemed to disappear completely. Had Franklin cut himself and staggered for the back door? How did that make any sense?

"Hey, Eddie."

"Yeah?"

"Is there anything out in the yard?"

"How do you mean?"

"Trash bags, tarps…piles?"

After a few seconds of quiet, Eddie called back, "Nope, there's nothing out here. Is everything okay in there? Is there a body?"

Is there a body?

He hadn't gone any farther than the edge of the living room, which he had already seen was empty from the window.

Rocky walked back outside to the patio and scanned the area for blood. There was nothing else that stood out. Eddie stared at him. The kid was chewing his nails, all cocksure teenagerness knocked out of him at the grim prospect before them.

"You don't have to be here, kid. Why don't you head home? I can come over and let you know if I find anything."

"You sure?"

"Yeah, get outta here. I got this."

"You want me to call the cops or wait until you say so?"

"Just go home. I'll call them if I find anything else."

"Anything else? Don't you think that blood is enough?"

"Could be he cut his hand or something. Doesn't mean he's dead."

"Yeah, okay, if you're sure. I'll be right across the street."

Rocky nodded as the kid took off. He watched him give the yard one more look before turning away and jogging around the house and out of sight.

They hadn't checked the garage and Rocky didn't want the kid with him if he found what he thought he was going to find. He shivered. Leaving the sliding door open a crack, he stepped from the patio and walked to the side door to the garage.

Swallowing hard, he surveyed the door and the area surrounding it. His gaze stuck on the dark smear between the doorknob and the doorjamb.

That could be from anything. Franklin could have scraped his knuckles on his way in.

There was more dried blood on the ground directly below the doorknob. Whatever the case may be, this wasn't trending in the right direction.

Calling the police seemed like a good option. The right one. A car pulled down the street. The driver, some white-haired fella with blue blockers on, rolled by. Rocky watched him, waiting until the man and his Grand Marquis moved snail-like down the road before pulling into a driveway at the other end of the street.

He was sweating. It wasn't just the summer heat. His nerves were working overtime. Between what looked like blood on the floor and wall inside and now this bit here by the garage door, Rocky was ready to bolt. The thought of some whackjob copycat killer being drawn to town over that fucking TV special made him sick. Of course, a copycat killer would be a lot tougher to pull off than any Joe Blow psychotic asshole could know. As far as Rocky could tell, there wasn't an overabundance of actual monsters in the world. At least, not the kind responsible for what happened here before.

What if it's November?

No. She wouldn't.

But how do you know? Maybe she's changed. Maybe she's gotten worse, and the cravings have eaten away at her mind.

You don't even know for sure that she's still around.

Another vehicle turned onto the road.

He instinctively pressed up against the side of the garage. His breath quickened.

What if it's the cops?

It's not.

Rocky closed his eyes and listened.

What was it with everyone on this street? Was there a speed limit of ten miles per hour? The vehicle's engine was fairly quiet, but he could still hear it. He could hear the wheels on the tar – and then they stopped.

Fuck.

His car was still parked in the driveway.

Why the hell was it so quiet out here? What were these people doing?

All Rocky could hear was the thumping of his pulse pounding in his neck. His hands were shaking. They tended to tremble whenever he was worked up. Ever since Gabriel. Even when he was working for the Old Orchard Beach Fire Department. He hid the tremors well beneath his suit, and it didn't keep him from charging into a burning building, so no one ever questioned it.

Get moving already.

Something moved on the back side of the garage.

He held his breath.

The sound, like someone tiptoeing toward him, drew closer. Rocky opened his eyes and turned, slowly, clenching his shaky hands into fists.

A squirrel scampered by, startling him. Rocky quietly laughed at his own ridiculousness until the sound of tires on pavement grabbed his attention. He moved to the corner of the structure and watched the yellow VW van as it drove away.

What the fuck.

He watched until it took a right down Leland Street. He turned back to get the hell out of here and gasped.

"Fuck, man," Eddie said, holding a hand to his own chest.

"Sorry. Jesus," Rocky said.

"Did you see that? That was the hippie van from the other night."

"I did, yeah."

"Dude," Eddie said. "That's some messed up shit, right? I mean, who the hell are they, and why are they hanging around here?"

Rocky felt the same whirling dervish of questions swimming around his thoughts, but there was no need to get the kid all jacked up and paranoid. "Let's remember it's summer here. There's thousands of out-of-towners roaming around. I'm sure whoever these hippies are, it's no different. They're probably staying nearby and your street's a comfortable route for them. It's quiet over here."

"Yeah, or maybe they fucking killed Franklin and are checking to make sure nobody is dumb enough to come snooping around."

He placed a hand on the kid's shoulder. "Can you hear yourself? You think this is a movie or something? Jesus."

"Dude." Eddie shrugged Rocky's hand away. "It's at the very least a strange coincidence that we were talking about that van and then it fucking drives by us again."

"Okay, okay, well, we haven't even got a reason to get worked up about it. We still don't know that there's anything wrong with Franklin."

Eddie nodded toward the garage. "Did you check it out?"

"No. Honestly, I think I might come back tonight after it gets dark."

"What? Are you nuts?"

"Kid, listen, there's not much traffic here, but there's more than I need to see me going into people's houses uninvited. The last thing I need is the cops getting called. At least until after I've looked inside."

"So, you want me to meet you here later?"

"Absolutely not."

"You're gonna need a lookout."

"At midnight? I better not. There shouldn't be anyone else roaming around here. Besides, I got the sense you didn't want to be over here."

"Yeah, well, now I can't stop thinking about it."

Rocky appreciated the kid's curiosity and couldn't blame him. A lookout wouldn't be a bad idea. On the fucked-up chance that something fishy did happen to Franklin and whoever was responsible came by to see who might be snooping around.

"Okay," Rocky said. "You can be my lookout. If you see anyone though, I want you to let me know then get the hell out of here."

"Deal."

★   ★   ★

Rocky pulled out of the driveway and gave Eddie a wave as he drove away. Tonight would prove one of two things: either something unfortunate had happened to his friend, or he and the neighbor kid were both fucking caught up in the Old Orchard Beach murder mystique and seeing shit where there was no shit to see. He shook his head and turned up Nirvana's 'In Bloom', blasting it on his way toward the pier.

He wondered about November again. Could she be around? And if so, was she capable of becoming something she hated? There was no doubt she was capable…but it didn't *feel* right. He thought of his dad and of Uncle Arthur. The photograph of November with her teeth in his uncle's neck.

Gripping the wheel to keep his hands from shaking again, he pulled over into the first empty parking space he could find. The memories of that summer flooding back triggered too many emotions for his daylight and sober mind. Tears welled in his eyes as a part of his soul reached back….

Old Orchard Beach
Summer, 1986

It was June, the first day after his cousin Axel had left for England. The pounding opening beat of John Cougar Mellencamp's 'Rain On The Scarecrow' played from the radio somewhere in the neighborhood, a song that was standing up for the farmers of the country who were having generationally owned family farms foreclosed upon. Rocky had less heavy things on his teenage mind. Usually, the top of that list was late nights of MTV and video games. This morning, though, there was another thrill coursing through his heart. There was a girl – November. She was gorgeous. Everything about last night felt like a dream. He didn't even think she'd be hanging around town, but not only was she there, they'd kissed. The goofy, mile-wide smile returned to his face. He'd gotten in a little trouble for coming home too late, but it had been worth it, and she was here for the rest of the summer. He'd seen a thousand movies about summer love. It didn't seem real that it was going to happen for him, but after last night, he'd die if it didn't.

He hoped she'd be around the beach or the square today.

Rocky's dad had left him ten dollars this morning. He'd earned it by mowing the lawn last weekend and helping his dad deliver a load of wood to Uncle Arthur's house for the porch his uncle was building. Rocky's mom was convinced her brother was only building a useless add-on to his house as an excuse to get his dad over for beers. Rocky didn't care the reason; he was just excited to be part of the project. His inclusion at the behest of his uncle made him feel like one of the men. The money would be nice, but any reason to hang at Uncle Arthur's was worth it. His uncle always had MTV on or some Chuck Norris movie. Rocky was always allowed to watch whatever was on and got to see his fair share of movies with boobs and sex. And kicks to the face and bloody murders, too. He could swear without worry, he could drink as many Cokes or Sunkists as he wanted, and there was a stack of *Playboy* and *Hustler* magazines right in the bathroom.

Rocky was jumping on his bike ready to go find November when Mr. Briggs yelled to him.

Rocky and Axel had accidently busted Mr. Briggs's window earlier this month. Mr. Briggs had never been nice, but since they damaged his property, he'd been downright mean.

"Yeah," Rocky said from the seat of his bike.

The man stalked over to the edge of the property, his gray work pants hiked up to his nipples, a matching scally cap over his stringy white hair. His squinty blue eyes were somehow squintier as he looked Rocky over.

"You stronger than you look?"

"Um, I don't know, I guess, maybe. Why?"

"I...." He dropped his mean gaze. "I need a hand moving something. I saw you out here and figured since you broke my window, you might as well help me out."

Rocky had paid Mr. Briggs for the window. It had taken most of his savings, but if helping him out meant fewer dirty looks from the guy, maybe it'd be worth it. He really wanted to go find November, so hopefully this wouldn't take long.

"Sure. What are we moving?"

He followed the old man into the backyard. A long box sat at the edge of his back door.

"You can see I got it to the door, but I can't get the damn thing up over the steps there. It's too awkward."

"What is it?"

"Not that it's your business, but it's a record player."

"That giant thing is a record player?"

"It was my sister's. She passed away last month, and I guess she wanted me to have it."

"Sorry about your sister."

"Ah," he said, waving Rocky off, "she lived a good life. Growing old is a gift, son. Don't you forget it. Not all of us make it to my age. Anyways, we used to listen to a lot of records together when we were your age. And over the years, when I'd go over with Evelyn for dinners, we'd listen to newer stuff like Elvis, Dolly Parton, Charley Pride, and the Beatles."

Rocky didn't know how Elvis and the Beatles counted as 'newer', but Mr. Briggs seemed suddenly less Grinch and somehow more human, so he let the man reminisce.

"She wanted me to have it and I just need to get it inside, so come on."

And just like that, the Grinch returned.

They walked over to the record player, and each took an end. It was heavy, but Rocky still managed to lift his end. He was shocked that Mr. Briggs seemed to lift his end just as easy.

It only took them a couple of minutes to get it up the short set of steps, through the door, and into the living room.

Rocky had never been inside his neighbor's house. It smelled like coconuts and smoke. The place was tidy. That bit didn't surprise him. Mr. Briggs's yard was immaculate, so it seemed a fair guess that his house would be, as well. They eased the record player down and slid it against the wall beneath a portrait of a young couple.

"Is that you?"

The old man looked up at the photo. "Yep. Me and Evelyn. We must have been in our twenties then. She married me in forty-six. A year after I got back from the war. She was my everything."

Rocky watched him gaze into the photograph, lost in time with a girl he might never see again.

"When did she, um, pass?" He wasn't sure he should ask, but he suddenly felt compelled to know. The man looked so happy in this picture.

"She had a heart attack when you and your family first moved here. You were just a little guy, still stumbling around in the yard in your diapers. She thought you were the sweetest thing."

"She said that?"

The man didn't look away from the portrait. He just nodded.

"She loved children, but we couldn't have any, due to some medical issues. She could have left me for a man who could give her that, but she never did."

Rocky felt a little awkward at this intimate admission, but just stood still and let the man speak.

Mr. Briggs took a deep breath and then pulled a handkerchief from his back pocket and wiped his eyes.

"You meet a girl like Evelyn, you'll understand all you need to about love."

He thought of November. One kiss didn't guarantee a lifelong marriage, especially when the girl was leaving in a couple of months, but his heart swelled whenever he thought of her. That was certainly the closest he'd ever come to true love in his life.

Mr. Briggs stuffed the handkerchief in his back pocket and said, "Well, you better get back to whatever you were doing. Riding into town or whatever."

"I'm going to see a girl."

He didn't know why he said it. The words jumped out of his mouth.

"Well, in that case, you better git. Women don't like to be left waiting."

Mr. Briggs smiled.

Rocky couldn't believe it.

He started for the door and was halfway out when the old man called after him again.

"Thank you, son. I think this makes us square."

Rocky believed his Nintendo money had already done that, but he held his tongue. "You're welcome, Mr. Briggs."

"Good luck," he said.

"With what?"

"The girl."

"Thanks."

Rocky was on his bike when he heard Dolly Parton's voice float through Mr. Briggs's open living room window. Rocky's dad was a huge Dolly fan. Even his mom said Dad watched *9 to 5* and *The Best Little Whorehouse in Texas* too much. His dad loved something huge about the singer, that was for sure. Rocky thought of true love, about Mr. and Mrs. Briggs, about November as he sat there for a minute, listening to Dolly sing about how we used to walk fields of green, sit by clear blue streams, and about other memories.

★　★　★

Talking to Eddie about Mr. Briggs had triggered him. Rocky was pulled over to the side of the road, crying. Christ, it had been years since he thought about Dolly Parton. After his father died later that summer, he couldn't listen to her or Elvis. Anytime they came on the TV or radio, he had to change it. Mr. Briggs passed away the next winter, stroke or something, Rocky couldn't recall, and as for his own true love…November hadn't stopped haunting him since. The one burning question that refused to leave him alone remained even now, running through his mind again as he wiped his eyes. Could you truly love and hate someone at the same time?

Yes, Virginia, there is a Santa Claus. And yes, you can love and hate the woman who, in one way or another, killed the two most important men in your life.

The radio had been playing the whole time, but he hadn't heard a word. He put the car in Drive and pulled from the curb, the ghost on the radio claiming all apologies.

PART TWO:

FESTER & DECAY IN THE LAND OF SUNSHINE

CHAPTER SEVENTEEN

Scott Jorgenson decided to swing by Franklin Tibbetts's place on his way to the station. He hadn't heard from Franklin in almost a week. The guy was notorious for hanging around the station, and he hadn't been around since that woman in the Volkswagen van stopped in looking for Rocky Zukas. He had no reason to connect the woman and Franklin's absence, but they just coincided with the man's sudden all-out vanishing act.

A full forty-eight hours awaited him at the station. It was a grueling job, and when they did have a real blaze to handle on his long shifts, it made them even more demanding. Scott was always exhausted. It was a state he simply accepted as the norm. Dreams consisted of an alternate tired version of himself doing mundane things like fixing his bathroom sink or driving to the mall. Lately, though, his dreams had changed. Several nights this week, he dreamt of the gorgeous woman asking about his friend. Instead of being half-awake, he'd been charged up, excited, even. They all started the same, with the woman showing up at the station. From there, she would flirt with him and Franklin. At some point, Franklin vanished, and Scott would begin to look for him, but the woman would grab hold of him and draw him in with an intoxicating kiss. They would make love in the station, and he would forget all about his friend. The visions had been so vivid, he'd had two wet dreams from them. Luckily, his girlfriend, Lisa, was in Florida with her mother and sister, visiting her dying grandfather, otherwise his nocturnal emissions would have been embarrassing. Instead, Scott just enjoyed them.

Somehow, these dreams seemed like a distraction. As if the world was trying to misdirect him. It felt every bit as foolish as it sounded when he'd mentioned it to Edgar Ansel and Bryce Collins at Barbara Ann's the other night after his Jack and Cokes loosened his mouth enough to share the strange visions. They didn't care. If anything, they were both jealous that they hadn't been there when the woman showed up and went on and on about what they'd give to have wet dreams.

The whole thing wasn't sitting right with Scott. The woman had lied about her connection to Rocky. She hadn't admitted as such, but Scott had lived in Old Orchard Beach his entire life and gone to school with Rocky the whole time. That woman had never been to the North East before, let alone this town. Scott had her pegged as a Left Coaster, a North Westerner. He'd detected a slight accent but couldn't recall just what it had been now. He only remembered thinking Seattle or Vancouver. Scott had been in the Army for two years straight out of high school. One of his roommates had originally been from Vancouver before his family moved to Portland, Oregon. Henderson, tall white guy with some Native in him. He'd talked the same way.

As he pulled onto Smith Street, the silence struck him. The yards, the sidewalk and the porches were all empty. It was almost noon on a hot August morning. He supposed they could all be parked inside by their air conditioners – Mainers were notorious for being babies about the heat. Once the temps got up to eighty-five or above, the six-months-of-winter people acted like it was the arrival of Hell on Earth. They disappeared into their homes, taking the tension-filled diatribes about outlanders with them.

Here and now, pulling into Franklin Tibbetts's driveway, offered up a different type of tension. It wasn't just uncomfortable or bizarre, it was both of those outlined in something he only felt before braving a house on fire – fear.

It's because I'm worried about Franklin. What if the poor bastard went and had a heart attack or an aneurysm?

That's not it, and you know it.

It's because of that woman and your dirty dreams.

Scott parked his Jeep and stepped out into the midday heat. Even the air out here felt tainted. Not quite like the pre-storm ozone-tinged air, but something just as noticeably *different*. Like it could bite.

He walked to the garage first, peering through the little set of windows there. A van, Arletta LePage's Dodge Caravan by the look of it, sat there with its hood open and engine exposed.

Abandoned.

Shut up.

Scott walked to the front door and gave a quick knock. He couldn't shake the feeling of eyes upon him. When he'd been stationed in Korea, there was a bar he and the guys frequented called the Cat's Eye. They'd been warned about a gang that roamed the bar scene looking to make an example of drunk G.I.s. They called them the Mono Chrome Muscle. Straitlaced, buffed-up tough guys who loathed enlisted Americans. Like OOB's locals who labeled tourists as invaders, the Mono Chrome Muscle would spot you in a glance and God forbid they caught you alone. Scott had never been cornered by the group of thugs, but his roommates hadn't been so lucky. Henderson, at six-six, proved too big of a challenge for the MCM to resist. They'd waited until Henderson was good and blitzed and snatched him off the sidewalk in the wee hours of the night. They broke three of his ribs, cracked his nose and left him concussed and bloodied outside the bar.

They wore white plastic masks, with twin rivulets of blood cascading from the corners of the masks' straight-lined mouth. Dressed in black from the neck down, they were indistinguishable from one another and completely unrecognizable outside of their uniforms.

Scott felt their presence from that night on until he finally finished his tour in Korea. That constant paranoia was visiting him here now.

The MCM might not be lurking but it sure as hell felt like something was.

No one was coming to answer the door. Scott glanced around; the neighborhood was still in hiding. He shivered, and tried the doorknob. It turned.

He nudged the door inward and cringed at the squeal that accompanied its movement. The odd smell – gym laundry, dirty dishes, and something sharp that stung the senses – met him as he stepped over the threshold and called out, "Franklin? You home?"

He closed the door behind him.

There was a small sink of dishes being bombarded by a swarm of flies like US fighter jets doing their damnedest to beat the enemy back, their buzzing and kamikaze dives the only sounds in the house.

Scott ventured further inside, quickly seeing the slightly but not exactly disheveled sofa. A blanket lay half on the cushions, half on the floor, plates of mostly finished food on the coffee table, discarded socks and shoes in a trail from the couch to the hallway beyond.

It was here, the dim space between the sunlit living room and the sliding glass door leading to Franklin's backyard, that Scott knew he was not alone. Every hair on the back of his neck became electric. His stomach suddenly felt spoiled.

"Hello," he whispered. He'd meant to say it loud and defiant, but terror strangled the word on its way past his lips.

"Why, hello again."

The amazing form emerged from the shadows. It was her, the woman from his dreams. The one asking about Rocky Zukas. He'd been right. She'd done something to Franklin.

Killed him.

"You came to find your friend," she said, stepping forward. The woman's eyes were mesmerizing, deep pits of sultry danger. Scott felt like he was being drugged just by gazing into them. Her hands found his shoulders and pulled him to her. He saw a vision of them naked and sweaty, caught up in a mad lust that blazed hotter than any fire he'd ever fought. In her arms, he didn't stand a chance, and he didn't care.

"I didn't realize your friend was so cared for. Judging from his place, he was alone every night of his life, but you're not the first to come checking on him."

Scott wondered briefly who else had been here...*Rocky? Maybe? Had she found him? Was he dead now, too? Is this all my fault?*

"I'd take my time with you, but I don't feel like it."

"What are you?"

Her smile revealed fangs worse than anything he'd seen on TV. Her features sharpened, her forehead wrinkling into an angry set of hardened lines over her skull like a topography map. The monster's eyes swelled to two black, viscous pools. The creature gripped him, tipped its head back, its fangs growing longer by the second. Scott wished it had been the Mono Chrome Muscle waiting for him, or even Franklin's decomposing body, anything but this. Its head flew forward and its fangs penetrated his neck with no resistance. The pain was quickly heightened as the fiend began sucking his blood in giant waves. Scott Jorgenson was dizzy within seconds. A few more and he was delirious. This was all...a...dream....

★   ★   ★

Kat drained the man in less than a minute. She pulled free of him and felt like her heart was going to pound its way through her chest. She needed to get ahold of herself. Everything around her was brighter, in razor-sharp focus. The rush of strength from the fresh blood was euphoric. If she didn't find a way to control herself, this could get dangerous quick. The craving was powerful...she could walk out the door and feast upon one after another – she flew to the corner of the room, fighting the undercurrent that could equal that of the strongest oceans.

Before she could stop, she was out the door, a blur through the backyard, and standing on the other side of a screen door, watching an elderly woman feeding a Milk Bone to her small lab. The dog whimpered and fled the room. The woman froze. The Milk Bone in her right hand fell to the hardwood floor with a small *thud*.

Kat watched a trail of urine run down her pale, varicose-veined calves and pool on the floor. The dog biscuit began to absorb some of the pee.

Kat opened the screen door and flew to the woman, taking her off her feet in a deathly embrace. Kat bit a chunk of her loose-skinned neck away, spat it against the television screen, splattering Victor Newman's rugged face with blood and flesh. She gulped the woman's blood in five full glugs.

The body had barely hit the floor before Kat had fled to the home adjacent and bled the man and two children there of their lifeforces.

Two more homes and three more elderly folks – a couple of slim, older gay women, and another senior who'd been fast asleep in his bed – later, and Kat was a complete mess. Her eyes were leaking blood, her hands were ferociously gnarled into claws. As she found her way into the basement of the man dead in his bed, she curled into a tight ball in the darkest corner and tried to focus on her breathing. She'd never fed so much, so fast. It was as if an insatiable monster were sitting upon her chest.

She needed to think. What did Vincent do when he was like this? Her thoughts were moving faster than the blood in her veins. She knew he'd come home more than once after overdosing on victims. How had he made it stop? What did he do? She couldn't think. It was useless. It was too much.

She couldn't even go to him for help. He was probably sleeping at the hotel, cuddling with that young bitch—

No, they aren't together.

Stop lying to yourself.

Kat let out a guttural screech that filled the room with her rage and pain.

Upstairs, the cats bolted at the terrible sound, and ran for the second floor.

CHAPTER EIGHTEEN

November still hadn't decided whether she was going to show up or not. Jason seemed like a sincere guy, kid, really. What did he say he was? Twenty? She wasn't that much older, but still. Lying in bed, Van Halen playing on her stereo, November thought about why she wanted to go in the first place. It was the same reason she took the radio show. She wanted some connection. She wanted more than anything to be seen, to be noticed, to be touched.

That line buzzed through her heart, and so did the boy attached to it. All the horror, *her* horror, the atrocity she'd committed whether it was forced or not, could not and would not ever be erased. There were some things *I'm sorry* couldn't handle. November had killed Rocky's uncle and he would never forgive her. Tears streamed over her pale cheeks as she let the hurt come flooding back.

And here she was, a monster in a human world, believing she somehow deserved another chance? She knew she should leave. She should have left years ago, but her stupid heart wouldn't let her. She'd turned herself into the fictional creature who pined for a love and a life they could never have. Why? It wasn't helping Rocky. It certainly wasn't doing her psyche any favors. She knew deep down. It was a penance. The loneliness was earned. It was her cross to bear for the misery she'd caused. She deserved worse. What she wanted was to evaporate and just to no longer exist. She'd considered running or suicide. The problem was a gut feeling that nagged at her when these thoughts arose. The feeling that something bad was coming, and Rocky was going to need her. She owed him that much, and so she continued. She existed. The radio show amounted to a special privilege allowed to her by the universe. Jason was not part of that benefit. It had been a nice thought, but not a smart move. He'd be disappointed, but he'd be fine. She'd apologize to him over the air and make up some really good excuse. There was plenty of time to think up something.

The album ended and November sat up from the bed, her eyes sore from crying. All the thoughts of Rocky made her want to check in on him. She often wondered if he felt her. It seemed like it sometimes. He'd turn and look around, like he was searching for someone or as if someone had called out to him.

She'd take a shower and then she'd go out. She was feeling nostalgic. A walk along the beach would be nice tonight.

The town was alive as ever as November stepped onto the beach. The sand burned her bare feet, but she liked the heat on her skin. Her sneakers were tucked safely away in the bag she carried over her shoulder. Her headphones were hanging around her neck. She'd stop and sit down for a bit to people-watch once she discovered a little nook where she wouldn't be noticed.

It was late afternoon, the waves rolling, children still cackling and crying as parents continued to burn beneath the sun. She saw a couple, maybe her and Rocky's age, maybe younger, sitting on a blanket, the woman tracing her fingers along his arms, smiling smiles of a love unbound. She couldn't help but imagine them being her and Rocky. In some crazy different world, would that be them? Maybe he wouldn't even like her now. She wasn't the cool mysterious girl she'd been then, was she? Not really. Pulling her gaze away, November wandered farther down the beach. Keeping the ocean and its worshipers to her left, the amusement park, food, and the town's multiple, filled-to-the-brim parking lots to her right, the pier at her back, she found herself walking the very path she'd taken after her and Rocky's first kiss.

The walk was nice. She didn't mind the drain of her power under the sun. She relished the feeling. To her, it had always been more like taking a mild sedative that relaxed every normally hyper sense. Most importantly, it made her vulnerable, human, even. At night, things were far too intense. Every sound seemed to cut through her moments of peace. The only thing to do when it grew dark was to crank up the radio or put on headphones. Music was a saving grace. She had no idea what other vampires did to counter these problems. Did they just attack, feast, run, hide?

The prospect of seeking out others like herself was nothing new. It just always ran into the same wall – Rocky. Once, she rented a car and drove as far as New Jersey. Her stop? Asbury Park. Yes, another seaside beach town. This one made famous by Bruce Springsteen.

There had been a girl – long, jet-black hair, sunglasses glued to her slim, pale face. What had made her stand out to November was the umbrella she used to walk under the light of day as she went from shop to shop, across the beach, and eventually to a motel called the Captain's Quarters. November had followed her the entire day and sat outside the motel until night. The girl came out shortly before midnight sans umbrella and hurriedly walked back to the nightlife. November had been sure the girl was like her, and trailed behind, waiting for her to either notice that she was being followed or for her to attack someone. Sometime shortly after two in the morning, with no visible blood spilled, November finally confronted her.

"What are you doing?" the girl asked as November pinned her to the wall along the shaded side of the Captain's Quarters. "What do you want?"

It was then and there November realized she'd made a mistake. This young woman was not a vampire. She had no powers at all. The pale skin, the pink eyes – the girl was an albino. That was why she'd traveled the day beneath the umbrella.

"I'm sorry." November tried to leave it there, she had every intention of walking away.

"You're one of them, aren't you?" the woman said.

November looked away.

"You are. This has happened to me before."

Suddenly, there was a burning gaze coming from the girl's eyes; there was a hunger, a desire.

"Please," she said, reaching a hand out to grasp November's arm. "Turn me. Please, I'm begging you. You don't know what a relief it would be for someone suffering like me."

"I…I don't know what you mean," she lied. "I thought you were someone I knew—"

The girl launched forward, exposing her milk-white throat for November to see. "You're a vampire. I know your kind exist. Another found me, stalked me all day, same as you, only she fled when I confronted her."

The pulsating flesh demanded November's attention.

"Please," November said, trying to look away from her neck.

"You can help me in ways you don't understand. This life is…is terrible. I want to be like you—"

The anger moved through her body in a flash.

"No!" The rage-filled response came with the transformation, her true face exposed under the pale moonlight.

The girl screamed. They always did. There was nothing sexy or beautiful about her true form. This was not Hollywood. She meant only to scare the girl and prove to her that this was not something she wanted. No matter how difficult her own disease, this was a curse of loneliness.

November thought about striking her and knocking her unconscious, placing her back safely in her bed, but her teeth were already in that precious throat, drawing the girl's lifeforce, and feeding the monster.

Satiated, the power surging through her veins, November grabbed the dead body and flew her up and over the Atlantic Ocean. She dropped the corpse and let the beasts in the sea feast. They would devour most of the body. If anything made it to the shore, the cause of death would never be conclusive, but at least she'd ended the girl's suffering.

November returned to Maine, and never again went further than Boston. If her kind wanted to seek her out, she would be here...until she wasn't.

Now, with the sun disappearing behind the town, the weeds leading to her old pathway through the woods at the edge of the beach, November followed the trail and was surprised to find it still intact. In the shadows, she was brought back to the night Gabriel had followed her here. He'd appeared from the treetops, speaking as if he were a vampire from the Victorian age, teasing her and at the same time extending an invitation to join him in his nightly feedings. She had known then things were bad, but she still held tight to her naivety, that maybe once they left town and went back up north, he'd come back from his, for lack of a better word, sickness.

It was the beginning of the rest of her life. The start of her sentence.

She continued to the cottage.

Weeds stood alongside the oldest gravestones in the small cemetery next to the property. November walked through the dead, Gabriel's ghost trailing in her mind, the tall grass tracing her bare legs and arms on her way through.

The cottage was abandoned. The paint was chipped, multiple windows were cracked, and the small back porch where she'd spent many of her last days with her mother sloped, caved in next to the steps.

November sat on the bottom step, put her headphones on, and hit Play on the Discman. She turned the volume up and let a Collective Soul song, with its acoustic guitars and string arrangements, soothe her soul.

For a little while, she sat there in the fading light breathing old air and visiting a past that offered the only world she'd known.

CHAPTER NINETEEN

Karla play-slapped Eddie's chest as they lay together, naked from the waist down in the back of her father's eighties station wagon. "You met Rocky Zukas? And you didn't come get me?"

Eddie loved the feeling of the drying stickiness between them. Karla was only the second girl he'd ever had sex with after Tiffany Olson last summer. Tiffany was fun but the relationship's days were numbered from the start. They were at the same campsite in Acadia, and their families were parked two spots down from each other. The sex was quick and exciting, but it came with too many mosquitos and too little else. Not that he was complaining. Tiffany had been really cool and pretty, too, but he was madly in love with Karla. He knew she'd be excited to hear he'd met Rocky Zukas.

He reached up and tucked a strand of her dirty-blonde hair behind her ear. "Yeah, but you were at Nadine's house. It's not like I could just tell the dude to wait while I went and picked up my girlfriend."

"What was he like? Did you ask him about what happened?"

"Not really. He didn't seem too excited that I recognized him. He was mostly concerned about Mr. Tibbets, you know, my neighbor across the street? No one's seen him in a few days."

"So? He probably just went on vacation or something. A bummer Rocky doesn't like to talk about that summer. He wasn't in the documentary, either."

"Yeah, well, he almost got killed. I'm sure it feels a lot different for him."

"But he could make so much money."

"Not everyone cares about money."

A quiet settled between them. The silence spoke volumes of the separation of haves and have-nots that fueled Eddie's anxiety regarding his and Karla's future together. He'd worked his ass off for two years to get his car, whereas Karla got her brand-new Mustang as a *gift*. Yeah, his family wasn't on welfare, but they were miles away from anything Karla was used to. Of course, maybe he wasn't giving Karla enough credit. Maybe she really didn't give a shit about his station in life. Regardless, he hated feeling this insecure.

She sighed. "I'm sorry," she said. "You're right. I probably wouldn't want to relive a nightmare if it really happened to me." She leaned in and kissed him. "Are we okay?"

"Yeah, of course."

"So, what's he like?"

"He was cool, ya know?" Her face on his chest, Eddie stroked her soft hair, loving the flowery scent. "He's really worried about Mr. Tibbets. We're supposed to…."

She lifted her head and looked into his eyes with her beautiful baby blues. "Supposed to what?"

He wasn't gonna tell her, especially if she thought she could tag along. He didn't want her with them if the cops showed up or worse, if they found Mr. Tibbetts with his head split open.

"We're supposed to be cruising in your new car. Remind me again why we're in this jalopy?"

"You're a jerk. I already told you, my dad's Firebird is in the shop, so he wanted to show off the Mustang to his girlfriend of the week, Sally or Cindy, or whatever her name is. Besides…." She reached her hand down between his legs and curled her fingers around his penis. "We wouldn't have been able to screw in the back of the Mustang. You should be *loving* this jalopy tonight."

He wasn't sure whether not telling the truth was the same as lying. Keeping his midnight rendezvous with Rocky from her was for the best, but as he started to get hard again, none of it mattered. Nothing else mattered but that moment.

Eddie leaned forward, tasting her lips again. He'd figure out how to sneak away later. For now, he let himself get lost in Karla's eyes.

★   ★   ★

Rocky paced his living room. He didn't want to go through with the break-in, but he knew he wouldn't be able to sleep if he didn't. Franklin was still missing. A normal human being would call the fucking cops and let them handle this shit, but Rocky's life to this point wouldn't classify as 'normal'. So, why the fuck should he start now? He'd already decided he was doing this and that he wasn't going out of his way to get the kid involved. Eddie reminded him of himself at various points of his younger life, not that twenty-five was old, but the kid did have a similar curiosity and right level of stupid in him. He'd probably be at Franklin's waiting.

Zipping up his black hoodie, dressed the part with his black Levis and all-black Nikes, despite the hot and humid night, Rocky paused at the door. His answering machine's red blinking light demanded his attention. Rocky wondered how many interview requests were on there waiting to be turned down. He'd had twelve requests yesterday, everyone from the *Portland Tribune* to *Weekly World News* wanted to talk to him about serial killers, vampires, and conspiracies.

That goddamn special. Motherfuckers.

He'd cleared the machine this morning and it was already full again.

"Fuck it," he said, reaching down and hitting the *Erase All* button.

"You have no new messages."

"Damn right," he replied, before opening the door and walking into the night.

Outside, the sound of the ocean, and the sound of the pier – late-night drinkers and wannabe singers hooting and screeching their drunken hearts out – just down the street, welcomed him to the night. It wasn't unpleasant. It was *home*.

Smith Street lay just up ahead, the little green and white sign lit up in his headlights. As he approached, Rocky checked his rearview mirror for the tenth time in search of the vehicle he was positive would be stalking him. There was no sunshiny Volkswagen van, though. He was alone. He turned on his blinker and pulled onto Smith Street. An eeriness skittered across his skin. The only light was the front porch light to Eddie's house. Every home except the kid's was pitch black.

The Cranberries' *do bee da* intro to their fifties-sounding 'When You're Gone' slow-danced across the radio waves. Rocky turned the radio down and scanned Franklin's property for any sign of...*what? Other night prowlers?*.... And saw the Jeep in Franklin's driveway – Scott Jorgenson's jeep. He knew it by the firefighter license plate. The house was still dark. He decided to park on the curb farther down the street, hoping it would draw less attention from anyone passing by, not that it looked like there was anyone else even alive here. Better safe than sorry.

He killed the engine, silencing Dolores O'Riordan. He felt the hint of nervousness like a hundred tiny sparks somewhere in his stomach, but otherwise, remained calm-ish.

Bam!

Rocky jumped.

Eddie's face appeared in his window.

Rocky rolled it down. "Fuck, kid," he said, a hand to his chest.

"Sorry. You see the Jeep?"

"Yeah," Rocky said. "How long's it been there?"

"Not sure. It was here when I got home."

"When was that?"

"I don't know, man. Maybe about an hour ago."

"You seen anyone?"

"Nope. Must be someone, though, right?"

"The Jeep belongs to a friend of mine, Scott Jorgenson. He's friends with Franklin, too." Rocky leaned forward and gazed back at the house. "You didn't see them? Scott or Franklin?"

"Nope. No lights, either, but I was out with Karla since like five." Eddie looked over his shoulder toward the Jeep. "You think we should call it off?"

Rocky's heart was thundering. What was Scott doing here? Was he here? Did he find Franklin? If so, why hadn't the lights come on. If not, why not? Was he still there? Was he...*okay*?

"I mean, if you wanna call it off we can, or if you wanna go in still—"

"Yeah, yeah, cool it, kid, huh?" Rocky said. "We'll get there."

"I brought a couple beers," the kid said. He held up a plastic beer ring with three cans attached. "You want one?"

"Sure, yeah. Come sit in the car, at least."

Eddie tapped the window sill and hurried around the front of the vehicle before opening the passenger door and sinking into the car. He pulled a beer free and handed it to Rocky.

"Cold? Nice. Thanks, Eddie."

"Yeah, of course." The kid cracked his open and raised it toward Rocky.

"Cheers," Rocky said, clinking his can to Eddie's. "How old are you? Not that I care."

"Seventeen next week," he said.

"You see anyone else around the place today? Or anyone lurking nearby?"

"Nah, just the Jeep sitting there. To tell you the truth, I haven't seen *anyone* on the street tonight. It's like they're all gone on vacation. Or dead."

That last bit sat there wiggling between them like a maggot on a corpse. Rocky didn't want to say it out loud, but there were a lot of similarities to the vibes this whole scene was giving him and what he felt back when he and November were going to take on Gabriel. It was like something tangible. If there were a barometer that could detect the supernatural, he was pretty fucking sure the arrow would be bobbing back and forth like crazy. He hoped he was wrong, so he kept the thought to himself.

Eddie downed the rest of his beer and Rocky followed suit. As the kid reached for the last can, Rocky laid a hand on his forearm. "Let's save the last one for after. When we come here laughing at ourselves for being ridiculous, then we can drink to that."

"Yeah, yeah," Eddie said. "Good idea."

"Come on."

A couple of streetlamps cast their dim glow to vacant sidewalks. The houses on Smith Street were dark. Even this late at night, he'd expected someone to be up. Rocky's neck hairs prickled to life.

Once they got around the corner of the garage, Rocky touched the kid's shoulder. "All right. No fucking around. You're lookout. You see anything, headlights, a drunk swaying home, you let me know. Got it?"

Eddie nodded and motioned toward the driveway. "Got it. What about your other friend?"

Rocky didn't want to say it, but he wasn't getting fuzzy feelings from Scott's Jeep being here.

"We'll check the garage first, then worry about who is or isn't in the house. Okay, you stay right on the corner and let me know if you see anything."

"I can't see both sides from here."

Rocky looked over his shoulder. The deadlands. He shivered. The kid was right. "Yeah, better back up some, but stay in the shadows."

Eddie took four steps back, looked each way and then gave Rocky a thumb's up.

Rocky turned and focused on the doorknob. Pulling a jackknife from his pocket, the same jackknife he'd used to kill Gabriel, Rocky opened the blade, making sure it locked into place, and then jammed it between the door and the frame where he thought the latch would be. The thick blade and high quality of the knife, along with the garage door's cheapness, allowed him to pry it open. He gave the barrier a quick, hard shoulder, and it gave way, the door swinging inward.

"Nice," Eddie said from behind him.

Even the doorjamb remained intact. A detective might be able to tell it was broken into, but a layman wouldn't see shit. He turned his attention to the interior of the garage. Rocky pulled the flashlight from his pocket, flipped it on and began to scan the room. The minivan was still sitting just as he saw it before, hood up, a socket wrench and an oily red rag on the engine block, Franklin's yellow lantern hanging from where he'd hooked it to the hood. Rocky moved farther into the garage, guiding the beam over the floor. He saw a few oil stains, a few empty beer cans, plenty of sand, and more tools. No more blood. The lack of blood didn't make it any less creepy. All he could think about was when Jodie Foster's character finds Benjamin Raspail in *The Silence of the Lambs*. That movie had unnerved the shit out of him. As he approached the sliding door on the passenger side of the vehicle, he prayed he didn't find a jar with Franklin's head floating in it.

The light's glare off the glass notwithstanding, Rocky could see the backseat was free of any body parts, connected or otherwise. A red and green afghan covered half of the backseat; the rest of the blanket dangled toward a few Happy Meal boxes littering the floor.

The flashlight beam moved from the backseat to the trunk section.

Another perfect place for a body.

Or a spare tire and some roadside gear.

He went to the rear of the van and found the handle in the center of the tailgate. He held his breath at the soft hiss of the hydraulics, praying there would be no snakes and definitely no bodies.

When the door finished rising, he forced the flashlight beam into the space. Empty.

He breathed a sigh of relief, closed the door, did a quick scan of the rest of the garage — nothing out of the ordinary — and returned to the doorknob, where he'd seen the spot of blood earlier. It really could have been ketchup or barbeque sauce. Franklin's grill was just around the corner. Whatever the case, he wasn't about to smell or taste it.

"Nothing, huh?" Eddie whispered.

"Nope." He closed the door behind him. "Let's check the house." The kid looked freaked out.

"Look, Eddie," Rocky said. "I don't think anyone's coming to check on us tonight. Why don't you go home? You can grab that last beer out of my car. The doors aren't locked."

"Maybe you don't need to look, either. Haven't you seen enough, I don't know, fucked-up shit?"

The kid had him there.

"Yeah, but Eddie, I just don't know any better. If Scott's not here, I just want to check the upstairs, then I'll go. Maybe I'll call the police in the morning."

"Hey, man," Eddie said, holding his hands up in surrender, "it's your party, man. I'm out."

"Thanks for keeping lookout for me, though. I appreciate that. Go. Don't forget that beer."

"You can have it."

Eddie hurried across the road, and never looked back. Common sense and curiosity's abnormal relationship personified in the kid's hemming and hawing. He wanted to be here with Rocky trying to solve the mysterious disappearance of one Franklin Tibbetts, but some variables were just too damn sharp to ignore. If anyone got it, it was Rocky. You didn't want to solve the mystery and find out the answer's bloodlust has robbed every opportunity for you to do the *smart* thing and *run*.

Good thinking, kid.

Not that he was going to find a dead body or a bloodthirsty monster waiting upstairs. He shivered and walked toward the sliding glass door out back. The moonless sky above did little to illuminate the scene, but he knew the blood-speckled wall was still there, and the congealed mess in the crevices along the floor patiently festered and decayed. Rocky pushed the sliding door to the side and stepped over the threshold. The atmosphere was different. This morning, the place had been devoid of the one scent he expected. That aroma was now unmistakable and in full bloom. Death was here.

His feet refused to move.

There was no one here. No one alive, anyway.

He clenched his shaky hands, took a deep breath of the thick, fetid air, and forced himself onward.

No open windows, no place for the day's hot, humid air to escape. He may as well have been stepping into a sauna. The difference being that this one smelled like it was filled with ghouls. He covered his mouth and nose with his hand. Each step further inside cranked up that conflicted voice within.

What's in here?

Death.

Get the fuck out of here, right now.

The mystery versus the danger.

"I should have followed Eddie."

His voice sounded too loud in the quiet. There were no sounds at all. No creaks, no air conditioner running, no fans. He clicked on his flashlight and let the beam scour the areas he'd already searched this morning – the fruit fly battlefield at the kitchen sink, the abandoned dishes on the coffee table in the living room, and a pair of loafers by the door. The portrait of a life interrupted. It was eerie.

The first floor was clear. As he reached the bottom of the stairwell and glanced up, the scared kid in him seemed to claw at his insides like an unborn baby that knew better.

Mommy, don't go up there.

His foot ignored his gut and made the first move.

As his hand found the handrail, goosebumps rose to life all along the backs of his arms.

He took the next step, and then the next, the beam of light revealing a few feet of the darkness at a time, his senses refusing to acclimate to the putrid scent. Rocky couldn't back down. If his friends were here, he needed to know.

It wasn't until he was two steps from the second floor that he found more blood.

Don't be stupid.

Still, his feet betrayed him.

The landing was carpeted, and the large dark trail was impossible to miss against the beige rug. He stood on the second floor and followed the gory trail with the flashlight beam, dust motes climbing through the light, also trying to get away from whatever evil waited within. The trail stopped at the closed door farthest from him.

Rocky took three deep breaths and started forward.

The flashlight wobbled as his hands began to shake. He made sure to walk alongside the trail of blood, not wanting to get any on his shoes. He stopped when he reached the door.

Last chance to run.

He didn't want to touch the doorknob. He wasn't sure if getting his fingerprints on it would matter, but he used the bottom of his shirt to turn the knob, just in case. As soon as the door cracked open, the smell came pummeling out like a monster all its own and nearly knocked him to the floor. He took two steps back and then reached forward and shoved the door open further.

There was a bed, unmade, clothes on the floor, and more blood. The beam of light found two shoed feet sticking out from the other side of the bed.

A dead body.

It should have been enough. Instead, his curiosity and need to know compelled him. The shadows surrounding his light threatened to unleash the killer upon him. There were fangs ready to puncture his neck, claws set to reach out and slice his Achilles' tendons, whispers of sweet, lovely death ready for him to join the choir of the deceased.

And then, there was only the pale, exsanguinated corpse of Scott Jorgenson, his throat a ravaged clot of cracked and ruined flesh, his shirt a congealed blood map.

The sense that someone or something was suddenly in the room with him spilled over Rocky's skin like heavy cold cream.

Trembling, his bladder warm and heavy, Rocky gritted his teeth and turned.

A dark shape dropped from the ceiling, swatting the flashlight from his hand. Before the light could thump upon the carpet, the shape swung a fist as unforgiving as a concrete block to Rocky's jaw.

The world fell off its axis and Rocky was knocked into la-la land.

CHAPTER TWENTY

Vincent stood up as Kat stumbled into the room. Her hair was matted to her flushed face, her crimson-rimmed eyes crusted with dried blood – he knew this look. It's the closest thing vampires had to being hungover, only she looked far worse. Kat was in bad fucking shape. A smile broke out across his face as he brought a cigarette to his lips.

"Rode hard and put away wet, huh?" he said, lighting the smoke.

She held on to the doorjamb for support. "Help...me...." She collapsed.

Fiona appeared in the hallway behind her. "What the hell happened to her?"

Vincent crossed the room and knelt on bended knee, reaching down and cupping Kat's cheek in his hand. Her lids were heavy; her eyes shed bloody tears. "She fed too goddamn much."

"Her?"

"Apparently."

"Is she going to be all right?"

"Yeah, she should be strong enough to pull through," he said, and took a long toke before exhaling and blowing the smoke from the corner of his mouth. "She's going to need a night or two of pure darkness, though."

Fiona crouched beside them and took the cigarette from Vincent. Before she could bring it to her mouth, he leaned forward and gave her an open-mouthed kiss.

When their lips broke, she smiled. "What if she sees?"

"Don't worry. She won't remember anything. She's drowning in blood. It's a high like nothing you've ever felt."

"And you have?"

"More times than I care to recall."

Vincent remembered his first night out alone. He killed and feasted on so many people, he thought for sure he was dead. Kat had found him and buried him. He thought she figured him for dead, but later realized it was to help him pull through.

"She's tough."

Fiona blew smoke rings, and then raised an eyebrow as she trailed a finger from Vincent's exposed chest to his belly button. "She won't remember...*anything*?"

Vincent met Fiona's gaze. His pulse rolled like an avalanche, slow and heavy at first before picking up speed and becoming unstoppable. Despite their coming together the other night, he felt starved of desire. He looked to Kat, lying comatose. The bloodlust overdose was scary as hell, life-threatening, but she was strong. Another half an hour wasn't going to hurt.

Fiona placed her finger under his chin and lifted his face and he knew he needed her right now.

He took Fiona's hand and pulled her over Kat's motionless body. As their tongues intertwined, their clothes came off, Vincent and Fiona became one, moving like hungry beasts with no control.

Vincent left Fiona smoking a cigarette, the smell of their sex permeating the room. Dressed in jeans and his boots, Vincent held Kat in his arms and carried her into the hallway. He still loved her, but it was different. It had been for some time. He lied to himself the day he spotted Fiona. He thought he would help her out of a jam; the abusive loser she'd been seeing had damaged her. Vincent figured he'd eliminate the scumbag, become her hero, and then feast upon her. He didn't know he'd keep her. She would die. Only she didn't. And seeing that hero gaze in her eyes, it was far more powerful than he'd expected. He smiled as he brought Kat down into the hotel basement. He laid her gently on the concrete floor. He wiped the knuckle of his forefinger across her cheek. She was gorgeous. Even as a blood-smeared, near-corpse vamp. He leaned forward, placing his lips to her eyebrow.

There were four other storage rooms down here. Behind one door, he found several extra mattresses and lamps, a few end tables, and other small bits of furniture. He took the five mattresses and brought them to the darkest corner of the basement. He laid one down on the floor, leaving room on the sides for two of the others. He went to Kat and carried her over to the mattress on the ground. Vincent centered her on the mattress and then placed one more on either side and placed one on top, creating a small mattress cave like he'd made as a child. Now, it was more like a makeshift coffin for her. He used the final mattress to seal off the open end. Vincent used some spare blankets to cover the small basement windows, leaving the entire space in darkness.

"Sleep well, my love. We'll see you in a couple of days."

Vincent closed the basement door and returned to Fiona.

CHAPTER TWENTY-ONE

Eddie pulled the curtain back, squinting hard against the sun at Mr. Tibbetts's house across the street. The Jeep was still in the driveway. Worse, Rocky's Accord was still parked against the curb. Eddie hadn't meant to fall asleep last night. His mother asked him what the hell he was doing on the couch this morning, and at first, he couldn't even remember. She said something about leaving money for lunch on the kitchen counter and then kissed his forehead, told him she loved him, and headed out to work. He'd fallen back to sleep and into a dream about getting up on stage to sing 'Alive' with Pearl Jam at the Boston Garden. When he woke up, it was hot, and he was sweating like crazy.

He immediately recalled the mission last night and how he'd chickened out and left Rocky to search inside the house by himself. Eddie kicked himself for being such a pussy, especially seeing now that Rocky hadn't left.

Call the cops.

He knew he had to, but he wanted to peek outside first. If the police came and found Rocky alive and surrounded by the dead bodies of his friends, he didn't want Rocky facing that kind of heat. Of course, they could all be dead. And the killer could still be there.

Eddie, dressed in the same clothes he fell asleep in – a black t-shirt and jeans – laced up his Reeboks and went outside. The heat began cooking him as soon as he stepped into the sun.

"Fuck," he said. Just looking at Franklin's place soured his stomach. He craned his head toward the Accord parked at the curb and saw a shape slumped against the window in the front seat. He hurried over and found Rocky unconscious behind the wheel.

"Dude," he said, reaching in through the open window and shaking

Rocky's shoulder. "Dude, wake up. Are you all right?"

Rocky moaned. A trail of saliva hung from his bottom lip. An ugly dark purple bruise dressed his chin. As he leaned forward, Eddie noticed the dark clump on the back of his head and the congealed mess on the headrest behind him.

"Shit, dude," Eddie said. "Your head...."

"Wh-what?" Rocky reached his hand up and felt the sticky spot.

"Are you okay?" Eddie asked again.

"I think so." Rocky stared at the dark blood on his fingers. "Someone...there was someone else there...."

"Who was it?"

Rocky looked past him. "I don't know. But Scott Jorgenson is dead."

"What?"

"Call the police."

That sick feeling crawled up Eddie's insides.

"Go. Now!" Rocky said, more forcefully.

"Yeah, yeah," Eddie said. He ran to the house and practically fell through the doorway to get to the telephone.

He dialed 9-1-1. And told the guy on the other end there was a ton of blood on his neighbor's back door and to send the police and an ambulance to 3 Smith Street right away.

He saw Rocky walking up Franklin's driveway.

"I gotta go," Eddie said into the phone. "Just send them, quick."

Before the man on the other end could say anything else, Eddie slammed the green receiver down and hurried out the door.

"Hey, hey," he shouted at Rocky. "What the hell are you doing, huh?"

Rocky didn't answer. He walked around the garage and out of sight.

"Shit."

Eddie didn't want to go anywhere near the house, but he didn't want anything else to happen to Rocky. His head was fucked up right now. The dude wasn't thinking straight.

Eddie hurried around the garage just as Rocky opened the sliding glass door and walked inside.

"Dude, the cops are coming. Get the hell outta there!" Eddie waited on the porch. No way was he stepping foot into a crime scene. "Rocky!"

He stepped to the doorway and craned his head past the door. He listened but heard nothing.

What if the killer is here?

Come on. Come on.

A few seconds later Rocky appeared at the bottom of the stairs.

Sirens sounded out, coming closer.

"Dude, come on. The cops are almost here."

"He's gone."

"What?"

"Scott's body…it's not there anymore."

"Well, shit, man, come on, we can figure it out over at my house."

Eddie reached in and took Rocky by the wrist. He led him out of the house, off the porch and across the road just as two police cars came pulling into view and turned onto Smith Street.

It was high noon. Eddie helped Rocky clean the bloody mess from the back of his head. The actual wound didn't look as bad cleaned up, just a small gash. He and Rocky told the cops about not hearing from Mr. Tibbetts for a few days and about how, being concerned for his well-being, they went around the back of the house and discovered the blood on the sliding glass door. They made no mention of entering the house and most certainly nothing about Rocky finding the now-missing dead body of Scott Jorgenson upstairs. Rocky knew one of the officers, Officer Langdon, and the cop promised to keep him informed on whatever they found. Officer Langdon had yet to return.

Eddie poured cold coffee into a mug and heated it in the microwave. While the coffee was being nuked, Eddie found the bottle of Tylenol in the cupboard above the sink and shook a handful out for Rocky. A minute later, Rocky took the cup and the pills with a slight smile and a nod. The brew was from Eddie's dad's morning coffee. If the sludgy four a.m. coffee tasted like shit, it didn't seem to bother Rocky one bit.

"Thanks," Rocky said.

"How's your head?"

"Been better, but I think I'll survive."

Watching the pseudo-celebrity sip from a World's Best Mom mug in his living room was surreal. Forget about the fact that together they seemed to be caught up in an all-new murder mystery of their own.

Eddie crossed the room and fingered the venetian blinds. The cops were busy cordoning Franklin Tibbetts's driveway, garage, and porch. It was like watching a movie.

Rocky set the mug down on the coffee table and joined him at the window.

"What did...what did it look like?" Eddie asked.

"What?"

"The body."

"Jesus, kid."

"Never mind," Eddie said, directing his attention back to the crime scene. "I shouldn't have asked." Eddie couldn't even imagine what seeing the dead body of someone he knew would do to him. "What do you think happened? Where do you think it went?"

"I don't know."

"Do you think Mr. Tibbetts killed him?"

"Franklin? There's no way. He wouldn't hurt a soul."

"I don't know, man. *Somebody* killed him, and Mr. Tibbetts is MIA. You gotta admit, it doesn't look good."

"How long have you lived across from him?"

"I don't know. Three years."

"And in all that time, has he ever struck you as violent?"

Eddie let go of the blinds and looked at Rocky. "Well, no."

"Exactly. He didn't kill Scott. End of story."

Eddie didn't know Rocky well enough to push it any further, but the guy had to see how bad this looked for his friend.

"We don't know shit," Rocky said. "Franklin could very well be…he could be dead, too."

Tight-lipped, Eddie stepped back and sat on the arm of his dad's recliner. He hung his head, his knee bouncing like crazy. "Or he could have been the one who attacked you in there."

"That wasn't him. It was—"

A knock at the door startled them.

Eddie opened the door and let Officer Langdon inside.

"Garrett," Rocky said. "What's going on?"

"The house appears to be empty."

"Whose blood did we see?" Rocky asked.

"We won't know anything for a couple days. You know that's Scott Jorgenson's Jeep over there?"

"Yeah," Rocky said.

"It's possible he and Franklin went somewhere, maybe didn't tell anybody. People do that."

"Franklin doesn't drive, though. He doesn't even own a vehicle."

"Do you think Franklin would have any reason to attack Scott? Or vice versa?"

"What? No, of course not."

"Didn't he want to join the fire department? Hasn't he been trying for years?"

"Garrett, that's no reason to fucking kill someone. Come on."

"I know, I know, but these things happen. People snap."

"Not Franklin."

"Look, just do me a favor, Rock. If you see either of them, or hear from them, call me."

"Yeah, fine."

Officer Langdon looked at Eddie. "You too."

Eddie watched the cop leave and closed the door. "Hey, I like Mr. Tibbetts too, but it really doesn't look good. He could have felt caught last night, knocked you over the head, and taken the body."

"Thanks for the coffee, Eddie." Rocky patted him on the shoulder and opened the door.

Eddie followed Rocky outside. "Dude, what's our next move?"

Rocky turned and poked a finger into his chest. "*We* don't have a next move. You're going to enjoy what's left of your summer. If you do see Franklin or anything at all happening across the street, you call me."

"If it wasn't Mr. Tibbetts who attacked you last night, then who the hell was it? The boogeyman?"

Rocky turned and headed toward his car. "Never mind, Eddie, just go hang out with your girlfriend."

★   ★   ★

Rocky remembered the shape upon the ceiling in Franklin's bedroom. He should be dead next to Scott Jorgenson. But he wasn't. The killer, the thing moving in the dark, allowed him to live to see another day.

He could think of only one person who would spare him.

November.

Unless....

CHAPTER TWENTY-TWO

"Jason," his mom called from the bathroom. He finished drinking the milk from the bottom of his cereal bowl and placed the cheap plastic container in the dishwasher. He didn't want to ruin his appetite. He was hoping to buy Midnight some dinner at the drive-in. He closed the dishwasher door and walked down the hall to the bathroom. His mother was putting on mascara.

"What's up, Mom?"

She stopped and inserted the brush back into the slim tube of makeup. "I wanted to remind you to have fun tonight." Her gaze scanned him from his sandals to his backward Jets hat. "Put on some sneakers and lose the hat at least. I know it's summer, and this is a beach town, but you can leave the beach bum here while you take this girl out, huh?"

She was right. Always was. "Yeah, you're probably right. Thanks."

Jason walked two doors down to his room and kicked the sandals off. He had a pair of newish black and blue Nikes. He sat on the bed and pulled the sneakers on. He tossed his hat to the end of the bed and rubbed his shaved head. The decision to cut his hair off before the trip was one he thought he'd live to regret, but at a moment like this, it sure as hell made things a lot easier. He got up and checked himself in the mirror for the hundredth time. "You're a handsome devil."

He walked out to find his mom standing at the door. "Here," she said, handing him two twenty-dollar bills.

"Mom, I already have money."

"Just take it."

He did and pulled out his wallet. He placed the crisp bills in with the others and put the wallet back in his pocket.

She ran a hand over his head. "You look much better."

"Thanks, Mum."

She gave him a quick peck on the cheek and wiped away the little splotch of lipstick left behind. "Your father and I probably won't be back until after eleven. Don't wait up for us." She smiled and Jason gave her a quick hug.

"Love you, Mum."

"Be a gentleman. Be sweet."

"I will."

Jason stepped out the front door. He heard the sounds of summer fun – a radio playing some old Elvis tune, kids screeching and laughing, cars revving their engines on the road that led to the pier, the ever-present waves splashing on the shore – and saw Mary and Gil sitting on the porch next door sipping iced teas.

Jason gave them a wave.

"You have a good night," Gil said.

"I will. Do you guys have any big plans for the evening?"

"I'm going to take her for a walk along the beach," Gil said, turning to Mary and kissing her cheek. He placed his free hand over hers.

"That sounds perfect to me," Jason said.

"Don't be nervous, hon," Mary said. "You've got this."

Jason felt the heat warm his cheeks. "Thanks, Mary. You guys have a good night. I'll fill you in tomorrow."

"You better," she said. They both raised their drinks to him. Jason gave them a wave and jumped to the sand, ready to roll the dice. His heart pounded like a steel drum, as he got into his mom's Geo Tracker and headed for Saco.

He imagined Midnight being a mix between Winona Ryder and Mia Wallace, Uma Thurman's character from *Pulp Fiction*. Cute, mysterious, and way too fucking cool for him. Green Day's 'When I Come Around' chugged along from the radio as he left Old Orchard Beach behind and hit Route 1.

★　★　★

November pulled her hair back in a ponytail. After thirty seconds of thinking she looked like a little girl, she pulled it out, and shook her head, letting her black hair cascade over her shoulders. She'd cut her bangs last winter, and they'd grown back to her chin. She parted them and tucked them behind her ears. She didn't usually wear makeup but stared at the blush and lipstick that she'd picked up yesterday. There were butterflies in her guts, and that hadn't happened for the longest time.

She puckered her lips and applied the dark red lipstick she'd chosen. It looked like two dying rose petals against her pale skin, but she liked it. She decided against the blush. She forced a weak smile and put on her sunglasses. It would be light out for another few hours. She left her black sweatshirt at the end of the bed and grabbed her bag. She hesitated at the door, listening to her neighbors in 22b arguing over who was or wasn't paying next month's rent and laughed when the four-year-old girl with the curly brown hair across the hallway, dressed in a tattered Snow White costume, peeked out and gave her the most precious grin. November smiled back and gave the little girl a wink. The girl put both hands over her mouth and giggled up a storm.

"Hyacinth," the girl's mom yelled from inside. "Close that door. What are you doing?"

"You better listen to your mom," November said.

The little girl gave her a big little-kid wave, the kind that starts at one of their shoulders and goes back and forth to the other. She disappeared inside and slammed the door.

November took a deep breath.

★   ★   ★

Jason pulled into the drive-in. The double feature was a showing of *Mission Impossible* and *The Island of Dr. Moreau*.

He wasn't sure if November was driving or walking or riding a broom. They hadn't planned on how they were going to meet up. She just said she'd find him. He pulled the Tracker to the side before the ticket booth.

"You okay?" the goateed guy at the ticket stand asked.

"Yeah. I'm just gonna sit over here for a few minutes. I'm waiting on a friend."

"Okay."

Jason was there for ten minutes before a yellow Volkswagen van, like something out of a Woodstock documentary, pulled up to the ticket booth. He couldn't take his eyes off the couple. The gorgeous redhead and Chris Cornell clone were like a rock 'n' roll power couple strolling off the red carpet and into real life. The Volkswagen was a throwback but made much more sense when he saw the couple. Everything about them was intriguing.

The redhead turned and noticed him noticing them. She slid her tongue across her lips and blew him a kiss.

The pulse in Jason's throat thudded heavy like a throbbing slug just below his jawline. He felt his penis move in his pants and had to reach between his legs to adjust himself in his jeans. She busted out laughing as Cornell leaned forward and gave Jason a nod. The VW moved along. Jason reached for the shifter and put the Tracker in Drive, following them inside.

"Hey, hey!" the ticket guy in the booth shouted, waving his arms to get Jason's attention.

Jason heard the guy and eased the brakes on. What the hell was he doing? He'd just started following these guys like...like...he couldn't not follow them. The Pied Piper came to mind, before the ticket guy came up to his window.

"It's ten bucks, man."

Jason put the vehicle in Park, took a twenty-dollar bill from his wallet and handed it to the guy. "If my friend shows up, her name's Midnight. This covers us both."

"Sure, man. What's she driving? What's she look like?"

"I don't know. This is our first date."

"Um, okay. Sure. Midnight? That's her name?"

"Yeah."

"Sure, man. Good luck."

Jason put the Tracker in gear and pulled in, looking for a good spot without realizing he was scanning for the yellow van, as well.

He couldn't find it, which didn't seem to make sense. It should stick out like a Bell Biv DeVoe fan at a Nine Inch Nails concert, but they seemed to have vanished. Jason pulled into a space close to the snack stand centered in the lot and shut the vehicle off. His mind should have been racing with thoughts about Midnight and what it was going to be like to actually meet her, but he couldn't stop thinking of the redhead.

"Hi there," a woman's voice whispered in his ear.

He turned to find the amazing ginger standing next to him.

"Hi," he said, his voice cracking like he was turning fourteen all over again.

"Mind if I join you?"

"I, uhhh…I have someone…."

"Me too, but I like to play around, and he doesn't mind."

She leaned in and gave him an open-mouthed kiss. Her tongue slithered in and wrapped itself around his, swirling in circles and making him dizzy.

When their lips parted, Jason thought he tasted blood.

"Why don't you come in my van?" she said. Her voice floated through his head like a dream.

The yellow van was parked beside them. Chris Cornell was nowhere to be seen.

"Yeah, sure, for a minute…I guess that would be fine."

She opened his door and took him by the hand.

He heard the door of the Tracker slam shut and then felt himself thrown into the back of the van. He landed on the carpeted floor and spun around, looking at the impossibly beautiful woman climbing in behind him and shutting the side door. It was very dim inside despite the blazing sun outside. His gaze fell upon her stiff nipples poking through her tight yellow t-shirt.

"You want to see my tits, huh?"

He nodded, his mouth hanging open. His hard-on demanding release.

She crossed her arms. Her hands fingered the bottom of the t-shirt and lifted it off her perfect flesh, over her head.

"Come closer," she said.

Some small voice, like a tiny man stuck at the bottom of a gargantuan hole in the Earth shouting but barely audible, asked him what in the hell was happening. Jason stared at this amazing woman's breasts and shushed his inner voice. There was nothing else but this moment, there was no one else but…her.

He sat up, pulled his feet behind him, and put his mouth on her glistening right breast.

She ran her fingers through his hair, down the side of his neck, and to the front of his pants, where she gave his penis a hard squeeze.

She moaned softly. Her lips next to his ear trailed to his ear lobe, and to his throat.

Before Jason could let his hormones rage any harder, a quick, sharp pain came to life in his neck.

Did she just bite me?

Her hand on his hard-on continued to numb his thoughts.

He was dizzy all right. This was the most fantastic thing that had ever happened to him.

Eat your fucking heart out, Laura.

The pain in his neck swelled like a wave. His penis didn't seem to get the correct message as he exploded under her touch. She let out a muffled moan. The sucking sounds hit his ear and the pain came to fruition.

Danger! Danger!

His mind screamed for him to abort this mission, but it was far too late. Jason tried to lift his arm and found he couldn't. He had zero strength.

The redhead pulled free from his neck, blood covering her lips, teeth, and chin.

Oh God.

Her face changed, shifted, tightened, and grew sharp edges. Her blood-covered teeth were too long. Her eyes burned through him, swirled into twin black pools.

Oh no, no, no...Mum. Mary...Midni—

The monstrous woman slammed her mouth back into his tender flesh and it all went black.

The driver's side door opened. Vincent, lit cigarette between his lips, two hot dogs and two Pepsis in his hands, climbed in and glanced over his shoulder.

"Did you leave anything for me?"

Fiona licked the fresh crimson lip gloss and said, "We've got tonight. And a beach full of lovers to feast upon."

"I fucking love the way you talk to me." He set the food on the dashboard and set the drinks on the floor between them. He leaned back and as they kissed, he lapped at the man's blood around her mouth.

He pulled free, his lips and insides tingling. "Let's have us some fun."

CHAPTER TWENTY-THREE

November saw the sign for the Saco Drive-In and kept walking. She couldn't do it. She was too chickenshit. Passing the entryway to the place, she slowed, just for a second. A strange sensation, the faintest voice within tried to tell her something. It could be the secret of the afterlife, the truth in creation, whatever it was she swallowed it down and hurried along. It was probably just fear. And she learned to avoid things that made her fearful. She'd been stupid to come this far.

The feeling dissipated as she got further down the road. Traffic, which was always heavy this time of year, fell into the background as she pushed Play on the mix CD she had made. Burning CDs wasn't something everyone had access to, but they had a burner at the school's radio station. All the DJs had been making mixes all summer. November's mix consisted of all her favorite eighties hard rock songs. Blackie Lawless howled in her headphones about being a wild child, as she left the main road for a break in the trees.

She wished she'd ridden her bike. Flying before the sun went all the way down was never a good idea. Still, she used the patches of woods to mitigate the chances of being seen. She could fly low, skimming the treetops on her way toward the beach. Her bigger concern was whether she might drop and break her Discman.

Try as she might to keep him out, Rocky slithered into her thoughts. What was he doing right now? How was he handling all the attention of the press from that damn prime-time special? She decided to check on him.

Surely, he was different. The adorable, shy guy who blushed on command, who worried his back brace would somehow make her lose interest in him, the boy who was the first and only that she'd ever...

well, they were each other's firsts. Rocky still moved like Rocky – shoulders rolled slightly forward, brown hair still a floppy mess on top of his head, which hung more than it should have. He'd become a hero after he'd returned home from his year and a half in New York City. She'd almost lost track of him, but discovered that he and his cousin, Axel, had enough musical talent to last in the big city, at least for a little while. It was just that the big city turned on them and took Axel down with it. Rocky came home, mourning the loss. He eventually ended up at the fire department. She'd had a hard time watching as he rushed into infernos and rescued men, women, children, and pets. From afar, he looked every bit the part, but she'd also seen him after hours, drowning his sorrows, and keeping himself away from everyday people. Away from love. And with each day, month, and year that passed, November felt more responsible for the way Rocky seemed to be coasting through life. Tonight was one of those moments, like many before, where she felt if she could talk to him, she could somehow save him.

She felt compelled to see him. Approaching Old Orchard Beach, she thought, *Oh man, here we go again.*

CHAPTER TWENTY-FOUR

Kat awoke in total darkness, cold and still. The smell of dust and mold surrounded her. As she rose, the soft walls around her came down. She was in a basement, but not the last one she remembered. The memory of her bloodlust, the killings, and the resulting state of complete ruin she'd found herself in came rushing over her head like a tsunami.

God, the things she had done. She'd never fed like that before. She'd been so reckless, so hungry, so unstoppable. Until she crumpled in upon herself. She remembered her master, the monster he'd become. How she'd deemed him too far gone. How she'd let him die. Yet, here she was, alive. Vincent had chosen to save her ass. Vincent had done for her what she refused to do for her master.

Shame swelled within her.

And as she stood there alone, she recalled something else.

No, no, that was just the overdose.

Vincent and Fiona.

No.

Kat found the stairs and followed them up. She had no idea what day it was or what time, but it wasn't dark yet. How long had she slept? Hours, days? She made her way up to their rooms and found Vincent and Fiona gone. The sheets on the bed had spilled to the floor, and the scent of sex permeated the room.

She didn't know which feeling was stronger, the hurt or the rage. She made her way to her closet, picked out a black knee-length skirt and a black crop top, and wondered how long the two had been betraying her. She stuffed the outfit in a bag. There was another inn just down the street. They had a lobby bathroom she'd used to clean herself up earlier this week, but tonight, she wanted to get away. She would just rent a room and take a nice long, hot shower. Then, she was going to Duke's to track down Rocky.

Another vague memory came to her...Rocky.... She could swear she saw him while she was still high on blood at the end of the world, or at least that's what it felt like. Hmmm. She couldn't be sure it wasn't just a fever dream, but still....

After rinsing most of the blood from her face and hands with a couple bottles of water, Kat checked in at the Betty's Island Inn, went straight to her room and climbed into the steaming shower. The sensation was nothing short of ecstasy. She allowed herself extra time to enjoy the feeling before getting out, drying off, dressing, and getting her hair just right. Her curls were natural, and she felt blessed that they always looked best towel dried.

Out the door, strutting down the sidewalk toward the lit-up Ferris wheel, Kat felt amazing. It was like she'd felt as a kid the day after being sick with a stomach bug or the flu. It's like you were suddenly electric. Everything just felt better than good.

Whatever the situation was with Vincent and Fiona, she was going to have fun tonight. She'd deal with that shitshow when she was good and ready.

Although she knew she should be sated after devouring the feast of all feasts, the pulsing, throbbing heartbeats all around demanded her attention. So many hot bodies, so much more blood. Her head swooned; she stopped, a man behind her bumped into her and excused himself. She told him it was okay and stood perfectly still. She closed her eyes and focused on her directive. Find Rocky, get him to drop his defenses, and talk to him. It was straight and simple.

Her mind redirected, Kat crossed by the fountain in the square and made her way through the throng of night people down the pier. Duke's stood out with its giant faux palm tree and the big smiling cutout of the owner/operator. When she entered the packed bar, she noticed Rocky right away. Sitting closest to the wall and sucking down a pint glass of beer, Rocky Zukas in the flesh. Her stomach fluttered.

What the hell? Why am I nervous?

Maybe it was the flood of emotions and the wild blood ride she'd just been on. Whatever it was, she felt off, not her normal in-control self. He was cute, but it wasn't like he was some movie star or anything. The nervousness continued despite her self-assurances that this was just a normal guy. So why wasn't it working?

He set the empty glass down and ordered another. He turned his head and saw her standing there, or so she thought. Kat looked behind her and only saw random people walking by the door. When she looked back to him, he quickly averted his gaze and grabbed his fresh glass of beer.

What in the hell, Kat? He's just a fucking guy. Get on with it.

She made her approach, forcing smiles for the few men and women that noticed her. A couple sitting next to Rocky put cash on the bar and got up from their stools. The man slid his arm around the blonde's waist and the two moved ahead.

Rocky was stealing glances as she moved in and took the seat beside him.

"Hi," she said, hoping she'd brushed away the scent of blood and decay.

He smiled and tipped his glass. "Hey," he said. "Drink?"

"Sure, what are you having?"

"Piss beer. Why, you want one?"

"Sure."

The big bartender looked in their direction. Rocky held up two fingers and the bartender nodded.

Kat was grateful for the tall glass of beer. The sweating pint glass gave her something to hold, something to focus on.

Goddammit, you're a monster and this is just a guy.

He had a single dimple in his right cheek when he smiled like he was doing right now. She noticed his hands shaking as he reached up and scratched the stubble on his chin. At least he appeared to be nervous, too.

"Do you know who I am?" he asked, sipping his drink.

"Is it so bad if I do?"

"That depends."

"Oh yeah, on what?"

Rocky finished his drink and put the glass down, signaled for another, and turned toward her. "What you're after."

"Okay," she said, nodding. "Okay, I'm sorry. My name's—"

"Why should I care who you are?"

"Uh…." She couldn't look him in the eye. This was not going according to plan. "All right, I'm sorry to have bothered you. I'll leave you alone."

Kat finished her beer, set the glass down and got up. "Thanks for the drink."

She made her way outside and walked to the end of the pier.

Swing and miss.

She was out of practice. It was to be expected, although she somehow didn't see it coming. The dark waters swayed beyond, slapping the posts below. Intermittent raindrops speckled her bare arms. One hit her nose. Rain wasn't a frequent West Coast thing, not in SoCal anyway. It had been a while and she hoped it would pour. She could use the cleansing right about now. Thinking of her feast this week, the resulting near-death experience and about Vincent and Fiona…well, she wondered if coming out here had been such a great idea. Rocky didn't strike her as a vampire killer of any sorts. A bit of a jerk, maybe, but not a killer.

"Hey," the voice behind her said.

She turned and saw him smiling, the single dimple on full display. He sidled up next to her and gripped the railing.

"I'm sorry about that back there. I'm not good with people. And I've had a pretty shitty couple of days."

"Yeah," she said. "I got that."

"So, what's your deal? Just a true crime fanatic or a journalist maybe?"

"Wow, so I'm not the first. Damn, I'm losing my mojo."

"If it's any consolation, you're in the top three cutest."

"Cute, like a high school girl?"

"Well, now you just dropped out of the top three."

"What, you don't like full-grown, professional women?"

Rocky laughed and it gave her butterflies.

"Yeah," he said. "I guess I'm not doing a very good job apologizing."

He stood straight and held out a hand to her. "Hi, I'm Rocky. It's nice to meet you."

"Katherine Collins. The *Scene* magazine."

"Katherine from *Rolling Stone*. Really?"

"Uh-huh, but you can call me Kat."

"Hiya, Kat. So...." He folded his arms on the railing and leaned toward the ocean. "Are you looking for an exclusive interview or a drinking buddy?"

She smirked and copied his posture, leaning forward on her arms. "To tell you the truth, I'm not sure what the hell I'm doing."

She wasn't lying. This whole excursion east had been a mess.

"It's going to start raining for real in a minute," he said. "Do you want to go back to Duke's? Or we could go to my place. I live just down the road."

"We just met and you're already trying to take me home?"

"The other girls in my top three already said no."

She guffawed and gave him a mock slap. He held out his hand.

He's just a stupid human boy.

The mental statement did little to quell her growing desire to be close to him. She took his hand. The summer nighttime rain began to come down harder.

"What's it going to be?" he asked as they neared the entrance to Duke's.

She really wanted to be able to sit down and talk to him. Duke's was crowded and loud.

"Your place, but don't get any ideas."

He gave her hand two quick squeezes and began to lead her through the thinning crowd. People were vacating the pier, either filtering into one bar or another or hightailing it from the beach altogether, an exile from the storm.

"Come on," he said. "Faster."

It was pouring by the time they hit the sidewalk. She allowed Rocky to pull her along. Off the main strip they hit one side street and then another until he pointed to a small apartment building on the next corner.

The downpour felt terrific on her skin. She could have stood and soaked in the deluge for hours. The sound was hypnotic, like a rushing stream on high.

As they got to the steps, Rocky undid the carabiner from his belt loop, found and inserted the key and opened the door for her. She stepped through and instantly worried about dripping all over his floor.

"No, no," he said, closing out the storm and slipping past her. "Don't worry about the floor, come in, come in."

Never welcome a vampire into your home, silly boy.

She nearly laughed at the thought.

★   ★   ★

November found Rocky heading straight for the edge of the pier. She tucked a loose strand of hair behind her ear as she approached him. Her smile fell when he began conversing with a woman standing there alone. November stepped back so as not to be seen by either of them. She took up a stool, placing her back to them, glancing over her shoulder to further assess the situation. They were definitely flirting. She could smell the pheromones from here. Blood was flushing Rocky's face, his heartbeat actually thrumming along for once. The slight bit of happiness for him was quickly doused by unwarranted hurt. He wasn't her boyfriend. He hadn't been in years, and even then, it had only been a few weeks. Still, her heart was pulled down by the undertow of Rocky and this pretty woman's undeniable chemistry.

November was ready to leave them in peace, when something about the woman kept her in place. November could sense and feel Rocky's heart rate, his blood, his excitement, but...the woman was giving off…nothing. Which, of course, was not possible. Not unless she were a— Nope, not possible.

But why not? If November was here, alive undead, hanging around a summer beach town swarming with people looking for Rocky, why couldn't another vampire find its way here?

And that was the feeling taking over her senses. Like the girl in Rhode Island? She watched Rocky and the woman turn toward the Atlantic. His sneakered feet were fidgeting with the bottom of the railing, tracing the wood there with the toe of his shoes. The woman couldn't seem to keep her foot from the back of her leg.

She's not a vampire.

Then why can't I feel her?

As the rain picked up, she saw Rocky holding his hand out for the mysterious woman. November rose and hurried down the pier and out of sight. Her heart suddenly felt bruised. She'd been ready to…to what? Talk to him? Run from him? Be given the cold shoulder again?

Rocky didn't owe her a damn thing.

As she left the pier and moved beneath it, lurking in the shadows of the wooden structure, she watched Rocky and his new friend hurry along toward his place. November knew she should leave them alone and just go home. She wished she had the radio show tonight. She could use the distraction.

Go find Jason.

She wasn't going to do that. She wasn't going anywhere until she knew Rocky was safe. Keeping her distance, she pursued them down the road and to Rocky's place. As they disappeared inside, Rocky glanced out into the rain. She felt as though he were staring right at her. She stepped back into a shadow. He closed the door.

★   ★   ★

He wasn't sure what this was or where it was going, but it felt good. Kat was beautiful and funny. And she hadn't told him to get lost. She could have. He hadn't been very nice.

"Go ahead and sit on the couch, it's fine," he said as he watched her looking around the room, trying to figure out who he was.

"Are you sure?"

"Yeah, yeah." He stepped into the hallway, walked to the linen closet and grabbed a couple of towels. He returned to the living room and handed one to her. A stack of *Maxim* magazines sat at the edge of the coffee table; her gaze followed his. She looked at him and smiled. It was gorgeous.

He shrugged.

"Single guys have needs too," she said, wiping her arms with the towel.

"We certainly do, we certainly do," he said. "Can I get you a beer? A margarita?"

"Beer's good."

He watched as she shook the rain from her black curls. She caught him staring, and he ducked into the kitchen for their drinks. Grabbing two Budweisers from the fridge, he looked for a snack, but outside of the leftover Pepperidge Farm coconut cake, some blueberry yogurt, and a package of bologna, he didn't really have anything to offer.

He snagged the half-empty bag of Doritos from the counter and carried it out with the beers. "I need to do some shopping, I guess. Nothing to eat." He offered the chips. "Doritos?"

"Sure. Thanks."

Taking the seat next to her, he opened their drinks and slid one in front of her.

"So," he said. "Do you have a tape recorder or a notepad hiding somewhere?"

Her forehead creased, her eyebrows knitting close together. "Oh," she said, her eyes widening. "Yes, no. Um, I do." She started to dig through her bag. After a few seconds digging through her things, she came out with a small notepad and a pen.

"Well, doc," Rocky said. "You've got me on the couch. Fire away."

"Are you sure?"

"Yeah, but if I say something that makes me sound stupid, at least I can say you tried to seduce me."

"Yeah, yeah, okay," she said. After taking a gulp from her beer bottle, stuffing her face with a few of the cheesy tortilla chips, and wiping her fingers off on the towel he'd given her, she scribbled a few things on the notepad and composed herself. "First off, you grew up here, right?"

He nodded, sipping his drink.

"And you left after high school and came back."

"Sounds right."

"Why?"

"Why?" he repeated. He knew why, but he couldn't exactly say it out loud. "Well, I guess I just like it here, ya know?"

"But after what happened…the memories? How do you deal with…it all?"

He held up his brew. "Beer, for starters. Honestly, I'm a sucker for distractions. I came home, joined the fire department, did that for a while, and then, this documentary happened and here we are."

"Uh-uh, not good enough."

"What do you mean? That's it, really. I mean, as far as I can tell without actual psychotherapy."

"What about girlfriends? You said you love distractions. Wouldn't a girlfriend be the ultimate distraction?"

He loved the way she was now nibbling on the end of the pen.

Talk about distractions.

"Um, that's personal, but since I agreed to do this, I don't know. I've gone out with a few women, but no one really right, I guess."

"Are you looking for someone specific?"

He saw November in her sunglasses, calling him Heat Stroke as she vanished into a crowd of beachgoers.

"No. Yes. I don't know." He stood with his beer in hand and started to pace.

"Okay, maybe there was someone?" she said. "We'll just leave it be for now. How about the incident. How old were you at the time?"

"I'd just turned sixteen."

"And people were going missing. Being murdered. It must have been frightening."

"You know, you're really starting to sound like a therapist."

"Thanks," she said, jotting something else on the pad. "So, how did the murders affect your summer?"

"I was aware of them, but I don't...." He thought back. He'd seen the reports on the news. "My mom and dad didn't want me out after dark. I still went out, at least for a little while."

"What stopped you?"

"My uncle Arthur and my dad...they were both, well my uncle was killed. My dad had a heart attack."

"I'm sorry."

He swallowed the last of the beer and wiped his mouth with the back of his hand. "Do you want another?"

"Sure."

He got the drinks and placed hers on the table next to her first. "Do you care if I put some music on?"

"Not at all."

He hit the power button on his component stereo system, and Play on the CD player, not remembering what he'd last been listening to. Soundgarden's *Superunknown* came on. He turned it down and sat next to her again.

"So," she carried on. "Your uncle is a victim, and your dad dies of natural causes. How long was that before the Beach Night Killer took your mom and sister?"

"A Polaroid picture...."

"What?"

Shit. Did I just say that out loud?

Rocky still had the picture that had been left by Gabriel that night. The image of November's teeth in his uncle's throat seared there for eternity. The most real horror he'd ever seen, and it was still in a box beneath his bed. Rocky knew that Gabriel had made her do it or he was going to kill their mother and probably the rest of Rocky's family, too.

The photo was still scorched into his brain. He would never be able to look at November the same again. Whether she wanted him to or not.

"I had a Polaroid camera when I was younger," he said. "I don't know why I said that. I just thought of it for some reason."

"It's okay, how long was it before the killer took your mom and sister?"

"It must have been a couple weeks, maybe a month."

"Was he targeting you?"

"What? Who?"

"Why you? Why did Gabriel Riley keep your mother and sister alive? Why did he wait for you? Why not just kill them. Kill you?"

He placed the bottle to his lips and tipped his head back, until the beer was gone. He closed his eyes and saw Scott Jorgenson's body on Franklin's bedroom floor. He saw the shadow moving toward him. His hand went to the fresh cut on the back of his head. This was all too much. Without a word, he was up and fetching another.

"I'm sorry," she said when he returned from the kitchen. "You wouldn't know why this killer did what he did. It's just that it has always felt like there was something…a connection…something missing from the papers, the TV news stories. I just thought you might be able to fill in the blanks. I didn't mean to upset you."

As he thought of the Polaroid, the note, that final night, he chugged the beer.

"I should probably go, I'm so sorry," she said, putting her notepad and pen away and rising from the couch.

"No," he said, feeling the buzz form the alcohol climbing over him. "I'm sorry. I just haven't really dug into this stuff in a while. How long are you in town?"

"I'm not sure. I've been interviewing some of the locals who were here then. I have a few more. I was planning on staying for a week or two."

"Could we try this again in a couple nights? Maybe have dinner first. My treat?"

"Yeah, I'd like that."

"Cool." He walked over to the door and opened it. "Still raining, but not very hard. Do you need a ride back to your hotel?"

"No, I'll be fine. It's actually not too far from here."

"At least let me walk you then."

She acquiesced and he grabbed a sweatshirt from a rack by the door and tossed it to her.

"You're slowly becoming quite the gentleman," she said, zipping the black hoodie.

He stepped aside, allowing her to leave. "Don't tell anyone. I have a reputation to uphold."

She laughed. They started back toward the square. This time, she reached for his hand, and he took hers.

They walked in silence. The soft drizzle was warm, nice. His beer buzz grew, enfolding him in the familiar carefree fog he spent most of his nights in. Holding Kat's hand like this, her in his sweatshirt, he wanted to kiss her.

"Home sweet home," she said as they stopped in front of Betty's Island Inn. "Isn't that a song?"

"Yeah, I love that song."

"It's a hair metal band, right?"

"Mötley Crüe."

"Oh yeah, well, I guess this is good night."

He was normally quite the coward when it came to end-of-the-night goodbyes, but he was lured by Kat's charm.

"Can I kiss you?" he asked.

She turned toward him, her nose six inches from his own, and nodded.

It was open-mouthed but sweet and innocent. Perfect.

When their lips parted, she said, "Good night, Rocky."

"Yeah, good night." He put his hands in his pockets and started to back away. "Wait, how do I get ahold of you?"

"Meet me at Duke's Thursday at seven p.m. We'll have a couple drinks before dinner. Then you can take me wherever you want."

"Cool. Bye, Kat."

She gave him a wave and he watched her walk into the cheap-looking hotel's front lobby. He thought a bigtime journalist for someone like *The Scene* would be staying at one of the classier inns along the shore, but she didn't strike him as the stuck-up, show-off type of girl. She didn't seem much like any girl he'd met. Well, maybe one.

He turned away and walked home in the drizzly night. Rocky was smiling for the first time in a long time.

★　★　★

From a distance, November walked Rocky home. Once he was safe inside, she returned to Betty's Island Inn. She walked into the lobby and waltzed up to the desk and the blonde woman standing there with elephant earrings and a pretty smile. "I'm looking for a friend of mine. She would have checked in in the last week or so, long black curly hair, pretty, just got back twenty minutes ago."

"I'm not able to give out that—"

Staring into November's heavy gaze, the woman, Angel, her name tag read, stopped.

After a few seconds, Angel looked at her computer screen, tapped a few buttons, and said, "She only checked in tonight."

Interesting. Where had she been staying before? She'd been here longer than just tonight. "Her name, please."

Angel went to the Rolodex of room information on the edge of the desk. "Kat Williams. Room 210. She's here for the next three nights."

"Thank you, Angel. You have a great evening."

She was tempted to go up to the room right now, place her ear to the door, see if she could get more vibes…but she also wondered if she were being a jealous, overprotective lunatic.

Rocky had been smiling.

And with that, she called it a night. Maybe her feelings were getting in the way of her powers.

She put on her headphones, pushed play on the Discman, launched into the air, and let the metal mix CD accompany her flight home.

CHAPTER TWENTY-FIVE

"Mary?" Jewel Marlon asked through the screen door. "Have you seen or heard from Jason today? He went to meet a girl on a date last night and never came back."

Mary placed the rack of freshly baked chocolate chip cookies on the counter and walked to the screen door. She placed a hand over her mouth. "Oh, dear."

"It's not like him to not at least phone. I don't know. He's twenty, but he's still my baby. I know it's possible he spent the night with her, I'm not old-fashioned, but it feels all wrong."

"Come in, come." Mary opened the screen door and allowed her inside. "I was gone in the city today. I'll go ask Gil if he's seen Jason."

Jewel stood just inside the door. She couldn't sit, the anxiety roaring through her like a thousand angry fire ants had her ready to explode or completely fall apart. Either way, her restlessness would put her out of commission soon if she didn't find her son.

Mary came back from the little hallway to the right of the television with Gil in tow. He was shaking his head behind her.

"Sorry, Jewel. I wish I could tell you he was here or that I saw him today, but I haven't. Did you contact the police?"

She brought a hand to her lips and shook her head. Her eyes grew watery.

"Come on, hon," Mary said, taking her by the elbow and leading her to the sofa.

Jewel didn't want to not be proactive, but at the thought of contacting the police, her knees suddenly felt weak, and the tears fell.

"Oh God," she said. "What if something's happened to him?"

Mary sat next to Jewel. She put an arm around her shoulder and let her lean against her.

"Where's Anthony?" Mary said.

"He's in town asking around."

"Gil," Mary said. "Could you get the cordless phone?"

By the time they had the Old Orchard police on the line, Jewel was picking at her fingers. Mary did most of the talking until Jewel could compose herself enough to finish the call.

Anthony returned just before dark, defeated. The Hersoms joined them next door, so as not to miss Jason coming home or any potential phone call.

He did not make it home that night.

Around the start of the second film of the Saco Drive-In double-feature, about the time Anthony Marlon had broken out the whiskey to help alleviate the fear and anguish he and his wife were being swallowed by, Gil Hersom had one drink himself, and Jason Marlon awoke from a deep sleep. A gorgeous girl had wrapped him in a tangerine dream… or was that a band on the stereo? Whatever the case, the heavens had opened and brought him home to a place that he'd never seen. Warm sand, sweat, and a sort of sexual residue covered his skin. The moment slowed and sped up, slowed and sped up, a bizarre waltz filled with even stranger rhythms and odder sensations. A thousand tiny legs trundled beneath the flesh of his throat…and then…the dream was over.

Jason opened his eyes to the moonlit sky above, and the warm ground beneath him. He gazed upon trees and heard the night critters all around. Meeps and peeps, skitters and scratches of smaller and smaller legs traipsing across the earth. He lifted his right hand and wondered where the hell he was right at this very moment.

The smell of popcorn and hamburgers, French fries and pizza wafted toward him. And the sound of…applause? He heard a familiar sound effect, *chick-eeewwww*…and a monologue he recognized. Jason sat up as the crazy laughter of a drunkard in the cemetery during one of the first few scenes of Tobe Hooper's horror classic *The Texas Chain*

Saw Massacre echoed from a hundred car stereos nearby.

The Saco Drive-In had classic horror double-features on Wednesday nights. But that was impossible. He was here to meet Midnight tonight.

His right hand found the wound on his neck. And it all came back to him. And it was then he knew he should be dead but wasn't.

Jason stood and shuffled from the woods, the lights of the big movie screen illuminating his way. Tears streaked his cheeks. As he wiped them with his forearm, he saw the dark trails they left on his skin. He was crying blood. And the tears came harder, blurring his vision as he walked on, leaving the trees and the forest surrounding the drive-in behind him.

Jason stumbled out of the shadows and onto the blacktop.

Headlights exploded into life like a prison spotlight as screeching tires filled the night. Jason never saw the truck until it smashed him into roadkill.

Lying there, half on the hot pavement, half in the dirt, his lifeforce oozing from a dozen compound fractures and gashes, Jason thought of vampires and eternal life and his mom and Mary Hersom.

What's going to happen to John Coffey on the Green Mile? Is he gonna be saved in time?

And he thought no more.

PART THREE:

FLESH & BLOOD: SACRIFICE

CHAPTER TWENTY-SIX

Fiona wondered if this was how they should have been living all along. The blood and the sex, the killing and the power, it was all so damn titillating. And having Vincent to herself, a partner in it all, the way she imagined it could be ever since he walked into her life back at the university, only made it that much better.

She wished now that she had stayed in her dorm room that night and witnessed Vincent's fury as it was unleashed upon her rapist boyfriend. Vincent never even told her what happened that night, just that he'd killed the asshole. It had been a while since she last tried to talk with him about it. Fiona would try again to get the full details from him when he was awake.

Getting up from the bed, last night's victim sprawled out on the floor of the hotel room, Fiona carefully stepped around it, and wondered if Kat was ever going to come up from her makeshift coffin in the basement. They'd been extremely careless the last few nights. What would Kat do if she rose to find them like this? Even in the early dawn light sneaking in from the sunrise across the beach, she could see the bloody mess. Reckless, overindulgent, fun as fucking hell, but still.

As she moved across the floor to stand in the window and gaze at the sun coming up, she wished more than anything for a steaming mug of coffee. It had been one of her favorite things. Waking up before her family when she was at home, her friends when they partied late into the night, or her roommate before Vincent came along. To get up while the rest of the world was asleep and welcome a new day full of unwritten stories, unlimited possibilities.... Well, maybe with the amount of money she'd had back in those days the list of possibilities would be shortened, but it was exciting to know you had a head start that lit a fuse inside. All your friends were wasting precious time.

As the brilliance of the sun grew, Fiona wondered for the first time in a long time what her ideal future was now. Where it once had been total domination of the indie punk scene, spreading her unique rebellious take on the world and its oppression of the soul, of gender, of class.... That had all been changed. But it wasn't becoming a vampire that initiated the change. No, her unraveling began with Roland. She had handed her balls over to him. Like a stupid, pathetic school girl. She had handed in her punk rock badge then and there as he slapped her around, treated her like a hooker, and promised her nothing.

Anger spilled into her. She felt the tears in there too, but it was the rage that fired her engines now.

Vincent stood behind her.

"Good morning," she said.

His hands found her bare shoulders. "What's on your mind?"

"Tell me about that night."

He leaned forward and kissed her neck.

She put a hand on his. "Please."

"What does it matter now? We're here, together."

"How long had you been watching me?"

"What do you mean?"

"Before you showed up to kill Roland. How long had you been following me?"

"I'd seen you in the park and I came to you." He continued kissing her.

She stepped away and crossed her arms over her chest.

"Oh, come on," he said, shaking his head and looking at the ground. He raised his gaze to meet hers. "What is this? Huh? What, are you having some crisis of the soul, or something? It's a little late for that, don't you think?" He gestured toward the body on the floor.

"Obviously it doesn't change anything," she said, turning back toward the sunrise. "I just want the truth. All of it."

He sighed behind her. And she knew she'd won.

"All right," he said. He walked up and wrapped his arms around her.

★   ★   ★

Near the end of that summer, Vincent wandered. After a year in Los Angeles, Kat had brought him back to her homeland. He'd never been to Canada when he was human. He'd never made it out of California. Why would he leave? It was Hollywood and the Sunset Strip, the land of opportunity and dying dreams. There was hope and desperation, promise and decay on every corner. Canada was different. Vancouver was still a city, it was busy, yet somehow retained its soul, a trick L.A. would never learn. He thought he'd be bored to death, but instead, he found a thousand nightspots to haunt, and a thousand more places to roam in the daylight. The campus was interesting, lots of young flesh to gaze upon, and plenty of out-of-town bodies to drain. He'd enjoyed his time there, but he had days when he was out on his own, while Kat was doing her own thing, when he felt off. It was as if he was missing something. It was on one of his off days when Fiona walked onto his path and changed everything.

Her fiery hair matched her burning soul. The scent of her body, not strong or bad, just *her* scent, lured him as she walked by him that first day. And if she had noticed him at all, she showed zero interest. This also made him want her more.

He came back to the park to see her every day after. Kat never asked where he was going and never had any inkling to join him. So he came out and observed Fiona. She would have headphones on and be belting out wild punk songs. Or at least, lip-syncing to them and thrashing around without a care for those around her. It was hypnotic. Her energy was beautiful. As the school year got under way, she spent more time near the coffee shop at the edge of the common swallowing down caffeine and checking the flyers posted to the door or to telephone poles. He recognized this daily routine for what it was, as he had done the same back home. She was searching for a band. She certainly had the voice for it, but every day was met with disappointment. And within a couple weeks, she began to act different.

The fire muted to a fading ember. Something had changed.

It was then that he found her with the other man. And then that he began to worry for her.

Roland had trapped her in the old familiar way. Flowers and romance. It shouldn't have worked on a girl like Fiona, but isn't that the way? The tough-girl façade was penetrated by this coward, this true fiend. And Roland Torrence was just that, a monster preying upon a type. And give the son of a bitch credit, he saw a weakness in Fiona that Vincent had missed. And within a matter of weeks, the bastard not only exploited her insecurities but managed to multiply them until they consumed and deteriorated every ounce of her self-worth and confidence.

She no longer sang her way to the coffee shop. Her stride was reduced to a chin-down, shoulders-slumped march of obedience and defeat. She was quiet and meek. It was the most painful thing he'd ever witnessed. And he knew he had to save her. To rescue her before this man took what was left and ruined it for good.

The next week, he approached her, and that night, he stopped the decay.

★   ★   ★

Fiona's heart swooned. She wrapped her arms around Vincent's neck and kissed him. He embraced her, and she'd never felt safer.

"Thank you," she said.

"I couldn't watch you disappear," he said, stroking her cheek. "You're my angel."

She knew he meant every word. No matter what happened with Kat now, he was hers and for forever, she would be his.

"I fucking love you, Vincent."

"Yeah, I know. And you've got me until the end."

Sunlight surrounded them, bright and glorious as the heavens. Even its draining effect couldn't piss on their moment. Fiona held him tightly, her cheek to his shoulder. They stood that way for a long time, reveling in their love.

162 • GLENN ROLFE

CHAPTER TWENTY-SEVEN

He spent the entire day feeling things he hadn't really felt in ages. Kat was so fucking cool. And working for *The Scene*? How rad was that? If anyone was worthy of getting an exclusive interview, it was *The Scene*. Rocky still had a hell of a collection boxed up right here in his apartment. So many cool covers. U2, Slash when Guns N' Roses were still tracking the *Use Your Illusion* records. Prince, Madonna, Nirvana, Green Day, Pearl Jam. He was half tempted to go dig them out and search for Kat's articles. Of course, she may not have anything in the ones he had. They were a little bit older.

Rocky took a shower, shaved, and threw on some black jeans and a plain black t-shirt. Looking in the mirror, he considered switching to something less, well, dark, but he didn't think Kat would care what he wore.

And there she was again, in his head.

The machine in the living room picked up as someone was leaving a message:

"Hello, Mr. Zukas, this is Kris Rufty with the Portland Tribune, *and I was hoping you might be willing to meet me for lunch sometime this week. It's obviously to discuss the network special surrounding Gabriel Riley, but I also wanted to get your thoughts on the recent rash of disappearances. My number here at the office is...."*

Disappearances? Rocky hadn't heard or seen anything reported on Franklin or Scott. He wasn't about to talk about any of it to anyone besides Kat, but his curiosity was a blazing inferno right now.

Disappearances?

He stepped outside into the last of the August warmth. It wasn't cold by any means, but the days of melting heat were finally on the run, a telling tale that summer was packing up. It felt good. His thoughts returned to Scott Jorgenson's desiccated body and shredded neck. The body that had vanished. Rocky had spent the last two days in a drunken stupor trying to forget what he thought happened.

November, please don't let this be you.

Bayley's Book Store was a few minutes' walk. They always sold copies of the *Portland Tribune* and *The Scene.* He wanted to see what he was apparently missing. What if Scott *and* Franklin were dead? What if it went beyond that?

Don't get ahead of yourself. Just chill out. Relax.

He stepped past a couple of bleach blondes, maybe legal age, maybe not, dressed in string bikinis. He averted his eyes from their curves and walked into the little store. He said a quick hello to Pamela, the elderly lady that always worked the morning weekday shifts at the shop, and grabbed a copy of the *Portland Tribune,* paid Pamela, and folded it under his arm without looking at it.

Outside, he stopped at Bruno's Pizzeria and ordered a slice of pepperoni and a Pepsi.

That's when he glanced at the front page and the headline:

Missing Persons in Old Orchard Beach Area. Police Asking for Information

He read the article while waiting for his order.

If you have seen any of the persons in the pictures below, or have knowledge regarding their whereabouts, please contact the Maine State Police or detectives at the Missing Persons Bureau. You may also contact the local police.

Rocky recognized Franklin and Scott. There were several others pictured he didn't know: Cyndle Rials of Saco, Jeremy Tripp of Old Orchard Beach, and Jeffrey Gallagher of Biddeford. One out-of-stater was listed. A Kasey Tetu, from Waltham, Massachusetts.

There were no details about the missing persons in the front-page article, just the faces and names, and numbers to contact. This hit far too close to home.

Someone tapped Rocky on the shoulder and said, "Hoss, that you?"

Rocky felt disoriented. A muscly dude with slicked-back black hair, dressed in a sleeveless undershirt and black Adidas shorts and way too many gold necklaces, pointed toward the pizza and soda sitting on the ordering counter. The guy was chewing on his own slice with cheese stretched out from his lip to the piece in his hand.

"Oh, yeah, thanks."

The guy nodded at the paper and wiped his lip. "You guys got some kind of killer on the loose 'round here, huh?"

"I don't think so," he said.

"Yeah, well, maybe you got a shark problem, huh? Your mayor gonna close the beaches?"

"What?"

"Nothin', bro, I'm just bustin' your nuts." The guy elbowed him. "Still strange, though, all them people missing. Enjoy your pie, huh?"

The guy walked off, yelling after some girls down the block.

Rocky didn't know what was going on, but Scott and Franklin were definitely connected. And after all that Rocky had been through, he couldn't deny the further possibilities regarding the others being missing too. He suddenly wanted to talk to someone else about it, but he hadn't spoken to this particular someone else in a long time.

He wondered if Kat had heard about the missing people.

If she's any good at her job, of course she has.

If only she'd given him her phone number last night.

CHAPTER TWENTY-EIGHT

Jason hadn't come home last night, either. Jewel knew her baby boy was in trouble. She made another call to the Old Orchard Beach police and was told to come down to the station. Jewel and Anthony Marlon thanked Mary and Gil for their hospitality and kindness. The Hersoms truly were the most amazing people, not just to them, but to Jason especially, Mary in particular. Her connection to their son through their shared love for Stephen King was something special. Jewel appreciated the Hersoms' sincerity more than they'd ever know.

Anthony was driving like a madman.

"Slow down," Jewel said, holding the oh shit bar. "It's just down the street. We don't need to get ourselves or anyone else killed getting there."

"I'm sorry. I just…."

He didn't need to finish his thought. She was already there with him.

"I know. Me too," she said.

He slowed down. The Old Orchard Beach police station came into sight just ahead.

"Do you think he's…."

Anthony grabbed her hand.

"No," was all he said. The silence expanded between them, somehow growing so loud in her heart that it made her feel like screaming her lungs out.

Anthony stopped across from the station parking lot and tapped the steering wheel, anxious to go as the early evening traffic refused to let them through.

166 • GLENN ROLFE

Jewel leaned out her window and said, "Come on, let us through, you fucking beach-going yuppie assholes!"

Two cars later, a Ford truck stopped, the old man behind the wheel wearing wire-rimmed spectacles waved them in.

"Thank you," Jewel said, much calmer.

Anthony pulled in and directed the vehicle into the first open spot. He put the car in Park and looked at her. "Are you ready?"

She nodded.

The small police station was buzzing like a hive full of agitated worker bees. The edginess in the air was suffocating. The vibe didn't make her feel any better.

"Excuse me," Anthony said to the nearest cop, standing by an empty desk.

"Sir?" the officer said. His name tag read: Peppers.

"Hi. Our son, Jason, hasn't come home in a couple of days. We called and were asked to come down to talk with someone."

"How long has it been since you last saw your son?" Peppers asked.

"He didn't come back the other night from a date, to the—" he turned to Jewel, "—the uh, drive-in, right?"

She nodded.

Anthony turned back to Officer Peppers and continued. "And before you say anything, yes, we considered he went home with the girl, but it is totally unlike Jason not to call and at least leave us a message."

"He wouldn't do that," Jewel added. "Jason always calls. Even if he's just running late."

"The drive-in, over in Saco?" Peppers said.

"Yes," Jewel answered.

The cop stood up straighter and looked over his shoulder, seemingly searching the room for something. His gaze found whatever he was searching for and he looked to Anthony. "Stay right here."

Jewel clasped her hands around Anthony's. "Oh my God. What do you think happened? What's he doing?"

Officer Peppers met a buzz-cut blond man across the room and was leaning in talking into the man's ear. She wished she could hear them, or that she could read lips.

The blond man – short, stocky, and dressed in khakis and a white short-sleeve button-up, looked in their direction before nodding at Peppers and picking up a folder from his desk.

He walked over to them as Peppers went in the other direction. "Sir. Ma'am. I'm Detective Sipowicz."

"Hello," Jewel said.

"I'm sorry," Anthony said, his irritation getting the best of him. "Can we please skip the introductions?"

"Of course," the detective said.

"Do you or do you not already know something about Jason?" Anthony said.

Sipowicz opened the file.

"Your son, Jason, was at the Saco Drive-In night before last?"

"Yes," Jewel said.

Anthony clenched her hand and put his other arm around her shoulder, pulling her close.

"I need you to look at these photos. They're not nice. We can go into my office if you'd prefer more privacy."

"Oh God," Jewel said, her knees weakened.

Anthony tightened his hold of her, and said, "Yes, I think privacy would be best."

Sipowicz's office was devoid of decor, important or otherwise. The walls offered no signs of recommendations or awards, no pictures of the detective smiling alongside people of importance, just pale green paint. A couple of three-drawer filing cabinets and a desk covered in paper, folders, and a tiny desk fan. His nameplate was the only thing in the room that gave his position.

"Please, have a seat," he said.

"Can I just see the photos?" Anthony said.

Jewel took the vinyl seat closest to him, already pulling tissues from her purse.

Sipowicz handed over the folder. "These were taken last night on Route 1, about five hundred feet from the drive-in entrance."

She watched as Anthony took the folder and began going through the photos within.

On the third one, he broke.

"Is that your son?" Sipowicz asked, placing a hand on the man's jerking shoulders.

Anthony nodded.

Jewel's cries filled the room.

CHAPTER TWENTY-NINE

Eddie tried to keep Karla away from his place; he knew she'd talk him into sneaking into Mr. Tibbetts's house. Ever since they talked about what happened when he was with Rocky Zukas, she had been obsessed and convinced it was some kind of murder.

"There," she said, slapping a newspaper on his kitchen table. "There *is* something strange going on around here. Look at those people."

He gazed down at the pictures of six people under the ominous Missing Persons headline.

The front door opened, and his father came through. "Hey, Eddie," his dad said, placing his lunch pail on the kitchen counter. "Hiya, Karla...right?"

"You got it. Hard day at work?" she said.

"Always is." He reached into the fridge and pulled out a beer, twisted the top off and took a sip. "What are you kids up to?"

"Just investigating some disappearances in the area," Karla said.

"Sounds like nonstop fun."

Eddie wasn't sure his dad even heard what she said.

"You get that note from your mom?" his dad asked.

"Yeah, we were gonna go for a walk—"

"Investigating?" his dad said, giving Karla a wink.

"Yeah. We'll stop in and check on Mrs. Beverly while we're out."

"You better. You know how your mother worries about her and most of our neighbors. She thinks this street should be rechristened the Smith Street Retirement Community."

"Yeah, but that would make us and Mr. Tibbets the caretakers, wouldn't it?"

"Yeah," he said. "I guess it would, if he's okay." His dad walked to the living room window, peeking through the Venetian blinds. "Still can't imagine anything bad happening to him or Scott." After a pause, his dad turned back toward them. "You two steer clear of his place, okay?"

"We will," Eddie said. He turned to Karla. "You ready?"

Out on the sidewalk, Karla took his hand. "Do you think they're both dead?"

"I hope not."

He thought about telling her what Rocky said about Scott Jorgenson's dead body but decided not to give her any reason to ignore his father's request to stay away from Mr. Tibbetts's house. Eddie hadn't told a soul about the body. Truth was, he didn't want to go anywhere near the house across the street again. Just looking at it now with the yellow police tape around the porch was giving him the willies.

He noticed a shape in the upstairs window. He froze.

"Did you—" he started.

"What?" she said.

He stared at the empty window. Whatever had been there was gone.

"Nothing," he said. "Let's get going."

Eddie gripped her hand tighter and moved a little faster along the sidewalk. Mrs. Beverly lived two houses down from Mr. Tibbetts.

The old woman's brick walkway was lined with pink and purple azaleas and yellow dahlias. His mom liked to talk about what a 'green thumb' Mrs. Beverly had. When Eddie first heard that, he thought it meant there was something wrong with the woman's thumb, like it was infected or something. He envisioned it rotting off like something from the eighties horror flick *From Beyond*. Later, he learned it meant that she could grow anything.

They walked to the door. Karla knocked.

Eddie let go of her hand, cupped his over his eyes and peered through the little window in the door. There was no movement. It was dead quiet. Still looking inside, he pulled one hand away and knocked harder.

"That's her car, isn't it?"

He looked at the spot in front of her little garage. The red Ford Escort sat in the sun.

"Yeah, so she's got to be here. Unless somebody took her out someplace."

Karla took a turn peeking through the window, and then turned to him with her finger pointing at her temple like a gun. "Or someone just took her out. Should we try the door?"

"What? Why? She's probably just gone shopping for arthritis cream or walking her poodle, Cooly."

Karla turned the knob. The door creaked open just a crack. But that crack was enough. The smell wafting out was horrendous.

"Oh shit," he said, covering his nose.

Karla did the same as she pushed the door open further.

Eddie could see the small pool of congealed blood on the kitchen floor. It wasn't Mrs. Beverly, though. It was Cooly.

"What the hell are you doing?" he asked.

"We have to see if your neighbor's all right," Karla said.

It wasn't just Mrs. Beverly's place that had been quiet this week. It wasn't even just her and Mr. Tibbetts. The whole damn street felt off. It felt...*dead*.

"No, I think we—"

Karla entered the house.

Eddie gave the car a second glance. Beyond the Escort, he noticed most of the others on Smith Street were also home. Usually, there would be a number of people tending their yards or on their porches sipping lemonade or beer. This afternoon, despite the nice weather, there was no one.

"Are you coming?"

He looked into her beautiful blue eyes and took her hand. "Yeah, but if we find anything else, we're going straight back to my place and calling the cops."

"Deal."

They stepped to the kitchen. A tea cup sat on the little Formica table against the far window. A magazine lay open next to it. The dog's dead body looked deflated. It could have been some kind of realistic-looking blow-up Halloween decoration.

Each with a hand covering their mouth and nose, the other clenched in one another's, Eddie and Karla moved from the kitchen to the living room and down the small hallway.

There were three rooms, each one with the door closed.

Eddie let go of Karla's hand and opened the first door.

A little white room, white walls, white carpeting, was filled with white shelves lined from wall to wall with life-like dolls.

Karla peered over his shoulder. "Creepy."

"Yeah, nope. Nothing to see in this one."

Eddie shivered. He had an aunt that collected creepy dolls with glass eyes. He always imagined them coming to life and crawling after him. Mrs. Beverly's collection was no different.

The next room was a very pink and frilly-looking bathroom. They moved to the last door. It had to be her bedroom. If she was dead, this is most likely where they'd find her.

"You sure you want to do this?" he asked.

"We have to, don't you think?"

He did not think so. Yet, for her, and because it was the last door, he reached forward and turned the knob.

Karla screamed.

Goosebumps busted out across his arms as his stomach hit the floor.

He stumbled backward and turned away, pressing Karla's head into his shoulder.

"You two really shouldn't have come in here."

Karla screamed again. The gross, decayed-looking body on the bed no longer mattered. Eddie spun, placing Karla behind him, to face the woman now standing at the end of the hallway.

"Who are you?" he asked, his voice quavering.

"It really doesn't matter, does it? Neither of you is going to be leaving."

"Karla," Eddie said. "Run."

He raised his fists as the woman flew toward him. He felt the wind and a force that hit like 'Stone Cold' Steve Austin and he was slammed sideways into the doorway where he crumpled to the floor. His head swam with a thousand impossible thoughts. Karla's screams brought him around.

"Eddie, help me!"

He climbed to his feet and heard the woman suckling at Karla's throat before he saw them on the bed next to Mrs. Beverly's ghastly body. He looked around for a weapon and found a doll sitting upon a small wooden chair. He knocked it aside and grabbed the chair it was sitting on.

The woman slammed into him again and clenched him by the throat. His feet came off the ground; the chair fell from his hand. He could see Karla's lifeless eyes gazing at him from where she lay next to Mrs. Beverly, her neck a crimson mess.

He looked to the killer and wet his pants at the sight of her monstrous face. Her forehead protruded slightly, lined with bumps and cracks. Her eyes were pure onyx pools, and her blood-covered mouth housed sharpened fangs.

The creature stared its death-filled eyes straight into Eddie's soul.

"Really," the monster said. "This isn't me. You just really shouldn't have been here."

Eddie's scream was cut short when the thing bit into his neck. The excruciating pain quickly waned to a warm fuzzy feeling. His body went limp; he became putty in her embrace until his thoughts drifted into nothingness.

CHAPTER THIRTY

Kat felt like a million dollars. She'd never fed so much in such a short period of time. A weak voice in the back of her mind was concerned about her growing hunger, but the parts of her that felt electric managed to stuff those worries down deep enough for her to enjoy the moment. Stumbling upon the teenagers on Smith Street was an accident. She had come back to take inventory of her kills and begin the cleanup job she knew she'd been too fucked up to do properly the last few times she was here. The young couple shouldn't have been there, but she was certainly glad that they were. The fresh blood was invigorating and made her feel invincible.

She had her next date with Rocky to think about.

She made her way back to her room at Betty's Island Inn. Showered and dried off, she gazed into the mirror. Her ringlets framed her face nicely. She'd picked up a navy-blue pencil skirt and a cute short-sleeve navy blue-striped shirt that made her breasts look amazing.

God, she had been nervous around Rocky. A vampire, fucking nervous. It seemed so ridiculous, but the slithering worms in her stomach had been undeniable. The fresh feeding had swallowed those butterflies and left her with a dose of swagger. She wanted him and, tonight, she would have him.

And if it turned out Rocky was a vampire killer?

Well, that seemed highly unlikely. The guy didn't look intense enough to kick a drunk dude's ass, let alone take on a monster and live to talk about it. She still had to press him on *that* night and be certain.

She grabbed her bag, double-checking to make sure she had her tape recorder, notebook, and pen, and made her way out of the room.

Angel stood behind the reception desk. The blonde smiled. "How is your stay?" she asked.

"Oh, it's been perfect. Thank you."

Walking up the pier, she spotted him standing there grinning, in a plain white t-shirt and jeans. He held out his elbow for her to take. She did, and a thrill ran up her arms at the touch. Rocky surprised her by leaning in and giving her a peck on the cheek.

"You look amazing," he said.

Kat was tempted to back him to the wall and kiss him for real right here, right now. The kiss the other night had been sweet but simple. She wanted more. Instead, she smiled and let him lead her to Duke's.

It was busy, but not as hectic and loud as it had been the other night.

"Aloha," Duke greeted them. "I have your table reserved. Follow me, please."

"Is he always this charming?" Kat said.

"Yeah, he's a local legend, and he lives up to every story."

"Sort of like you."

Rocky's smile faltered. Just for a moment. "Yeah, well, I'm not on Duke's level just yet, but I'm still young."

Duke held out a chair for Kat. She sat down and let him slide her seat to the table. He placed two simple one-page laminated menus before each of them. "Beers to start?"

"Sure," Rocky said. "I'll have Sam Adams Rebel."

"Oh, going with an IPA tonight," Duke said.

"Well, it's a special dinner, I guess."

"And for you, gorgeous?"

Kat looked over her choices. "I'll take anything sour."

"Coming right up."

Kat studied him. Something was off. He'd grin whenever their eyes met, but his forehead was creased in the moments in between. She recognized the look. He was contemplating something heavy.

"I know we agreed to have our drinks first," she said. "But can I ask you something now?"

"Sure."

"You dropped your guard with me before."

"Too many drinks."

"Could be," she replied. "Or it could be that you like me."

"You're all right, I guess." The corners of his mouth lifted.

An attractive young woman in pigtails brought them their drinks.

"Here you go, Rocky," she said. Kat could see the twinkle in the girl's eyes and felt a pang of jealousy.

"Thanks, Emily. This is Kat."

Kat gave a quick wave and forced a smile. The girl was much closer to Rocky's age and as cute as a Hollywood actress. She hated her.

Emily smiled and said, "Hi, Kat. I love your curls."

"Thank you."

"Do we need another minute?" Rocky said to Kat.

"Actually," Emily said. "Duke has something special for you two, if you're up for it."

"Sure," Kat said.

"Thanks, Emily."

Emily took their menus and pranced away.

"I wonder what Duke's got cooked up for us," Rocky said.

"For someone who strives to be Batman, you sure have a lot of Bruce Wayne going on."

"Hey, comic book references will only get you whatever you want. And besides, I'm not always dark and moody, I can be outgoing, too."

"Yeah, when there's cute girls waiting on you."

His smile fell as he looked over her shoulder. She tracked his gaze to the TV behind the bar. She couldn't hear it, but there was a picture of a woman with MISSING in bold white letters beneath her smiling face on the screen.

"Someone you know?" Kat asked.

"No, it's just…."

"What?" she said again, reaching across the table and putting a hand over his.

Rocky stared at their hands for a moment longer, and then cleared his throat, but left his hand with hers. "Have you heard about that?" He nodded toward the TV. "There seems to be something going on."

"What?" She looked back and the picture on the screen was now a weather map of the Maine coast. "What's going on?"

"Obviously," he began, taking his hand away and using it to sip his beer. "You're here like the others. You're trying to jump on the Gabriel Riley train and capture some of the buzz created by that bullshit documentary—"

"Rocky, I—"

He held up a hand to stop her. "Relax, Kat. I like you. I'm talking about…." He glanced around like someone might be spying on them. He leaned forward and she did the same. "People are going missing. It's fucked up, don't you think?"

"Are you connecting these missing people with what happened to you? Rocky, that was a decade ago. Gabe Riley is dead and a bunch of reporters descending upon the beach doesn't lead to a population decrease."

"Not exactly, but what if it's, I don't know, what if it's some kind of copycat killer?"

She knew they had been sloppy. She'd killed too many herself. There was no telling what Vincent and Fiona had done on top of the deaths she'd accumulated on Smith Street. She'd been lucky, so far. Fiona and Vincent weren't the subtlest creatures.

"It's totally possible. But to what end? Notoriety?"

"I mean, it wouldn't surprise me. This kind of media blitz on tragedy always brings out the pyschos. The world is full of sick puppies who just need a little push to go over that slim edge. Don't you think?"

"What if…" she said. "What if it's more than a crazy person?"

"What do you mean?"

"The rumors…."

His face soured, his eyebrows came together, his lips tightened.

"Here we go!" Duke said, appearing beside them and easing the tension. Emily set down a small stand next to their table and Duke placed a tray with two steaming plates of delicious-looking food down upon it.

"Whoa," Kat said. "This looks great."

"Loco moco," Duke said. "Mahalo, Emily."

The waitress bowed in a very dramatic and theatrical way, then took the tray and stand away. Kat didn't miss the smile she gave Rocky before making her exit stage left.

Duke's energy and cheerfulness were contagious. He beamed with pride. "It's rice with hamburger, eggs, and gravy. It's magnificent, if I do say so myself, and I do." His laughter filled the room. "Eat, eat. I'll leave you two to it."

"Mahalo," Rocky said, picking up his fork.

"Aloha!"

Kat dug into the meal, choosing to keep her mouth occupied and allow Rocky time to digest the course of their conversation. He wasn't stupid. He knew she would ask. How could she not?

Halfway through the meal, and two beers later, he finally spoke.

"I'm sorry. I know you have to ask about…the more bizarre aspects of what happened. I'm just on edge, I guess. I wanted to let myself believe I was out on a regular date with a gorgeous woman, and that was naïve of me."

Kat used a napkin to pat some of the warm grease and gravy from her lips. "Honestly, I had every intention of grilling you. I didn't care. I normally don't. I'm paid to get the story, but if it's any consolation, this is the first time I've actually felt guilty and a little dirty digging in. You don't deserve the aggravation."

"Thanks, but—"

"But, yeah, I wouldn't be very good at my job if I didn't push."

"Well, how's this. We enjoy the rest of our food like this is a real date, and when we get out of here, I'll give you the real story. Deal?"

She agreed. Most brainless decision she'd ever had to make. She wanted to keep up the façade just as much as he did.

After paying the bill and thanking Duke, they made their way down the pier to the beach, just starting to feel a good buzz from their beers. The time for revelations was upon them.

"Why *are* there rumors about monsters?"

He was holding her hand. It felt good.

"People don't like to think that humans are capable of such brutality," he said.

"So, you're saying there's no truth to the creature of the night angle."

"For real? You?"

"Hey, it's been rampant in the dark corners of the alternative media world."

"Yeah, where? The *Weekly World News*? *Coast 2 Coast AM*?"

"Well, of course, but these types of rumors tend to have a truthful spring. Where did this one come from? If anyone knows, it must be you. Maybe your mom or your sister?"

"My family stays out of this. Okay? They moved away from this place, these memories."

"Okay, but you gotta give me something."

He thought about Scott and Franklin. About the others in the paper. Jeremy, Cynthia. And the shape in the dark at Franklin's house.

It can't be her...but who else?

"Rocky?"

"Sorry, what was the question?"

"Come on," she said as they stopped, suddenly out of reach of the light from the closest bars. The ocean breeze, cool and briny, the sound of waves lapping the shore. No more pussyfooting around. She threw this pitch straight down the barrel with every ounce of heat she could muster.

"Level with me, Rocky. Why do you really think people are saying Gabriel Riley was a vampire?"

Rocky let go of her hand, took a deep breath, and turned to face the dark silhouette of the Ferris wheel. The scene of the final showdown. It was all very dramatic and if she really were a journalist writing this up for *The Scene* or any other publication, it would be sensational, but here alone with him, Kat's supernatural feelers were beginning to rise.

He brought his gaze back from the Ferris wheel and looked directly in her eyes, and said, "Come home with me."

CHAPTER THIRTY-ONE

November had no claim over him. Watching them was wrong, invasive, inappropriate. Still, she couldn't take her eyes off them as Rocky and the dark-haired beauty fled the beach before falling into each other's arms, a passion unleashed, their lips and tongues meeting under the streetlights halfway to Rocky's place. She should have left it there, allowed them their moment, but she followed. They stumbled through his front door, already undressing one another. When the door shut, November found herself outside his slightly open bedroom window.

Old Orchard Beach was motoring. Engines revved; music boomed from multiple establishments. Live bands, DJs, karaoke and open mics, it was all the same thing every night of the summer – *alive*. There was a time when November craved that same energy. Back then, whenever she could slip away from the watchful eyes of Mother or Gabriel, she'd get as close to it as she could. And when she finally got the courage to join in, her heart beat like theirs. The rhythm of life in progress was addictive. Where their cursed gifts became her brother's compulsion, the need to be among *them* was hers. The summer she met Rocky validated everything she thought she knew at the time. True love was not only attainable, but it was an absolute promise. She still remembered Rocky passing out from heatstroke the day they met, then, later that night leaving him breathless on the beach in neon green swimming trunks, days and weeks sharing their love of music, Rocky showing her around town, and the night they slept together....

The intimate sound of smacking lips, skin on skin, and a headboard booming against the wall brought her back from the past and delivered her face-first into the fate Gabriel assured her was waiting at the end of her fantasy.

You will never be one of them.

When they were younger, before Gabriel turned into the hideous creature that destroyed everything, he told her to always remember three things: lay low, feed when you can, and never make friends.

Her heart dropped into her stomach as she slowly stepped from the window and turned away.

She found herself on the beach, shoes in hand, feet in the cooling sand, shoulders slumped, tears ready to spill. Suddenly, everywhere she looked, there were couples. Two goth couples around a radio, listening to alternative music; a beautiful young blonde in a flowing white dress walking hand in hand with an older guy with a sky-high mohawk, dressed in cargo shorts and Chuck Taylors. Farther down, closer to the water, she noticed another couple just behind a stumbling woman, weaving back and forth before the apparently drunk lady wound up on her hands and knees at the farthest-reaching waves. November watched as the man and woman bent down and appeared to check on her. After a moment, the couple helped the woman up, each taking an arm as they led her away from the cold Atlantic.

It was sweet.

The gesture made her start to feel better until she saw the man and woman clocking their surroundings, their movements so slight that no one would notice...no one human. She knew what they were before the woman bit into the inebriated lady's neck, the action a blur to the naked eye. The female vampire moved with stealth and speed.

All these years November wondered if she'd ever witness another creature like her again. And here they were. Two of them on *her* beach, in *her* town. Right here, right now. She'd never felt territorial, but something was stirring inside her. An urge to protect this woman. Common sense muted the impulse. There were two of them and one of her. No telling how powerful they were. No, she wouldn't be able to save the woman, but she could follow along and see what she could find out about these interlopers.

Interlopers.

The word, even though she hadn't spoken it out loud, was something pretentious and exaggerated her brother Gabriel would have said.

I'm not like him.

No, November was not a bloodthirsty murderer, not yet, but she wasn't who or what she wanted to be, no matter how hard she tried or how much she wished.

Moving away from the shore and into the shadows closer to the thinning number of hotels and seaside inns, unnoticed, she followed the vampires and their victim. The blood-hungry couple carried their slumping meal, feigning a struggle until they reached an alley between a closed night club and the Captain's Biscuit, a shitty pub only lonely locals hung around in. The foot traffic here was next to nil. If they were going to feast, this would be the spot.

Sure enough, she watched the man and woman as they looked around, saw that they were indeed alone and dropped the woman's body to the ground. November witnessed a passion spark between these two fiends. A long kiss shared between them as they sunk down, tongues still touching as they lowered the body. They broke their lip-lock, smiles dressing their pale faces, their mouths widened, revealing gangs of sharpened teeth. Together, the monsters did what they did best. She could hear the familiar sounds of punctured flesh, the drawing of blood, thirsty suckling and gulping. Her own hunger stirred, dropping her to her knees. She had to tear her gaze from the scene, biting the side of her own hand. She could feel her own body begging her to join in.

She took deep breaths as the couple drained their victim. When they finished, November felt a knot pulled tightly in her guts when she tried to stand. She needed to find out where they were going next. Surely, they had a place nearby to sleep. The man turned toward where she stood. Holding her breath, she hoped he was just scanning their surroundings and not actually sensing her presence. He stood still, looking right at her, or so she thought. Her cold skin prickled. Just when she was certain he would come for her, he instead met his partner's gaze and motioned toward the desiccated form at their feet. The woman laughed and playfully slapped his shoulder. November breathed a sigh when he took the woman's hand. The couple gazed skyward and flew into the night.

"Shit," she muttered. She set into flight, being sure to stay low and trail behind without losing sight of them. Pursuit while in flight was more difficult, especially if you wanted to remain undetected. She chose to hurry across rooftops where she could, from shadow to shadow.

A few minutes later, the couple descended upon a boarded-up hotel not far from where her own family had once stayed. A road off East Grand Avenue, Wilton Street, was until recently, home to the Avalon Hotel. The Avalon surprisingly closed its doors two weeks ago. Rumors around town were rampant regarding Roux's gambling debts and bad habits. Whispers of 'the mob' possibly being the ones who forced Roux to sell and were now holding the deed to the profitable property weren't far behind. Small towns have big imaginations, though, and November highly doubted that any greedy new owners would close the place before the end of summer. After following the vamps here, she now knew what happened to Jonathan Roux and the Avalon Hotel.

The couple entered the building via an open window on the fifth floor. November landed on the roof and pulled the door open. As she descended into the darkness, a thrill rushed through her. She crept down the stairs, through nearly pitch-black hallways and down more stairs until she reached the fifth floor. Slowly, November opened the door and peered down a long corridor. In a room not far down the hall, and for the second time in this short night, she heard the unmistakable sounds of people fucking.

"Great," she muttered.

Not eager to eavesdrop on the fornicating vampiric duo, or to be caught by them, she decided to leave the floor and make a quick check of the lower floors before heading out.

In short order, she found the other floors vacant of other vampires but not of bodies. The couple had been busy in their short time here in town. As she suspected, the body of Jonathan Roux was here among at least a dozen others. Jonathan's blood-drenched white dress shirt adorned his shriveled body. His name tag was still pinned to his chest and read:

Jonathan Roux
owner/operator
The Avalon Hotel

She didn't recognize any of the others but had a feeling investigating any recent missing persons with the police department or local paper would prove extremely enlightening. She had no such desires. What she had now were more questions, and one giant decision ahead of her.

She let herself out one of the broken entrances on the ground level. With the hulking hotel of death behind her, November knew what she had to do. This news was too big to keep to herself.

And she knew the only person she could tell.

186 • GLENN ROLFE

CHAPTER THIRTY-TWO

"Thank you," Rocky said. He reached up and tucked one of Kat's loose curls behind her ear.

She leaned in and kissed him. "You won't be mad if I have to leave, will you?" she said.

"I won't be *mad*, but do you really have to go?"

"I don't, but it's sort of a deal I've made with myself. You seem like an amazing guy, I mean, I know in my guts you are, but I never allow myself to stay overnight with someone new. We don't know what this is, if it will happen again, or really if it even should."

He took her hand. "I'd like to see you again."

She dropped her chin, and he loved her even more for it.

"Listen, I do like you. Okay? We can definitely see each other again—"

"But..." he interrupted.

"But...I intend to keep to my promises."

Now it was his turn to look crestfallen.

"I never got that all-access exclusive, so I have to come back, at least one more time."

He met her gaze and kissed her smiling lips. "We could do it right now."

"No way."

"Why not? Look at me. I'm all naked and vulnerable."

"Yeah, but after what we just did, I'm afraid I might be too easy on you. Let's schedule it for tomorrow. Does that work for you?"

Rocky kissed her again. "I guess it'll have to."

"You're really sweet, you know that?"

"What did I tell you about that kind of talk? I've got a reputation to uphold around here."

She got out of bed. He watched her beautiful rump in the moonlight that came in from the bedroom window and already wanted to hold it in his hands again. She dressed and stepped into her shoes before leaning over him as he lay on his back.

"Your secret is safe with me." She kissed his forehead and moved to the door. "See you tomorrow, Rocky."

"Good night, Kat."

And just like that, the greatest girl he'd met in a decade was gone.

He put his hands behind his head and stared at the ceiling. He couldn't keep the grin from his face. She'd be leaving soon, though. She had a job to do and then, just like a ghost, she'd be gone, and he'd be back to being the Incredible Haunted Man. The push and pull played inside of him like magnets in his heart and mind. What universe had she come from? How did she end up falling to his planet? And why did she have to go? He turned onto his side and pulled the pillow she'd laid upon to his chin. He inhaled the lingering scent of her hair – something fruity, nice. His smile was a guarded one, even here alone in his bed. He hugged the pillow tight and closed his eyes. The momentary happiness crashed like the waves upon the OOB shore, again and again slamming into the inevitable heartache.

Rocky's mind quieted as a dream fog began to roll in. He was seconds from falling all the way in when the knocking on his front door pulled him back into the moonlit room.

She changed her mind.

He didn't even bother putting on his underwear before he walked to the door and cracked it open.

His jaw fell to his ankles.

November cocked her head at an angle, her gaze moving downward before returning to meet his. "Are you going to invite me in?"

He didn't know what to say. He couldn't think let alone talk or move. Maybe he was asleep. This had to be a fucking dream, right? She wasn't really standing on his steps speaking to him. No way.

"This…this is…."

"Listen," she said.

She was gorgeous.

"I know you just had company. I wasn't being a perv. I was coming to see you when I saw her leaving. She's really cute, by the way."

"This is a dream."

"Can I come in now?" she asked.

"You…I mean…."

"Listen, I'll stand out here. Go put some pants on or whatever. I'll wait."

I doubt it.

He stood a few seconds longer. "Yeah, um, yeah. Just…just wait there, don't leave."

"I won't. I promise."

"Okay, don't…don't go anywhere."

He looked her over again. He wanted to reach out and touch her, make sure she was real. Instead, he forced himself to leave her there. In his bedroom, Rocky did a clumsy dance-hop into his *Star Wars* pajama bottoms, nearly falling into the wall as he tried to control the manic thrumming inside his chest.

He'd left the front door open. He opened it further and gestured for her to enter.

"Thanks," she said.

She took a seat on his couch and looked around. "Seems about right. Looks like you."

He put his hands on his hips, dipped his chin, and harrumphed before bringing his head back up. "So, how long have you been in town?"

"I never really left."

"What?"

"You deserve to hear the whole story, but we don't have the time right now."

"You know, November, I really think we do."

"We don't. I came here to warn you."

"What? That there are vampires in town, and they want to kill me?"

"Wait, you already know?"

"What? No, I was being ridiculous. Weren't you?"

"Holy shit, Rocky, I don't know. I don't know what they want, or what their intentions are, but I do know there's at least two of them, a man and a woman, and they're staying over at the Avalon Hotel."

"The Avalon? As in the closed-up-all-of-a-sudden Avalon Hotel?"

"Yes."

"I need a drink."

He stepped toward the kitchen and lost his balance. She was up and holding him before he had a chance to fall.

"Sit down. I'll get us a couple drinks."

She led him to the couch, grabbed two beers from the fridge and set one on the coffee table in front of him. She opened the other and took a drink.

"I can't believe you're here," he said, opening the beer and swigging from the already sweating bottle.

"You don't know how many times I wanted to come see you."

He held a hand up to her, silencing her, and shook his head.

"Okay, I know," she said. "I'm an asshole, but you need to be made aware of what I just saw."

"You saw vampires?"

"Yes."

"Here. In Old Orchard?"

"Yes."

"Great."

"They killed the owner of the Avalon, and I'm pretty sure they've been killing people in town since they got here."

"How do you know this?"

"I saw them about an hour ago. On the beach. They took a drunk girl and helped her to an alley. Once they got her there, they fed on her and left her dead on the ground before flying back to the Avalon. They're staying on the fifth floor. I know. I followed them. On the lower floors is where I found Mr. Roux and the rest of the bodies."

Rocky sat back and swallowed the rest of his beer.

"And there's something else."

He looked at her.

"I don't have direct knowledge that it's true, but I have a niggling feeling that it is."

"What?" he said.

"I think…I think your girlfriend might somehow be involved."

"And why is that? Because I like her and she likes me, so she must be a monster?"

"Okay, fair," November said. "I know how it sounds—"

"It sounds fucking stupid. And you know what? I can't believe you. You say you've been in Old Orchard this whole time, and what? You wait until I find someone else I actually like, the first person that I don't automatically size up next to you and cast off as not good enough? And *then* you decide to knock on my fucking door?" He slammed his palms on the coffee table, startling her as he stood.

Her bottom lip was out, her watery eyes turned away from him.

Shit.

No, don't feel bad. She's the asshole here, not me.

Rocky swallowed his rage. "The rest of what you said…. They were definitely vampires?"

November nodded.

"Well, if they're here, it has to be because of the stupid TV special, right?"

"That makes the most sense."

"What makes you think they want me and not you?"

"Because you're the survivor, remember? No one even knows I exist."

She was right. He walked to the fridge. As if Rocky didn't have enough feelings crashing into each other. As if he didn't have enough craziness on his plate. The documentary special, Franklin and Scott, the kid, Kat, and now November…it was too much. He opened the fridge door and grabbed the last two beers. Returning to the living room, he handed one to November and sat down beside her. He remembered how she'd stopped his heart cold that June morning in 1986. He remembered the beach, the kiss, and later when she'd been his first time. Then there was the Polaroid. Her teeth in his uncle Arthur's throat....

It wasn't her choice. She did what Gabriel had made her do. He knew that. Had accepted it years ago.

"You've really been here all this time?" he said.

"I live over in Biddeford, but yeah. I couldn't leave."

"I kind of always knew," he said, sipping his beer. "I've felt you, like, like the wind or a change of wind, I guess. And in my dreams, you're always there."

"I'm sorry," she said, putting a hand on his. "For everything."

"You don't have to apologize. I just wish you would have.... I don't know."

He turned toward the wall, but he wasn't looking at anything in his house. He was traveling far across the Milky Way.

"Man," he finally said.

"I know. I'm sorry. I thought you still hated me."

He turned his hand to hold hers. "I never hated you."

She licked her lips and squeezed his hand. He wanted to turn back time. He wanted this to be that summer. The ocean played its lullaby as his pulse kept beat in his neck. It was hard to swallow.

Damn it. This isn't happening. This isn't real.

Still, here they were. Finally. Rocky pushed those old feelings down and tried to bring this back to right now.

"What makes you think Kat is involved?" he asked.

Kat, Kat, Kat.

November looked amazing. His gaze drifted from her eyes to her lips.

"I know it could be a total coincidence, and with the documentary stirring everything up, she could just be one of the many...."

"But?" Rocky was grateful to have heard what she was saying and for his ability to respond appropriately.

"That part's a little harder to put my finger on. She's not staying with them."

"Well, then that clears her, doesn't it?"

November eased her hand from his. His heart gave a slight ache. It was ridiculous, he'd just slept with Kat. Could this even be possible?

"Not exactly," she said.

She wasn't answering his thoughts. Still, it freaked him out enough to make him try and clear his mind. He didn't think mind-reading had been one of her abilities, but maybe it was like a super power that developed over a matter of time.

"Don't worry, I can't read your mind."

"Right, yeah, I didn't forget."

"So, this reporter, *Kat*?"

"Yeah." He couldn't take his eyes off her as she began to pace back and forth. The excitement or concern or both, whatever it was she was feeling, apparently made it hard for her to sit still.

"She shows up the same time as these other two."

"And everyone else."

"Right," she said. "Except she's at the Betty's Island Inn and the others are at the Avalon."

"I think we already established all that."

"The aspect that you wouldn't get is the feeling I got from her – Kat. Or more like the feeling I *didn't* get from her."

"Okay? Like a vampire tingle or something?"

"Sort of, yeah," November said, still pacing. "I saw you guys together on the pier and I could feel your energy, your heartbeat, I guess, and not hers."

"Or maybe you're just jealous." He was sort of joking, but not.

She stopped. "Yeah, maybe. I actually wondered that myself. I don't think so, but there's been so much happening over the last couple of weeks. I've been overwhelmed by it all."

Rocky sat up straighter. He thought of Franklin and Scott, and the others listed in the paper. "Like what?"

"There's the bodies I found at the Avalon. Seeing you with Kat. And I…was supposed to have a date, I guess, too."

"You guess?"

"Yeah, no, maybe. He wasn't a local. We were supposed to meet at the drive-in."

"What happened?"

"You. I had to make sure you were okay."

"Oh."

Rocky didn't really care who the guy was. She deserved someone, too.

"Back to your girl. I really don't know. I mean it. I've been messed up. My emotions are all over the place. What about you?"

"What about me what?"

"You slept with her. Did you get any vibes?"

"No. I don't…I don't think so. Other than she's the first girl I've really been attracted to since you. So, if I'm only into vampire girls…."

She rose. "I'm gonna go."

"What? Where?"

"Hey, listen. I don't know if Kat's actually part of this, but be careful, okay? I'll see what I can find out."

She walked to the door and opened it.

"Wait," he said, standing up.

But she was gone.

CHAPTER THIRTY-THREE

Kat's heart hammered. If Rocky turned out to be a vampire killer, well, she was going to have a harder time killing him than she thought. She could still smell his sweat on her body. Under the nearly full moon, she allowed the fresh memory of their entanglements a few extra beats before she felt the shadows move behind her.

She stopped. "I know you're there."

Vincent stepped forward, Fiona in lockstep just over his shoulder, death burning in her eyes.

Vincent turned his attention to the hotel sign just ahead. "This is how you repay me for taking care of you? You, what, just sneak out behind my back and hide? That's not really like you, Kat."

Fiona remained tight-lipped behind him.

"Well," Kat said. "I was wondering when the two of you would notice."

Fiona came out from behind Vincent. "And what's that supposed to mean?"

Kat turned toward Fiona. "I think you both know exactly what I mean."

"Hey," Vincent cut in, stepping between them. "You need to come home with us. There's something you might like to know."

Kat turned her back and started toward the inn.

Vincent grabbed her arm.

Her face soured.

"I said you're coming with us."

"Get your hands off me, Vincent."

He leaned in and inhaled just below her ear. "I can smell his stench on you."

"I was at his house getting the story—"

His grip tightened on her arm. "Don't fucking bullshit me, Kat. And don't go giving *me* shit when you're, what, fucking your way to the truth? Is that about the gist of it?"

Kat jerked her arm free. "Fuck you, Vincent."

"We're not the only vamps in town," Fiona said.

"What?"

Fiona stepped beside them. "We can act like a trio of bitter shitheads over who's fucking who when we're through with this little summer vacation. Right now, there's another vampire keeping tabs on us. And she needs to be dealt with first."

"*She?*" Kat said.

"She saw us feed, and then followed us to the hotel," Vincent said. "She doesn't know we saw her."

Kat scoped their surroundings to make sure they were still alone. "And you're so sure of this, why?"

"I'd know," Vincent said.

"Are you fucking kidding me, right now?" Kat said. "Like the way she *didn't* see you two sloppy idiots feeding and like the way she *didn't* find out where we're staying?"

"Yeah," Fiona cut in and poked a finger into Kat's shoulder. "Where *we're* staying. You think fucking somebody that's the number-one celebrity in town is laying low? You're a fucking hypocrite."

"Fiona," Vincent said. "Enough."

"Whatever." Fiona kicked an empty fountain soda container across the sidewalk and walked away.

Kat felt seething hatred toward Fiona. Not just because of what these two were doing behind her back – she honestly couldn't care less – but it was something darker, something new. This new loathing was intense. She imagined ripping the little bitch's heart straight out of her chest.

"She's not wrong, Kat. We've all been a little too laissez-faire about all this. We've never been this reckless. Especially you."

He had her there and the smug grin on his face only made it worse. She knew better. And even though Vincent didn't know exactly how she'd spent her free time lately, he would hold it over her forever if he did, he was right.

"Come home with us."

It was the last thing she wanted to do right now, but considering what they didn't know about this other vampire, sticking together would be best.

"I'll be back tomorrow."

"Good choice," he said. Vincent leaned in as she turned her head from him. His lips on her cheek, still warm with the fresh blood he'd drunk earlier, stirred the creature within. "Fine, be like that. Just watch your back." He looked around and said, "She could be anywhere."

Vincent turned and walked down to where Fiona was pacing like a hungry tigress. Kat wanted to beat the shit out of the little bitch, but that would have to wait. They were right. It was time to figure out what secrets this beach town was hiding.

When she was certain the dynamic duo was truly gone, she headed back the way she came. She *was* changing. She felt it inside. She was stronger. Hungrier. She went back to Smith Street.

CHAPTER THIRTY-FOUR

It was past noon by the time Rocky cleared the morning gunk from his eyes. Even though he'd slept with Kat last night, all he could think of was November. He sat up in his bed, sweaty, exhausted, and strangely ready for whatever the future had to offer. The very idea with everything that was going on – Franklin, Scott, Kat, these new vampires – it was all just something different. November was here. Sort of. He shook his head. How she could still have such an effect on him, he didn't know, but it was undeniable.

He slid his feet from the sheets and placed them on the floor. His head hurt a little from the drinks last night, but even that was nothing. He slapped his hands on his knees, stood, and walked to the kitchen, ducked his mouth to the faucet in the sink and guzzled straight from the tap.

When he was satisfied, he straightened up and wiped his lips with the back of his hand. Why hadn't she given him a way to contact her? Where'd she say she lived, Biddeford? He wondered if she was in the phone book. He found the book under his cheap coffee table, sat on the couch and fingered through to the Rs. There were Rileys, but no Novembers. Not surprising. He closed the book and pushed it away. He considered what to do. Try to find November? Not happening. She'd come around when she was ready. Call Kat? Was it required? Was it courteous? Was he a pig if he didn't at least try to phone her today?

He thought of going to check on Franklin's house, maybe see what Eddie had seen, if anything. Or maybe he could take a walk around town and stroll by the Avalon, see for himself what was going on over there.

No. That's the stupidest idea you've had in a long time.

Yeah, that was probably not a good choice.

Franklin's it was.

Rocky turned onto Smith Street, the gray summer day threatening to unleash some seriously righteous, wrath-of-God-type weather upon his beach town. The sky was darkening by the second, the first rain drops pitter-pattering against his windshield as he pulled up to the curb in front of Eddie's house and cut the engine. He instantly felt wrong being here. Franklin's house still had police tape around it. Scott Jorgenson's Jeep was gone. Looking to his left, he saw so was the kid's Mustang. Thunder cracked overhead, startling him as he prepared to step from the vehicle. He gave himself a weak laugh for being so jumpy and got out of the car. The rain turned to sheets of kamikaze bombers.

Of course.

He tried to cover his head with his arm, but it was laughable against the torrential downpour. Rocky scurried to Eddie's door, grateful for the small porch roof. He knocked and waited. The kid probably wasn't here, but he'd seen someone move by the window as he ran to the door. A second later, a woman opened the front door.

"Yes?" she said, her face pale. The bags beneath her eyes looked like they weighed twenty pounds each. "Can I help you?"

Rocky cleared his throat. "Yes, um, I'm a…a friend, I guess, of Eddie's. Is he here?"

"You're—" She stopped.

"Yeah, hi. I'm Rocky Zukas."

"How do you know Edward?"

"We met recently. I guess we're both interested in what happened to your neighbor, Mr. Tibbetts."

"Yes, it's a shame about that." She looked back into the house.

The rain continued to pelt the porch roof.

"Ma'am," he said. "I'm sorry if this is a bad time. Is Eddie around?"

A man with a full head of mostly gray hair, Eddie's father most likely, came up behind her, and opened the door wider.

"What do you want with my son?" he asked.

"Look, honestly, it's not that big of a deal—"

"He hasn't been home since yesterday," Eddie's father said.

"Oh, sorry."

There was a bright flash across the sky. Thunder boomed.

"He went off with his girlfriend. It's not that odd, but with everything that's been going on this last week or so…well, his mother and I are a little more nervous than we'd normally be. I'm sure you of all people would understand."

"Unfortunately, yeah. I get it."

"What did you want with him anyway?" The man nodded toward the vacant house across the street. "I heard you mention to Linda about Franklin. Is there something going on we should know about?"

Rocky looked over his shoulder. The storm made everything a touch more sinister. He turned back. "I'm not sure, sir, but I'd be lying if I told you it didn't scare me. I knew Franklin. I worked at the fire department with Scott. The whole situation is…bizarre."

"It's pouring out there," Linda said. "Would you like to come in for a cup of coffee?"

"Sure," he said.

The couple parted and motioned for him to enter.

"How do you take your coffee?" Linda asked.

"A little cream, a little sugar," he said.

"Name's Jack. This is my wife, Linda. Have a seat."

Rocky shook Jack's large hand and felt the man's strength in his grip. He took a seat at the table as Jack took the one across from him.

"Have you guys called Eddie's girlfriend's house yet?"

Linda stood still at the counter and craned her neck toward him. "No. Why? Do you think something's happened?"

"No, that's not it." But wasn't it? Rocky had been here before. In a situation in this town where strange and abnormal things happened. Franklin didn't kill Scott. He knew after what November told him last night what was responsible for Scott Jorgenson's death, and he feared Franklin's, as well. But what could he tell Eddie's parents?

Linda finished pouring his coffee and brought the mug to the table.

"Thanks," he said, taking the cup and sipping the fresh brew.

"I didn't like it last night when the kids didn't come back from their walk. I just figured they got carried away and probably went back to Karla's house. But no phone call since. They haven't turned up, and now you show up at our doorstep. I gotta tell ya, my gut's telling me something ain't right. Now, don't give me no bullshit. Do you know something that we don't?"

He couldn't do it. Vampires weren't real to most people. There was no way he was going to say it in front of them.

"I don't know what's up with Eddie and Karla. I'm sure it's nothing, but maybe you should try and get ahold of them, just to be sure. Do they live close enough to walk?"

"You live here. Just about anywhere is in walking distance," Jack said.

Rocky finished his coffee, set the mug down, and stood. "I'd try Karla's. See if they went there." He started for the door.

"Wait," Linda said.

Rocky was at the door.

"The news..." Linda said. "I saw on the news this morning that people are missing. Hannah at Jenner's Grocery even mentioned a copycat killer."

Jack stepped to her side and put his arm around her. "Now, dear, don't go listening to anything Hannah has to say. That woman believes aliens visited her through her dreams. She's a kook."

"Jack, she heard it from Blair Peppers. Her husband is a policeman. She's not prone to telling stories unless it's something she picked up from him."

"Doesn't mean a damn thing," Jack said. His voice grew meaner. "Everyone's all caught up in this because of that damn special."

"He's right," Rocky said. "It's easy for people to start connecting dots that aren't there."

"But there are people missing. Franklin, and now our son."

"You don't know that," Jack said, softer.

"I better go. If I see Eddie, I'll make sure he comes straight home. Thanks again for the coffee."

The rain was still in attack mode, and it seemed to have convinced the wind to howl and shove like a beast all its own. Lightning flashed across the sky. An AC/DC song crossed his mind. Rocky was young, and he sure as hell wasn't ready to die. He ran to his car and climbed in, the wind shutting the door for him. He started the car. The windshield wipers did their best, which wasn't hardly enough, to keep pace with the storm coming down. He put the car in gear. As he crept along at a snail's pace down Smith Street, a vision came to him. The yellow Volkswagen van. He recalled how the vehicle stood out not just because it looked like it drove through a time warp, but because of how *slow* it had moved. And...the beautiful dark-haired woman behind the wheel.

Beautiful dark-haired woman.

No, it couldn't have been her.

Kat?

★   ★   ★

Linda set the phone down on its cradle, her knees weak, her stomach turning. Jack's eyes told her she didn't have to say a word.

"What do we do?" she said.

"Give me the phone. I'll call the police."

Linda lifted the receiver and handed it to Jack, then moved to the sofa and tried to hold on. There was no proof that anything bad had happened. The kids were just that – kids. They could be shacked up anywhere making teenage mistakes. Just because Rocky Zukas, the young man from the Beach Night Killer special, suddenly appeared at their front door asking for their son, and just because Franklin Tibbetts had apparently murdered a fireman—

Shut up, Linda, she scolded herself.

Wait.

Breathe.

Despite Jack standing right in front of her, her husband's words to the police drifted in and out like a frequency she couldn't quite receive – "He hasn't come home…. He's not on drugs…he doesn't…he wouldn't…we know them. They're good kids…."

"I'm going out," Jack said, hanging up the phone. "Raymond is a fucking self-absorbed dickhead. He wouldn't know if Eddie and Karla were screwing in the next room."

"Jack."

"I mean it, he's a rich prick."

He grabbed his L.L. Bean windbreaker, his car keys from the counter and started for the door.

"I'm going with you."

"No. One of us should stay in case they come here."

He was right. Still, she didn't want to sit around and drive herself mad. "We'll leave a note."

"Fine. Let's hurry," he said. Jack opened the door as a flash of lightning lit up the sky. "It doesn't look like it's getting any better out there."

Eddie, wherever you are, please be okay.

Linda sent the thought to her son as she taped the note to the TV screen and joined her husband at the door.

She got in the passenger's seat of their station wagon, grateful for the shelter. Jack hesitated. After a few seconds, he ducked his head in and said, "Stay right here, I wanna check something out real quick."

"What? Jack, just get in."

"I'll be quick."

He shut the door before she could argue. Linda watched as he ran across the road and made his way over to Patty's house. She lost sight of him when he went up her walkway.

What was he doing?

The storm raged on. She never liked thunderstorms, not even the ones that rolled in and out of town quickly. This one was somehow more threatening. It was relentless and felt like it insisted on going on until the sun gave in and went away for good. It was a heavy, malignant feeling. She didn't like it one bit.

Thunder boomed and she shuddered.

"What in the world are you doing, Jack?" she said aloud. How long had he been over there? Five minutes? Ten?

She wondered if Eddie had run off with that girl. She seemed okay, but there was no way she was going to stay with her Eddie. Not when school started back up, and certainly not when they graduated. The Tisdales came from money. Karla was going to break her Eddie's heart.

If they're okay.

The voice wouldn't leave her be. All this crazy Beach Killer stuff was like an infestation on their community. It crept and grew, moldering beneath the surface of their sunshiny vacation town. And now, with the missing people, it was taking hold, making its move to become more, to manifest from whispers and rumors into a monstrous thing that would not be ignored.

"Come on, Jack."

Linda wanted to run back inside and lock the doors and hide beneath her covers. A little girl praying the bad storm away.

She couldn't sit any longer. She got out and ran to Beverly's. She sensed the danger as soon as she reached the door.

"Jack? Patty?"

Under the cover of Patty's porch, she shook her head and arms like she was a dog and went to knock on the door. It was open a crack.

A smell drifted up and stung her nose.

"Jack?"

She nudged the door and stepped inside.

A pretty, dark-haired woman stood smiling, blood rolling from the corners of her mouth. She held Jack in her arms like a lover on the cover of one of those cheesy romance novels Patty liked to read. She dropped Linda's husband to the floor, where he landed with a heavy *thump*.

"Ah, welcome," the woman said.

Linda began to tremble.

Before she could run or scream, the woman was between her and the front door.

"Are you going to kill me?" Linda asked.

Bumps rose to life on the young woman's forehead, her eyes went black, and her mouth seemed impossibly large.

"After I hurt you, yes."

Linda's screams were swallowed under the worst thunderstorm in Old Orchard Beach history.

CHAPTER THIRTY-FIVE

November sat on a metal folding chair. The corner office faced the Avalon Hotel. If the vampires left, she was going to follow their asses. She'd been so caught up in Rocky that she'd missed what the hell was happening around them. She'd picked up a paper and read more about the missing people in the Old Orchard Beach area. There was a Jason Marlon listed among the missing. She thought of the drive-in date she'd skipped. She'd never bothered getting his last name. She'd been so focused on what was happening with these creatures and Rocky that she hadn't even thought about Jason. Could it be him? A churning in her guts told her that there were more victims than anyone knew about. It was just like when Gabriel was here. And staring at the hotel-shaped coffin across the street through the downpour, she knew why.

The sun was hours from setting, but the dark clouds were heavy over the normally sunny beach town. If these two fiends were waiting for the night to fall, she'd stay vigilant. They were done bleeding her home. She wasn't sure she could stop both at once, but she'd do enough to save whoever she could. She'd considered going to the small inn where Rocky's reporter girlfriend, Kat, was staying, but she wanted to believe that the woman wasn't connected. She wanted to believe it for Rocky. The idea that the guy waited a decade to fall for someone else and that girl ended up being a vampire, too…it would be…heartbreaking.

A curtain moved on the fifth floor of the vampire hotel.

November leaned forward.

The redhead appeared, embracing her lover…only…. The vampire drew her mouth from the man's neck, her gaze drifting across the storm, daring November to try and stop her, her worst nightmare came true.

On her feet, November felt an ache in her soul.

"No...."

She was out of the office, out of the building, and across the street in a blur.

How could they have gotten him without me knowing?

Flying straight up to the fifth floor and crashing through the window was her first option, but it could be a trap. The bitch had looked right at her. She knew November was here watching them. *How* she knew was another question. November was done underestimating these creatures.

November entered the hotel through the roof access door. The world felt off kilter, like when she'd drank too much blood and got woozy. She pushed on, making her way up the stairwell as silently and quickly as she could. She hadn't experienced this mixture of fear and rage since the night Gabriel forced her to feed on Rocky's uncle Arthur. It was a mixture of overwhelming emotions she'd hoped to never feel again. The doors to each floor had been closed, but the door to the fifth floor was wide open. They were waiting. Even so, she didn't want to show up carelessly. As overwhelmed as she was, she needed to be smart.

She steadied herself as she walked the hallway of long shadows. Taking deep breaths, she continued toward the last room on the left. She knew that's where they'd been. The place was silent. Dead. November reached the end of the hall and stopped and stared at the open door before her.

She stepped across the threshold, ready for anything.

There was no one here.

Her gaze fell upon a pair of feet sticking out from beside the king-size bed.

"Rocky?" she said. Her voice sounded too loud.

She rounded the end of the bed and exhaled.

It wasn't him. The dead man held a strong resemblance to Rocky, but it was another beachgoing victim.

They were gone.

Another ruse.

Another set-up.

They wanted her distracted.

And all at once, she knew where they were going.

This time, the quickest way was the only way. She smashed through the glass and headed to Rocky's.

208 • GLENN ROLFE

CHAPTER THIRTY-SIX

Kat stood dripping from head to toe in a t-shirt and short blue skirt when Rocky opened the door.

"What are you doing out in this mess?" he asked, stepping aside to let her in.

She turned to face him as he closed the door. Taking him by the sides of his face, she stared into his eyes. "I couldn't stop thinking about last night."

"Yeah, it was…me neither. It was great."

He thought of November.

Kat brought her lips to his. His heart pounded; his thoughts swirled as he tasted something tangy in her kiss. She pressed her wet body against his. Her hands drifted down his neck, his chest, to his jeans.

Rocky tried to break the embrace but with surprising strength, Kat pulled him closer. She undid the button of his Levi's and slid her hand into his boxers. As she gripped his shaft, his need to slow down and figure everything out washed away. He placed his hands under her rump. She wasn't wearing any panties. His head buzzed with lust. Rocky squeezed her bare flesh and carried her to his bedroom. He laid her on the bed. She pulled him down and tossed him to his back, straddling him.

"Wait," he managed.

Kat placed a finger to his lips and said, "Shh. After."

She pulled his erection free from his boxers and eased down upon it. Her moist warmth surrounded him. Rocky bit his lip and, for a little while, forgot about all the monsters of the world.

"Tell me something," Rocky said, the afterglow glistening off both of them, radiant and magical.

"Anything," she said.

"You're not a vampire, right?"

A blankness settled across her gorgeous face. His body went cold.

"Yeah right," she said, a modicum of warmth returning to her face. "Maybe then I could get in a heavy metal video."

"Yeah, I thought I sensed that you were a bit of a freakshow," he said.

She slapped his shoulder. "Jerk."

Rocky leaned in and kissed her.

"Did you ever interview any of those freaky bands?"

"Like who?"

"I don't know. Marilyn Manson."

"I wish. Unfortunately, I'm the low man on the totem pole. I got Powerman 5000 instead."

"Who?"

"Yeah, I know. The singer's Rob Zombie's brother."

Rocky leaned in for another kiss when a loud *BANG* made him jump out of his skin.

"What the fuck?" he said, swinging his feet to the floor. A long-haired man rushed forward and slammed his fist into the side of Rocky's head. And then it all went dark.

★ ★ ★

November watched as the asshole vampires carried Rocky and Kat to the still-running yellow van.

The woman really was just a reporter. She wasn't sure whether she was more relieved or hurt that Kat wasn't a monster. Either way, the vampires had them. Despite the shitty weather, non-stop traffic continued to stream by. No one seemed to notice two limp bodies being loaded into a vehicle, or if they did, they didn't seem to care. The vampires were obviously taking Rocky and Kat back to the hotel. And they would be waiting for her to try to rescue them.

They were in a vehicle. She was not. She could get to the Avalon before them and maybe for the first time, get the drop on them. Hurrying behind the Tasty Freeze building, drenched in rage and pouring rain, November took flight.

CHAPTER THIRTY-SEVEN

Rocky opened his eyes. The night had swallowed him whole. He touched the side of his face and winced. The spot was tacky with drying blood. It all came back in a rush, and Rocky bolted upright.

"Kat?" he whispered.

Reaching out his hand, he sighed. Her naked hip was cool beneath his palm. He remembered what they were doing before the intrusion.

"Kat? Hey." He gently rocked her hip. "Are you okay? Are you hurt?"

"Yeah, I'm fine," she said. "You're naked too, huh? You okay?"

"Yeah," he said, leaning forward and giving her shoulder a quick kiss. "Come on, we need to get the hell out of here. I'll tell you everything I know. Everything."

Her hands found his. "Rocky, you're kind of freaking me out. What's going on?"

He took a deep breath. "Okay, okay. Just let me get it out. Gabriel Riley wasn't just a serial killer. I mean, he was, but—"

"Spit it out," she said.

"He was a monster. A real-life monster. He killed everyone that they said he did. He hid most of the bodies in a basement in town. He was responsible for what happened to my uncle...." He considered telling her about how it wasn't Gabriel who drained his uncle, but he decided to keep that secret to himself. It didn't matter right now. "He wanted me, so he took my mom and sister."

"But why you? What am I missing?"

"He didn't approve of my girlfriend."

The room was quiet as the truth hung between them. Kat sat in stunned silence.

"I've never told anyone that before," he said.

"There's gotta be more."

"Listen," he said, moving closer and bringing her cold hand to his chest. "She's still around. She came to me last night—"

"Your ex-girlfriend? When last night?" There was a meanness in her voice.

"After you left. There was a knock on my door, and I thought you'd changed your mind about not spending the night—"

"Did you sleep with her?"

"What? No. She just came to tell me about—"

"Do you still...do you still love her?"

He didn't need to answer.

Kat pulled her hand away.

"Listen," he said. "We're going to need her to help us fight them."

A door burst open to his left. Dim light spilled across the floor. Her silhouette seemed impossible. Twice in one week. She was right there.

"Rocky?"

"November," he said.

Lights blossomed to life. Rocky squinted and winced at the sudden brightness.

"Well, well, well," the male vampire said. "What a compelling confession of love and death."

The long-haired, leather jacket-wearing Soundgarden wannabe asshole that knocked Rocky out earlier stood against the far wall. The redheaded vamp next to him started toward them, but she was quickly sent flying to the side. She hit the ground, limp. November stood, fists clenched, between Rocky and Kat and the pissed-off vampire.

"Come on, you sweet little vamp bitch," the man said, his face suddenly grotesque. A vile forked tongue flickered from his mouth. "Let's see what you've got."

November lunged. The two locked up, hissing at one another, spinning around the room against the wall. Framed paintings were knocked to the side, one fell, the cheap wood frame smashing on the ground. Rocky sat crouched, naked, with Kat sitting up at his side.

He stayed low but got his feet beneath him. He gazed in awe and fear as November and Soundgarden made their way around the room in a blur and a whirl of whipping hair. Rocky's lip gave a slight lift when November smashed the asshole into the ceiling, knocking plaster to the floor. Soundgarden grunted as November headbutted him and flung him down.

Rocky had seen her in this monstrous state once before...but she looked even more bestial than he remembered. Was it an age thing? Did vampires grow uglier in their monster form as time passed, or had she become the thing she hated in the years since they were together?

"I am going to give you and your trashy ginger beast one chance, and one chance only to leave my town and never come back," November growled.

"Please," Soundgarden said. "Mercy."

"Leave these two alone." She nodded toward Rocky and Kat. "Go back to wherever you came from, and we'll call it good. Understood?"

Rocky wanted to pump his fist in the air. He wanted to stand behind her and tell this piece of trash to get fucking lost.

A blur and a quick blast of air stopped him cold as November was knocked away from the vampire. She rolled to a stop across the room. November rose just in time to be pinned to the wall.

Kat was no longer at Rocky's side.

"Kat," Rocky said, more shocked whisper than anything else. But she heard him, just the same.

Kat had her nails deep in November's neck in the blink of an eye. She was squeezing her throat. Rocky stood, set to get between them, when a lamp smashed against the back of November's head. Dead or alive, Rocky couldn't tell which, November dropped in a pile on the gold and burgundy hotel rug, a ragdoll left for dead.

Rocky scurried to her side, taking her in his arms. "November, please. Please be okay. Come on, come on." He slapped her cheeks and shook her shoulders.

"Fiona," Soundgarden barked. "Get up already."

The redhead climbed to her feet. "Fuck you, Vincent. She kicked your ass, too." She crossed the room and joined Kat and Vincent.

Kat.

She was one of them. All this time, she was a fucking creature of the goddamn night, and she played him like a fool. November's suspicion had been right. The trio of monsters *were* in this shit together, and November paid the price for protecting his dumb ass.

Rocky stood, seething through his clenched teeth. Kat's gorgeous face morphed into the true ugly thing beneath her lying eyes. "Why? Why the hell didn't you say anything? What was this all about?"

"We should kill him," Fiona said. "Her, too."

"Now, now, Fiona," Vincent said. "Let's have a little fun first." He turned to Kat and put an arm around her shoulder. "What do you say, Kat? For old time's sake?"

Fiona snagged Rocky, pulling him away from November. "Come on, Kat," Fiona said, "kill him."

Kat looked away.

"Oh, what is it?" Fiona said, mocking her, whining like a little kid. "Can you not hurt him because he's your little blood-bag boyfriend?"

"Shut the fuck up, Fiona," Kat spat. "We should have left your pale ass to die in Seattle."

Rocky reared his head and saw the wicked grin come to life on Fiona's face.

"Oh, sweetie," Fiona said. "You still think Vincent *found* me."

Kat's mutated forehead wrinkled.

"He didn't find me." Fiona dragged Rocky along with her, stepping to Kat's face. "He *chose* me. To replace your boring, *old* ass."

Kat turned to Vincent. "Is that true?"

"It doesn't change a thing, Kat. Besides, you're the one wearing human spunk around like some kind of slutty blood-bag perfume. It's disgusting. While you've been wasting your time letting this trash between your legs, we've been waiting."

"And fucking and killing," Kat said, her hands clenched at her sides.

Fiona grinned.

Rocky let his own anger keep him from thinking about his shitty predicament.

Vincent tilted his head and looked toward November. She still hadn't moved.

"You're every bit as much of a killer as either of us, if not more so, so please, keep your shitty excuses."

Kat had no retort.

Vincent turned back to Rocky. "Okay, Mr. Survivor, Mr. Prime Time Special. Since Kat's been useless, how about you tell us why we're here."

"You're a bunch of unoriginal copycat killers."

Vincent backhanded him. Rocky tasted blood in his mouth again.

"Let me tear him open," Fiona said. She ran her clawed finger down the side of his neck. Blood trickled along the path. "Right here, right now."

"How come Gabriel Riley wanted you?"

Rocky didn't say anything. What did it matter?

"Was she there?" He pointed to November. "How do you know one another? You got any other secret vampire friends?"

"Just you guys," Rocky said.

Vincent snatched him from Fiona and slammed him to the ground, knocking the wind from his lungs and the smartness from his mouth.

"You're going to tell me what I want to know or I'm going to turn *you* into one of *my* friends. How would you like that?"

The weight of his threat flooded Rocky with a fresh dose of fear.

"Yeah," Vincent said, gazing into Rocky's eyes with a new gleam. He meant to do it. "You could join the family. What do you say, friend?"

If November was still alive, they were going to make sure it wouldn't stay that way. Rocky needed to keep these creatures occupied long enough for her to recover. She was their only hope.

Knowing it was a bad, bad idea, Rocky spat in the monster's face.

Rocky's spittle hung from Vincent's nose. "Kat," he said. "Go on and get out of here. We'll talk about our personal shit when Fiona and I are done here."

"What are you going to do?" Kat asked.

"Something that you obviously can't. Now go."

★   ★   ★

He's right.

Kat couldn't do it. Even as Rocky's legs and arms squirmed under Vincent, a part of her wanted to stop him, to make him let Rocky go and to take Vincent and Fiona back home. She wanted to take it all back, but it was all too late. Rocky knew who they were. He knew *what* they were. It would be too dangerous to let him live. Kat swallowed the urge to help him and walked into the hallway. She closed the door and sealed Rocky's fate.

She wiped a bloody tear from her cheek. She'd fucked up. She really was no better than Vincent or Fiona. She'd gotten too close to Rocky. Emotionally, physically, she had been a total mess since the day they arrived in this cheery little seaside town.

Rocky's muffled groans echoed after her. She had betrayed him. No matter what she felt for him or thought she had felt, it was a lie. It could be nothing more.

It was a fantasy. It was all a part of her summer de-evolution. For all her years of carefulness, calculating every threat, every risk, every move she and Vincent made, Kat, for a moment, had let go of the reins and allowed her heart – not her head – to make the decisions. And it wasn't just her reckless choices with Rocky. Far more dangerous was her giving in to her hunger. Feeding off an entire street, leaving nothing alive in her wake. She lost herself over and over to the monster she had truly always been.

She slumped against the wall at the end of the corridor and crumbled like a pastry as she slid to the floor in pity.

"What have I become?" she whispered.

Commotion from down the hall brought her back from her despair.

★   ★   ★

November's eyes fluttered open. She knew the sound coming from across the room the moment she heard it – someone was feeding.

She turned and felt the heart-punch. Vincent was on Rocky, sucking at his throat.

Silent and with perfect precision, November moved faster than she thought she could, and collided against the creature. Their momentum carried them to the far wall, entangled.

The bastard had top control, pinning November beneath his weight. "Not dead yet?" he said. "We can fix that."

She moaned as his nails penetrated her flesh, just above her left breast.

"Let's see how long it takes you to bleed out."

She hadn't felt strength like this since Gabriel.

November raised her right arm, intent on fending him off, but Vincent, nails burrowing deeper into her side, easily deflected the strike. He countered with a fist as hard as steel, striking her in the face again and again.

The room began to spin.

In November's periphery, she watched helplessly as Fiona fell upon Rocky and set about finishing him off.

"Nnnnnooooooo!"

Vincent gave a deep, gleeful laugh and dragged his hand down the length of her torso, ripping into her from her breast to her hip.

He pulled his hand free and sat upright. "Get up from that, bitch."

The door to the room crashed open, smashing into the wall with a thunderous crack, as Kat burst across the threshold.

Stunned, November watched reality reach Vincent's shark-like eyes in slow motion. Kat, at Fiona's back, wrenched a clawed hand into the fiery curls on her head and yanked her from Rocky's tattered throat.

"Kat—" Vincent began.

November, her hands shaking, her arms weak, let go of Vincent as he rose. Unable to move, she could do nothing more than witness Kat's free hand becoming a blur, leaving a crimson trail. Blood like water from a broken dam gushed from Fiona's throat. Kat was a supreme fiend unlike anything November had ever seen. She was ferocity incarnate.

"What have you done?" Vincent said.

She dropped the chunk of Fiona's ruined flesh on the floor. The bloody piece of throat landed with a wet *plop* upon the carpet in the growing crimson pool.

"I killed your little whore."

Vincent stepped away from November as she bled out on the garish carpet. She placed an elbow on the floor, barely able to hoist herself up. She was growing frailer by the second.

"You stay right fucking there," Vincent said, reaching Rocky's prone body and kneeling beside him.

"What do you think you're doing?" Kat said.

"Eye for an eye. Now, stay the fuck out of my way."

November's eyelids were too heavy.

I'm so sorry, Rocky. Please, forgive me.

CHAPTER THIRTY-EIGHT

Kat fumed. Fiona's blood was still dripping from her fingers, the bitch gasping her final breaths at her feet. Kat watched as Vincent dropped to Rocky. She hated him. Kat knew it more surely than she'd known anything else. Whatever feelings she'd felt for Vincent – love, admiration, intrigue, trust – it was all broken. Everything they once had was no more.

Rocky may or may not have been responsible for the death of one of their kind, but so fucking what? They were the monsters. Her, Vincent, Fiona, November, and Gabriel. They were killers. They took and they took, and they fed, and they murdered. Some of them worse than others, but none of them deserved mercy.

He wasn't perfect, but Rocky was more innocent than any of them.

Whatever it took, Kat would not allow Vincent to kill him. She shot a glance at November.

It's up to you to save him.

She had no way of knowing for certain that November would pull through, or if she even had the strength to try, but Kat knew November had the will.

Kat reared her head and shot forward, sinking her teeth into the back of Vincent's neck. He shot up, knocking her backward but releasing Rocky.

Perfect.

Kat wiped his blood from her lips.

Vincent rubbed his neck, pointing at her with his other hand. "You just fucked up for the last time."

"I made you, Vincent. Out of nothing. Off the streets. From the grip of addiction and the precipice of death, I made you into something you never had a chance of becoming – more."

"You don't know how many I've killed since we arrived. I'm stronger than you."

"How many you've killed? And you don't think I have?"

"What?" he said, stepping closer. "Your little overdose? What'd you do? Feed more than once that night? Yeah, I'm scared. You ungrateful bitch. I should have let you die."

"It was more than a couple feedings, dear. I killed a whole community. And I finished off the last two survivors tonight. You think you're stronger than me, Vincent, but like always, you're just a goddamn fool."

His smug grin faltered.

"What?" she said. "Speechless for once? Good."

Fiona sputtered her last breath and died.

Vincent glanced her way before bringing his hate-filled eyes up to Kat's.

"Yeah, good riddance," Kat said, and spat on Fiona's corpse.

Vincent growled.

"I made you, Vincent, but it's time for you to die."

"Traitor!" he shouted, launching at her, claws out, teeth bared.

He stuck hard, knocking her off her feet, but Kat knew how to take a fall. Arms stretched to the side, she landed on her back, and managed to catch Vincent in the chest with her boots as he pounced. She sent him sailing through the air, but the monster landed on his feet and came at her again. Upright in a heartbeat, Vincent managed to drive her into the wall, half a foot deep.

He sneered. His lip curled like a junkie Elvis Presley. "I'm going to give you one chance to come to your senses, Kat. It's not too late for me to forgive you. Let's finish these two and get the hell out of here. What do you say, sweetheart? Truce?"

Kat sunk her nails into each side of his neck. Vincent gasped. Fear fully reached his stupid eyes. "Not a goddamn chance." She let out a banshee squeal and carried him through the air, smashing through the fifth-floor hotel room window. Shards of glass fell like fireworks toward the pavement below. Together, Vincent and Kat fell to the earth.

CHAPTER THIRTY-NINE

November opened her eyes at the loud crash. She tried to raise her arm, but she felt buried under a ton of stone.

Her eyes found him.

Rocky.

It all came flooding back. The moment he passed out on the hundred-degree pavement as he pursued her that summer day so long ago. The evening on the beach, tackling each other in the waves, coming up so close. A kiss beneath the fireworks as she left him lovestruck on the shore. Their first time together beneath the pier. Gabriel. His hatred and anger.

Her choices in their relatively short lives had put Rocky in this position. She stunted him, trapped him romantically, emotionally in the shell of the man he should have been. This was all on her. Even these creatures coming to Old Orchard Beach and releasing this new hell upon them. It was all her fault.

She pushed beyond the weakness in her body and began to crawl toward Rocky. There was only one way to save him now. Wrong or right, it was his only hope. She pulled herself closer and closer, the seconds like hours, an eternity to cross to be at his side.

"Rocky," she wheezed. "Rocky, wake up. Come on, look at me."

His eyelids fluttered, but they did not open.

Reaching out, she clutched one of his hands. It was cold to the touch.

No.

"Rocky, please, please…stay with me. Just a little longer. Do you hear me?"

He didn't move.

November held his hand and leaned her forehead against it. Her shoulders hitched; she could no longer hold back the emotions.

His hand twitched in hers.

"Rocky?" she said.

"Hey," he said, but his voice was like a ghost's floating in a quiet, dusty room.

"Rocky, there's only one way I can save you. I have to turn you. It's your only chance. I swear, I wish it wasn't, but it is. Do you want me to save you?"

Eyes open, his throat a blood-coated disaster, he managed the slightest of nods. "I always wanted...to forgive...you. I never stopped...wanting...to be...with you."

She kissed the back of his hand.

With no time to spare, November bit a chunk from her wrist, and placed the bleeding wound against his lips.

"Drink, Rocky. Drink."

His suckle was weak at first. By all accounts, he should have been dead already. His mouth tightened against her flesh, his suck harder, feverish even.

It hurt but she didn't care.

When he stopped, she pulled her knees up beneath her and gazed into his pale face.

"It's going to hurt, at first."

His mouth contorted, his eyes rolled into the back of his head, but he appeared too weak to move the rest of his body.

Something's not right.

"Rocky?"

He barely raised his arm from the floor before it fell limp again. He was breathing; the blood was doing its trick, changing him. November felt sick as she got an up-close look at his horribly tattered throat.

He needs to feed. He needs to feed now.

November willed herself to her feet.

Without thinking, she walked to the shattered window, the beach still alive with the late-night crowd, and leapt.

CHAPTER FORTY

Kat had underestimated Vincent's strength. The asshole had always been a pain in the ass, but he killed more than even she suspected. His strength easily equaled her own. Even after the hell she unleashed upon Smith Street, Vincent's past months and years of ruthless killings made him an incomparable brute.

Tangled together, they hit the vacant parking lot, both ignoring the pain of their landing. She landed two good strikes to his jaw, backing him off momentarily. Vincent grinned – that damn grin – and flew ahead, tackling her and hoisting her upon his shoulder as they bounced from the ground to the sky, over a small but active coastal inn and bar, and came crashing down next to a bonfire on the beach.

Screams erupted around them as they separated, glaring at one another.

The humans would have to be dealt with later. Kat needed to finish him.

She managed to strike him in the ear, staggering him.

Now or never.

Kat stepped over his outstretched leg, hooked an arm beneath his armpit, and swung him over her hip hard and fast, slamming him onto his back. His black eyes fluttered. She sprung upon him, grasping his trachea in her fingers. Teeth bared, she squeezed and felt his blood trickle up around her fingers.

A camera flash, then another flickered to life. Again and again the bright lights lit up the night around them, blinding Kat and momentarily discombobulating her.

She turned from the gathering crowd and tried to get her head on straight.

Pain exploded in her chest. A stake pushed further through her heart, one splintery thorn at a time, and she gazed at Vincent's glee-filled face, and then to his fist clenched around the shard of wood he'd managed to grab during their tumble.

He began to pull his fist back and the stake reversed its way out of her. Kat was dead before Vincent pulled the weapon free.

★　★　★

Vincent rose, Kat's blood running down his wrist and forearm.

The few remaining amateur photographers dispersed in an air-raid worthy set of shrieks.

The police would be coming. He needed to make sure the other vampire and her blood-bag friend were dead. There could be no survivors.

"I gave you a chance," he said, kneeling next to Kat's dead body, her pretty face back in place. He leaned in and kissed her cold lips one last time.

Stake in hand, Vincent flew through the night toward the Avalon Hotel. Landing in the room where this battle began, he saw November was gone.

Still alive. Whatever. She'll die like the rest.

Vincent walked to the only other bodies there and knelt beside Fiona. Her gorgeous skin and body were now lifeless. He remembered her as he'd first seen her, a beauty under the thumb of a worthless piece of shit.

"I'm sorry you ended like this, Fi. You were my favorite. And forever will be." Vincent kissed her cheek.

"You came back," Rocky said.

The blood bag was sitting up on his elbows, watching Vincent hold Fiona in one last embrace.

"You," Vincent said.

"Hi, asshole. I'd say it's nice to see you again, but I suspect you killed some of my friends, so how's about *fuck you* instead?"

Holding Fiona, Vincent sneered at Rocky and said, "You did this. You brought us here with your story, and now you've taken *everything* from me."

"I'd apologize, or get up and kick your ass, but I think I'm dying over here, so *you're welcome*. Now, get the fuck outta my town. How's that sound?"

Vincent squinted as he moved closer and stared into Rocky's eyes.

"Whoa, I don't swing that way, man," Rocky said. "Not that there's anything wrong with that...."

"She turned you."

"Yeah, I'm becoming an ignorant prick, just like you."

Vincent smiled.

"Listen," Rocky said. "I've killed one of you before and I guess I'll have to do it again. If that goes against your vampiric code, I really don't give a shit. You got it coming."

"Little man," Vincent said, rising, "you really don't look too good. Let me clue you into something, yeah? There are no vampiric codes. There's only love and blood. And guess what, wise guy, you took my girl, so, I think I'll leave you here to die, and go take yours, huh?"

The expiring new vampire looked like an angel fallen to the earth – suddenly wingless and, despite his brush with higher power, wounded and impotent.

Vincent walked to the broken window and looked out at the night. He knew the other vamp bitch was down there, close by.

"I have one last pretty lady to say goodbye to. One last deathly kiss," Vincent said. "Why don't you hold down the fort until you die, or the police come to see what you've done? Adios."

Vincent darted into the moonlit sky. Rocky's screams from below brought an unmatched joy to his dark, dark heart.

CHAPTER FORTY-ONE

November hovered over two women screaming at the top of their lungs. Swooping down, she crunched her fangs through the brunette woman's skull and sucked her body dry of its lifeforce. The fresh blood ran through her, delivering a high she'd not felt in years. There was no time to consider her moral standing. She snatched the blonde friend and tossed her over her shoulder.

November could feel her side. Her wound nearly closed, her strength slowly returning as she carried the woman down the beach. Another body by an unattended blaze on the sand stopped her cold. Kat's body lay motionless by the conflagration.

November hefted Kat's body to the other shoulder.

The drunk blonde stirred and began shouting.

"Oh my God, what are you? Please, Jesus."

November reared back with her elbow and knocked the blonde in the side of the head, rendering her unconscious.

"I'll thank your god for that."

Leaning forward, balancing the weight of the two bodies, she took a burning log from the bonfire and flew toward the Avalon, heading for the lobby doors just across the street.

In a blur, November pushed through the hotel lobby doors. The sparse room was empty. She continued down the first corridor and kicked open the door to the next room she came to, Room 120.

She laid Kat's corpse on the bed and lowered the torch. The sheets ignited almost instantly.

Carrying the knocked-out drunk girl to the stairwell, November stopped.

Vincent began to clap from his seat before the second-floor doorway. "Hey, bitch," he said.

The sirens were approaching. November dropped the drunk girl, and shook her head, her arms out to her sides. "You already tried to kill me more than once. Don't you think it'd be a better idea for you to turn and run?"

Vincent rose and tapped the wooden stake in his hands against the concrete wall.

"Why don't you bring that cute hard-to-kill ass over here and we'll see what you've got left?"

"My pleasure," she said.

A door down the stairs burst open. Voices echoed from below. *Police.*

November closed the distance between her and Vincent.

He tried to bring the stake up, but November kicked it from his hand, sending it to the bottom of the stairwell.

Vincent elbowed her in the chest, and managed to break her grasp and escape down the stairwell.

November followed. She wasn't about to let this dickhead get away. Vincent had his mouth suckled onto an older officer's neck. A younger officer lay at his feet, twitching but still breathing.

Without thinking, November grabbed the downed officer, sank her teeth into his throat and sucked him dry.

Smoke filled the stairwell. The heat from the fire warmed their final battleground.

"Nice to see you're not so squeaky clean," Vincent said. "I like that." He tossed the dead cop at her.

Dropping her own feast, November sidestepped the airborne body and tackled Vincent into the burning hallway of the first floor.

Rocky appeared at the first-floor door, covering his mouth with his elbow. He'd seen what she did, the way she drank the cop dry. But she'd worry about that later. Rocky either loved her for what she was, like he said, no matter what, or he didn't. Either way, Vincent needed to be put down for good.

Vincent rose and charged her. Again, November was able to slip away from him. She snagged his shirt and, using his momentum, flung him head-first into the concrete wall of the stairwell.

Rocky hobbled out of the way. She saw the stone-bottomed lamp in his hand as he raised it over his head and brought the heavy base down on Vincent's forehead.

Vincent raised his chin and screamed, spittle flinging out, as he tumbled backward.

"We killed one as sick as you before," Rocky said. "I guess it's your turn, asshole."

"Rocky," November said. "There's a blonde on the next level. You need to feed to survive. Go. Now!"

With his arm at an awkward angle behind his back, Vincent ignored Rocky and the wound the weakling had inflicted, and directed his venom toward November.

"Look at you," he said. "Look at what you've become. A monster just like Gabriel."

"Shut up," she said, stepping closer to him, ready to finish him. "I'm nothing like my brother."

"Oh, I think that you are, sweetheart," Vincent said. "You're a murderous, bloodthirsty fiend. You're no better than the rest of us. And congratulations, you'll be the next media sensation. The female serial killer…major headlines. Kudos, kiddo. You're a star."

November clenched her fists.

"Truth hurts, huh, toots?"

"Die, you fuck!" She dived down, nails set to puncture his eyes from his ugly face.

Vincent's crooked arm moved in a blur.

"No! Look out!" Rocky shouted as he hurried after her.

November moaned. Her arms and legs weakened at once. The stake stabbed into her. The monster laughed.

She reached forward and gripped the wooden spike running through her stomach and felt it poking through her back.

Blood dribbled past her lips.

Vincent turned his face as November's blood drizzled across his flesh.

★ ★ ★

Rocky launched at the fiend. His new vampire fangs chomped huge sections of flesh from Vincent's throat.

Vincent gurgled in shock. His eyes went wide as he saw the newly made creature of the night feasting upon his neck. Rocky spat the last glob aside and sank his teeth into the fresh flowing well of blood spurting from the vampire's throat.

Somewhere in his feast, power, energy, life flowing like nothing he'd ever felt before through his veins, Rocky stopped when he felt a tap on his arm.

"Here," November said. She offered Rocky the stake she'd pulled from her stomach. "Finish him."

She's not going to make it.

Despite his fear, ignoring the hurt rearing up to challenge him yet again, Rocky took the weapon and plunged it through Vincent's left eye, driving through to the creature's brain. He yanked the stake free and shoved it through his other eye. The monster was dead, but Rocky withdrew the wooden stake again and stabbed it through Vincent's blackened heart.

He let go of the stake and turned to November. Thanks to Vincent's blood mixing with his own, he could feel the surge of strength just as visibility fell to next to nothing from the fire burning around them.

"Come on," Rocky said, hefting her in his arms, racing against the smoke. His firefighter training went against carrying people up the stairs, but that's just what he did as he burst into the second-floor hallway, found the closest window, and jumped through the glass.

Old Orchard residents were usually just falling asleep about this time of night, but in the early a.m. hours, they were reawakened by sirens and shouting as everyone tried to figure out what was happening.

Rocky found himself half floating, half running from the parking lot, across the street, between a couple of run-down businesses and finally, into the woods.

Laying her down upon the ground, Rocky leaned into November's pale face.

"Hey, gorgeous. You're gonna pull through. You hear me, you're making it out of this mess."

"I'm dying," November said. "I've loved you...all these years...."

"Why didn't you come to me?"

"You deserve better."

"No."

"Do something amazing, Rocky. You're better than I am."

He reached down and pulled her to his chest. His blood-smeared and soot-covered face stuffed against her hair, sucking in her scents, Rocky cried. "No, no, no, no, no...."

He clenched his eyes tight, but the tears would not be held back. Sirens sang as the love of his life faded in his arms.

EPILOGUE

The fire at the Avalon Hotel and the remains discovered inside have since been attributed to an unknown copycat killer. A sadistic murderer who not only replicated several deaths by the Beach Night Killer, but managed to far surpass his body count. Thanks to the quick response by the surrounding fire departments, the building was mostly saved, making it possible for the bodies to be identified, including the owner of the hotel, Jonathan Roux, and his missing girlfriend, Maggie Mae Miller.

On Smith Street, a second batch of murders was uncovered. Like the house of Jim and Betsy Seger in 1986, the Segers' basement stuffed with surrounding missing members of the town, the folks of Smith Street were found, many in Patty Beverly's home drained of most of their blood. Scott Jorgenson was one of the bodies in Patty's basement. They also found Eddie Mulligan and his girlfriend, Karla Newton. They were all laid to rest two weeks later. I went to each funeral.

My sister Julie has called me every day since the morning after. I can't talk to her. I can't talk to anyone. My heart, like my damned soul, is blackened and devoid of all love and hope. November is gone forever. Kat helped save us and she paid the same price. My only solace is that Vincent and Fiona are dead and gone, as well.

Me, I'm now cursed. At least until I die.

Thank fucking God the movies are full of shit, and we aren't truly immortal.

I could kill myself, but November wants – expects – more from me. And that's why I'm sitting here on a cold December night, two weeks after Thanksgiving, scouring the internet for any deaths that include major blood loss and/or bizarre neck wounds.

There are more of these monsters out there. Feeding upon the innocent, getting away like stone-cold killers, free to move from one feeding ground to the next.

No one else knows what they are or what they can do. Just me.

Hi, I'm Rocky Zukas, vampire killer.

Husk of a man found in the park Monday morning. Police and MDs are baffled by the grotesque discovery. Local psychic Peter Nash claims the victim's desiccated body is the result of being bled dry by a creature of the night. A vampire. Fort Wayne Police Department say they are on the hunt for Dracula or Freddy Krueger. Anyone seeing someone suspicious should report to the....

I closed the laptop and slipped it into my computer bag. I'd never been to Fort Wayne, Indiana, but I was certain there was something there I had to destroy.

Are you coming with me?

FLAME TREE PRESS
FICTION WITHOUT FRONTIERS
Award-Winning Authors & Original Voices

Flame Tree Press is the trade fiction imprint of Flame Tree Publishing, focusing on excellent writing in horror and the supernatural, crime and mystery, science fiction and fantasy. Our aim is to explore beyond the boundaries of the everyday, with tales from both award-winning authors and original voices.

•

Also by Glenn Rolfe:
Until Summer Comes Around
August's Eyes

You may also enjoy:
Think Yourself Lucky by Ramsey Campbell
The Hungry Moon by Ramsey Campbell
The Influence by Ramsey Campbell
The Wise Friend by Ramsey Campbell
Somebody's Voice by Ramsey Campbell
Fellstones by Ramsey Campbell
The Lonely Lands by Ramsey Campbell
The Haunting of Henderson Close by Catherine Cavendish
The Garden of Bewitchment by Catherine Cavendish
In Darkness, Shadows Breathe by Catherine Cavendish
Dark Observation by Catherine Cavendish
The After-Death of Caroline Rand by Catherine Cavendish
Dead Ends by Marc E. Fitch
The Toy Thief by D.W. Gillespie
One By One by D.W. Gillespie
Black Wings by Megan Hart
Silent Key by Laurel Hightower
Will Haunt You by Brian Kirk
We Are Monsters by Brian Kirk
Those Who Came Before by J.H. Moncrieff
Stoker's Wilde by Steven Hopstaken & Melissa Prusi
Stoker's Wilde West by Steven Hopstaken & Melissa Prusi
Land of the Dead by Steven Hopstaken & Melissa Prusi
Whisperwood by Alex Woodroe

•

Join our mailing list for free short stories, new release details, news about our authors and special promotions:

flametreepress.com